MEETING LADY LUCK

Lucky Lawrence needed to get lucky—real quick. Marrying Melissa Grayson might be a temporary way out of the trap into which he'd been so neatly maneuvered.

"I didn't expect you to be . . . I mean, we've only corresponded by mail," Melissa had whispered to him behind her hand.

That was what he thought. She had sent for a groom.

"You're so different from what I expected. If I didn't know you were James, I'd ask who you are."

"And I'd say, I'm the man who's going to keep you out of jail, darlin'." He leaned close to her ear. "You must have caused a real ruckus in this town."

"You're wearing a gun. And you've grown a mustache. You look more like an outlaw than a scholar and gentleman."

"Scholars and gentlemen have mustaches."

"But they don't look like you."

Lucky knew that because he was using a false name the wedding ceremony wouldn't be legal—so long as it wasn't consummated. Consummation. That and the obvious curves of the woman standing close enough to be kissed might make that part of the solution a trial. . . .

SANDRA CHASTAIN

THE

MAIL ORDER

GROOM

BANTAM BOOKS

New York   Toronto   London   Sydney   Auckland

THE MAIL ORDER GROOM

A Bantam Book

July 2002

ISBN 0-553-58050-7

Published simultaneously in the United States and Canada

Bantam Books are published by Bantam Books, a division of Ran-
dom House, Inc. Its trademark, consisting of the words "Bantam
Books" and the portrayal of a rooster, is Registered in U.S. Patent
and Trademark Office and in other countries. Marca Registrada.
Bantam Books, 1540 Broadway, New York, New York 10036.

PRINTED IN THE UNITED STATES OF AMERICA

OPM   10 9 8 7 6 5 4 3 2 1

THE
MAIL ORDER
GROOM

1

September 9, 1888
Silver Wind, Colorado

"Not a man in sight."

Melissa Grayson let out a sigh of relief. She'd made it. She drove down Silver Street past Sizemore's General Store and the Lucky Chance saloon, then stepped down from her wagon in front of the Methodist church at the end of the street. She'd loop Arthur's reins over the fence post and with any luck she'd make it into the church before any of the single men in Silver Wind knew she was there.

A sudden burst of wind caught Melissa's bonnet. She shivered as she felt the unwelcome hint of winter curl around the back of her neck and tug at the ribbon tied beneath her chin.

At that moment the bell in the steeple began its Sunday morning summons to the three hundred permanent residents of Silver Wind, Colorado, and any miners or cowboys of a mind to attend services.

"Well now, will you listen to that bell, boys," a loud male voice called out from the saloon behind her. "It's time for church. Think I might just go. Been a long time since I heard any words from the Good Book. Morning, teacher."

Melissa groaned. She'd congratulated herself too soon. The voice belonged to the worst of her suitors, a miner who called himself Black Bart. She heard the laughter and the sound of the batwing doors as he and his fellow drinkers stepped onto the plank sidewalk that wandered crookedly alongside the buildings.

It was only eleven o'clock in the morning, but if the smell of whiskey had been gunpowder, a mountain lion would have picked up the scent and hightailed it out of town. Before she could get inside the churchyard, the miner stepped in front of her and grinned. "Morning, Miss Grayson. You remember me? I'm Bart Jamison. Folks call me Black Bart."

Melissa Grayson didn't respond. She knew him. Every woman in Silver Wind knew Bart. He'd been a nondescript, unsuccessful prospector until a dime novelist immortalized the real Black Bart, who was a silver-haired businessman and part-time stagecoach robber. At one time, he'd worked for her father. But that was before she'd come. She wasn't certain if the "black" attached to Silver Wind's Bart was because he was such a bully or because he was covered in dust.

Just what she needed. The city elders, including the preacher, had issued a stern warning the last time an argument ensued over her attention. Any more fighting over her and they'd have to take action. She'd stayed away from town hoping to avoid trouble, but this was Sunday and she always attended services on Sunday.

Melissa ignored Bart. She pulled her collar close around her neck and started forward. Two quick steps around him and she'd be inside the picket fence that surrounded the small churchyard. But before she could get to the gate, Bart put his hand out to prevent her from passing.

Suddenly a younger male voice called out anxiously, "Miss Grayson, we'd better hurry. We have to choose the morning hymn." The breathless voice belonged to the mayor's son, who appeared beside her.

"Thank you, Theodore," she said to her fourteen-year-old student, "but I'll be fine." In secret reassurance, she patted the recently acquired derringer she now carried in her reticule.

"Step aside, sonny!" Bart growled. "I ain't seen the inside of a church since I left Virginny. This morning the Lord's calling out to me long and hard."

"It ain't the Lord's call that's long and hard," one of the onlookers muttered and let out a chuckle.

Theodore Dawson pulled himself up to his full height of five feet and swallowed. "Mr. Jamison, I insist you let the lady pass."

"Go home, boy!" Bart growled and shoved Ted aside. He took Melissa's arm and stumbled into the churchyard. "Miss Grayson knows a real man when she sees one. Don't you, sweet thing?"

"Let her go!" Ted scrambled after Bart. Planting himself between the bully and the church door, he drew back and swung at the miner. Nobody seemed more surprised than Ted when his fist connected to flesh and a spurt of blood gushed from Bart's nose.

"Why you scrawny little . . ."

What had started out as a skirmish turned vicious, as Bart grabbed the boy by the throat and began shaking him. Before Melissa could intercede, a churchgoer jumped in and caught Bart's arm. A free-for-all was about to ensue right there in the entrance to the churchyard. If she didn't stop it, Ted could be injured. That would be another black mark on the town's tally of her troublemaking. No matter that Melissa was not responsible, her father's school could be closed and her promise to make his dream come true would be over. Grayson Academy would never be the finest boarding school in the West. In desperation, she reached inside her bag, snatched out the derringer, aimed for heaven, and pulled the trigger.

Fate was not kind to her that day. As the church bell swung outward, the bullet hit the bell, ricocheted downward, and struck Theodore Dawson in the arm. Of all the men who didn't deserve a bullet, she'd shot her defender—the mayor's son.

Ted let out a yell and collapsed against the fence.

"Oh, Ted," Melissa cried out, and hurried to his side.

The minister, the deacons, and the choir rushed out of the church staring aghast at the drunken miners, and Melissa, kneeling beside the wounded boy.

"Miss Grayson, what's going on here?" the mayor roared, then caught sight of the blood on his son. "Ted?"

"It's nothing, Pa," Ted said weakly. "The bullet just grazed me. I'll be fine."

"How'd you get shot?" one of the townsfolk inquired and looked directly at Melissa, still holding her gun. "As if we don't already know."

"Every time *she* comes into town there's a fight," another added. "I don't care if she is the best-looking woman west of the Mississippi, I say to hell—pardon me, Brother Weeks—with her. Let's just run her out of town."

"No need," Bart said, and grinned. "I'd be obliged to take her off your hands."

"Now, now," the minister cautioned. "We must not defame the Lord's day."

"It isn't the Lord she shot," an angry female voice shouted. "It's Ted. I say, since she's taken to carryin' a gun, it's time we take action. Ain't no book learnin' worth lettin' her shoot up our folks."

Melissa looked down at her gun. What had she done? She'd only bought it to protect herself from men like Bart. "All I did was try to stop the fight. I didn't shoot at Theodore."

"That she didn't," Obie Kinder, an onlooker, observed. "She shot in the air but her bullet hit the church bell. Musta bounced off and caught the boy." He pulled off his cap and lowered his head. "She didn't mean no harm. It was God's will."

The mayor and the minister lifted Ted and walked toward the church, followed by the other worshipers. That was when the bell fell and cracked into two pieces.

Mayor Dawson shook his head. "I think you'd better come inside and have a seat, Miss Grayson. You've been warned, but you're as stubborn as your father—and he was the most stubborn man in Silver Wind. Built that school way out on his claim—even after we offered him the use of the church for it."

"Somebody get Sheriff Vance," Mayor Dawson said. "Doc, you come in and look at my boy's arm while the rest of us figure out what to do about Miss Grayson and the future of Grayson Academy."

Melissa tucked the derringer back into her reticule, straightened her shoulders, and entered the church. The onlookers moved to the side, forming a corridor of stern-faced townsfolk. Joan of Arc couldn't have been any more heroic. After walking the gauntlet, Melissa took a seat on the back bench as the elders met behind the altar. She couldn't believe none of the women would speak on her behalf, but then again, these were older women who bowed to their husband's wishes.

How could this have happened? All she'd wanted was to make her father's dream come true. Back East he'd tried to care for her and his fragile wife, tried and failed. Soon after her mother died, he'd closed his small private school, sold the last of their possessions, and left Melissa in a boarding school where she became both student and teacher while he went West to make a new start. Melissa had feared the worst. She knew he had neither the physical nor the practical ability to live a wilderness life.

To Melissa's surprise, he'd gotten lucky. He managed to stake a claim that produced enough gold to allow him to build a new school, and he planned to send for her in the spring. Then, before they were reunited, he came down with pneumonia and died. Only after she arrived did she learn that there was no claim. The only gold he'd found had washed down from the hills of the San Juan Mountains above Silver Wind. But he'd left her his dream, Grayson Academy. The school was the only thing she had left of the kind, gentle man who'd been her father. Now all that would be threatened because

Western men had the manners of rutting buffalos and wouldn't take no for an answer.

Sheriff Vance huffed into the church. "What's going on up here?"

"Miss Grayson shot Ted," the mayor said, "and broke the bell."

"The teacher shot Ted? Why?"

"It was an accident," one of the onlookers called out. "She meant to shoot Bart."

The sheriff whirled around brandishing his revolver.

Reverend Weeks frowned. "Put that gun away, Sheriff. You're in the house of the Lord."

"Yeah," one of the church members said in a loud voice. "Besides, Vance is so blind he's liable to put a real hole in Ted."

The doctor pronounced Ted's injury a flesh wound and the mayor called the city officials to join them at the front of the church. Fifteen minutes later, after a heated argument between some of the members, Melissa Grayson was summoned forward.

"When your father died and left you the school, we welcomed you as the new teacher. But from the beginning, you seemed to be more interested in teaching our children art and poetry than reading, 'riting, and 'rithmetic," the minister said.

"We tolerated that because we didn't want you to get married and quit or go back East," Alfred Sizemore, the storekeeper, added.

"Then," Ida Sizemore added, "we wished you would go back."

"And now you must," Reverend Weeks said solemnly. "Ted wasn't killed today, but he might have been. And *you* are responsible. The bullet came from your gun. The sheriff is ready to put you in jail."

Mayor Dawson cleared his throat, signaling an announcement. "After careful consideration, we feel that choosing a husband is the only way to stop the fighting over a woman who looks like you."

"I'm sorry, but I have no intention of marrying," Melissa said firmly. "I'm a teacher, like my father. That's all I intend to be."

"You have no choice. If you refuse," the mayor said grimly, "I'll have Sheriff Vance put you under arrest for attempted murder of my son. I'd hate to do it, but I will."

There was a collective gasp from the audience.

"But Papa—" Ted began.

"The shooting was an accident," Melissa protested.

"So you say," the mayor went on, "but the city council has decided that any single man interested in taking you as his wife will meet here three weeks from now to make an offer for your hand. It's marriage or jail."

Melissa stood, her mouth open, all the air emptied from her lungs. "But this is 1888. You can't mean to force me to marry?"

"We mean to do just that."

"Suppose I refuse?"

"It is your decision, of course," the mayor said, "but you must understand the consequences. I'd hate to see that fine school building go to waste, but even if the law rules that you don't have to go to jail, we will withdraw our children."

Withdraw their children? So far, she hadn't had enough students to pay for her efforts. "You'd give up your children's education in order to force me to take a husband?"

"We will. We don't mean to be harsh, Miss Grayson. We respected your father. He isn't here to keep an eye on you and we've decided to act on his behalf," Reverend Weeks said formally. He then added softly, "Ah, Melissa, this is best. In the West, a fetching woman like you needs a man to protect her."

Melissa studied the faces of her well-meaning accusers. They didn't approve of her. They were her father's friends, the mothers and fathers of her students, the people in town she'd come to know and count on. She knew she was a good teacher. She taught the basics, but there was nothing wrong with inspiring hearts or minds with a little art and poetry. In this cold, harsh place, the people needed something that warmed their souls.

As for how she looked, she couldn't help it that God had made her petite, with sky-blue eyes and unruly hair the color of warm taffy. She'd taken great care to be cautious about her dress and demeanor. And she hadn't accepted so much as a hand to hold from a man since she'd been in Colorado. How could the town turn against her like this? And what was she going to do?

"Let me see if I understand," she finally said. "If I marry, you'll send your children to my school?"

"Yes, we will." The minister's wife nodded. "With a husband to protect you, those heathens will leave you be. Though our husbands still think you should leave off all that poetry you make our younguns read. But," she whispered shyly, "we're working on that."

"I can pick any man I want?"

"You may," the mayor promised.

Melissa had no choice. She nodded her head. "Fine. I'll announce my choice three weeks from today."

September 10, 1888

MASTER JAMES HAROLD PICKNEY IV
354 FIFTH AVENUE
NEW YORK CITY, NEW YORK

DEAR JAMES,

I know this will come as a great surprise to you, but it seems I must choose a husband in order to continue to operate Grayson Academy. As a single woman, I seem to drive men to mischief and keep the town stirred up.

It occurred to me that, though we've never met, I know you better than anyone here. The confidences your sister and I exchanged as schoolmates, and the year of correspondence you and I have engaged in, suggest that we might get on well.

I know you're frustrated with your weak lungs, and I've been told that the clear, pure air here in the Colorado mountains has proven beneficial to breathing problems.

To come to the point, would you entertain the thought of taking a wife in exchange for a chance at good health and an opportunity to teach? I would not, of course, expect you to be my husband in the physical sense. We would live as brother and sister.

Time is of the essence. I will not be hurt should you decline. If you choose to accept, please

telegraph me immediately, as I must name my
choice on the last Sunday in September and make
it known to the town fathers.

> *Yours in friendship,*
> *Melissa Grayson*

Melissa folded the notepaper and slid it into the envelope. She'd been sending mail to James since the first week she'd arrived. To the postmaster, this was just another letter. For her, it meant her life would be forever changed.

She held the letter against her chest and let out a deep sigh. Winter was approaching. The prospectors would close down their operations until spring. The farmers' crops would have been harvested. The cattle would be left to fend for themselves, and the weather would curtail many of the children's normal chores, which meant that the students would return to school if Grayson Academy was still open.

If she took a husband.

If James Harold Pickney agreed to her proposal, and she married a man she'd never seen.

Melissa paid for the postage, handed the postmaster her letter, and went back home to wait. With the railroads delivering the mail from the West Coast to the East Coast in only a matter of days, she would receive James's telegram in plenty of time to fend off the city council's sentence. In the meantime, Melissa avoided town, readying her classroom and gathering wood for the coming winter. She grew more and more nervous as time passed.

One week came and went. No telegram.

Two weeks, then three.

James hadn't responded; she grew anxious at the thought of having to choose one of the men she'd avoided for two years. On the Sunday morning of her deadline, she resigned herself to her fate. But the only decent single male in Silver Wind was young Ted. She gave a dry laugh. As a last resort, maybe they would let her pick the fourteen-year-old pupil. She was only six years his senior.

An hour before she was to meet with the minister and the mayor, the telegraph operator brought her James's answer.

Where rose the mountains, there to him were friends.
Illness delayed reply. I accept.
Will arrive 2 o'clock train—first Sunday of October.

                              James Harold Pickney IV

How like James. He'd not only accepted but also quoted Byron's poem *Childe Harold's Pilgrimage*. To James, whose health had kept him from a normal life, rescuing her would certainly be a kind of pilgrimage. She should have felt elation, but all she could muster was a vague sense of relief that she'd escaped the hangman's noose.

Pushing a nagging tinge of worry away, she made her way to the church. Every bench was crowded with men. It appeared as if every bachelor in Colorado had slicked himself up and gotten in line. The church smelled of lye soap and hair tonic. If nothing else, the washerwomen, the barber, and the trading post had profited by the town's plan to marry off Melissa. The Widow Sweeney shared her organ bench with the Widow Cassidy. They were both deep in whispered conversation, studying the congregation as if they were dividing the leftovers. If the tables had been turned, Melissa might have enjoyed what was about to happen.

Even if Melissa wanted to marry—and she didn't—the truth was, there really wasn't a single man in town who had one ounce of culture. She'd seen her mother's unhappiness over being poor turn a kind, gentle husband into a beaten man. Melissa vowed never to repeat her mother's mistakes. If she ever married, she'd accept her husband for what he was.

Pausing a moment to tug at her bodice, Melissa straightened her shoulders and jutted out her chin before marching to the front of the church, where she clapped her hands to quiet the crowd. "Please, may I have your attention. I appreciate very much your kind offer for my hand in marriage but I have already made my choice."

The silence was swift and ominous.

"What you mean? I come here fair and square" was the first protest.

"Me, too. I even took a bath."

"We're supposed to prezent ourselves here today and she'd pick," another argued.

Bart stood and took a small bow to those behind him. "Guess the lady took one look at you scoundrels and decided to choose me after all."

"No, Mr. Jamison," Melissa said firmly. "I choose none of you. The postmaster can tell you that I've been corresponding with a gentleman in New York City for over a year. What he didn't know is that Mr. Pickney is my fiancé He'll be arriving next Sunday on the two o'clock train."

"She's just making that up," one of the contenders called out.

"Don't matter," another argued. "She's supposed to pick one of us. We don't need to bring in some outsider."

The minister, sensing trouble, held up his hand. "Hold on. We didn't specify that she had to choose one of you, only that she choose."

"So, she's gonna marry some Eastern pansy," Bart Jamison said. "Miss Grayson, I think me and the preacher will be waiting on that depot platform to make sure your groom shows up. If not, a wedding is gonna take place—mine and yours."

"That choice is not yours to make, Mr. Jamison. Besides, Mr. Pickney will be there," Melissa said, assured that James was a man of honor, unlike Bart and the rest of these hooligans. "I have a telegram that says so."

Bart frowned. "And if he ain't?"

Silence swept the church.

"Then I'll . . . I'll choose one of you."

Bart grinned. "Let's head for the saloon, boys, and drink a toast to my coming wedding." He winked at her. "And the wedding night."

The preacher raised his closed eyes to the heavens as the men filed out of the church. Melissa was certain she heard the women of the town let out deep sighs of relief. Except for the Widows Sweeney and Cassidy.

"Excuse us," they murmured gleefully as they brushed past Melissa to follow the men. "These fellas deserve our attention," one said.

"Of course, we're obligated to do God's work," the other agreed.

"Certainly," Melissa said, and watched as they headed for the exit. Obviously, the two women were intent on their mission. The devil had a hold on half the men in the small church, and the widows were apparently convinced that the Lord expected them to be his messengers of salvation. If that involved marriage, they were prepared to do their Christian duty.

Bart's wink and his reference to a wedding night gave Melissa pause. She hoped that James truly understood their marriage was simply one of convenience.

She wasn't obligated to . . . anything.

2

September 26, 1888
Santa Fe, New Mexico

For over an hour, Lucky Lawrence had been waiting. The Lady Luck saloon was said to be a favorite of Cerqueda, the man who had taken an innocent girl as settlement for a gambling debt. Rarely was Lucky uncomfortable, but tonight he felt a strong foreboding.

This part of Santa Fe was known for its lawlessness. He just hadn't figured on losing his horse at the last saloon—not in a game but to a common thief. It hadn't taken him long to decide that any one of the patrons here would do far worse.

Though Lucky could use the silver-and-pearl-handled Colt revolver strapped on his hip as well as the next man, he didn't like killing. He didn't like men who hurt women either. Once he learned Cerqueda's reputation, he considered giving up the job and returning his fee. But to find Louisa, the ravished daughter of an old but foolish friend of his mother's, Lucky would take a chance. He rubbed his fingers across the diamond mounted in the center of his lucky gold coin and hoped the girl was all right.

After all, the Mexican was a gambler, and Lucky's talent was playing cards. He'd gambled with the best, and losing wasn't his style. He wouldn't mind taking the Mexican's gold along with the girl. All he had to do was outsmart him, get Louisa, and head for home.

Then, as if by summons, a tall dark man swaggered through the door, accompanied by two underlings and a dark-haired girl. A few questions to the bartender confirmed this was Cerqueda, the man Lucky was searching for. According to the saloon keeper, he'd frequently bragged that he'd won the girl in a poker game. She had to be the one Lucky had come to rescue.

In the mirror over the bar, Lucky watched in disgust as the man dragged up a stool and motioned for the frightened girl to sit behind him. She was pretty, or she would have been, had she been smiling. She wasn't. Defeat dulled her eyes as she sat, slumped and mute, shivering from the sheer fabric of the dress she was wearing and the cool September air that spilled through the cracks of the crude building.

Cerqueda pulled out a deck of cards and shuffled them listlessly. He casually scouted the crowded bar, settling his gaze on Lucky. Lucky didn't like the deadly challenge in his eyes.

"Hey, gringo! You, at the bar! You want to give me some of your gold?"

Lucky turned and leaned back against the wooden counter, resting his weight on his elbows. He hadn't

been able to save his sister from a man said to be a
ne'er-do-well. At the time he'd been just as young and
foolish, so intent on finding gold that he ended up in a
bar in Alaska, where he'd been shanghaied and put on a
ship heading for the South Seas. By the time he'd gotten back to New Orleans, his mother was dead and his
sister had run away with a fast-talking piano player on
his way out West. To search for her, Lucky had become
a gambler, a wanderer who made his money on cards
and by taking special assignments for those who could
pay. He hadn't found his sister, but he would never stop
looking.

This job was *déjà vu*. Rescue Louisa Hidalgo. The
difference was, Louisa hadn't gone with the gambler
willingly.

The man who'd hired him was a fool, a man so
caught up in the grief of losing his wife that he'd turned
to drink. He'd gambled away his Texas ranch, and in
one last desperate drunken attempt to regain his land,
he'd let his daughter become his bet to stay in the
game. The man had lost everything to a Mexican named
Cerqueda.

"What you say, gringo? Do you play?"

"Yeah," Lucky said, and moved slowly toward the
table. "But I'm thinking that your gold belongs in my
pocket."

Cerqueda laughed and shoved one of the players
aside, clearing a seat for Lucky. The first few hands
were even, with little conversation and no urgency. The
Mexican took two games and Lucky won two.

"You're a stranger. What business do you have in
these parts?" Cerqueda asked.

"My own."

"Don't talk much, do you?"

"Nope."

Cerqueda grinned and slapped the girl's leg. "Get us a bottle of whiskey, chiquita."

The girl didn't move fast enough.

"I said"—he reached out and caught her arm, shaking her vigorously—"get us whiskey." He shoved her so hard she fell to the floor.

Lucky sprang to his feet and helped her up. "Take it easy. The lady looks cold. I'll get the bottle."

"Leave her alone," Cerqueda snapped. "And she's no lady. She was once. Oh, yes, she was once too good for the likes of me. Once she was Louisa Hidalgo, daughter of the owner of one of the largest spreads in west Texas. It belongs to me now. So does Louisa."

"Please, don't try to help me," the girl whispered. "You'll only make it worse."

Lucky let her go and headed for the bar. "You don't look like a rancher," he said over his shoulder to Cerqueda. Then he returned with the bottle.

"I'm not," Cerqueda confessed. "I'm a gambler. I won the ranch in a card game in Austin. The owner was a fool. He wouldn't quit. The last hand was for his daughter. I always win."

"Why did you want her?"

"Because she didn't want me. I was a stranger who simply offered her a hand when she stepped out of her carriage. She spit on my boots. Now"—he grinned— "she polishes them. And more."

Lucky's rage boiled, so much so that he had to force himself not to lose his concentration. He quickly figured out that not only were the other players cohorts, but the cards were marked and his opponent was dealing from the bottom of the deck.

Across the table, the eyes of Louisa Hidalgo grew wider. Keeping the girl safe until he could rescue her was the only thing that kept Lucky from challenging her captor to an old-fashioned Louisiana duel.

Rescuing the girl was the important thing. Punishing the Mexican would have to wait. Lucky never cheated. But he could if the need arose. And it looked as if he was going to have to play dirty if he intended to free the girl.

Cerqueda never knew that Lucky deliberately let him win the next two hands. Making it look good was hard, for Cerqueda was a worthy opponent. Lucky couldn't help Louisa unless the pot was big enough to be a challenge. But he couldn't take a chance on letting his stake shrink any further, so he took the next pot and the deal. The time had come to make his move. He dealt Cerqueda a hand good enough to make him confident that he'd win.

"Last hand," Lucky said, stopping to light one of the cigars he favored. He took a long draw, fingered his cards, and said, "I'll see you and raise you"—he reached inside his coat pocket and pulled out his pocket watch—"this." The watch slid into the pile, dislodged the money and came to a rest on the table. Lucky leaned back in his chair and smiled. "It's worth a hundred dollars. What do you say?"

"I say you're bluffing. I don't need a watch and I don't think I trust you." Cerqueda pushed the rest of his money toward the center of the table. "Let's see what you've got."

Louisa was openly shaking her head behind her captor. She couldn't know that her future hinged on what happened next, that he'd promised her father he'd find his daughter and send her to New Orleans, the home of her Creole grandparents. Mr. Hidalgo would wait in New Orleans until Lucky found her.

But the girl was obviously upset enough to risk Cerqueda's fury. Her eyes were frantic. Lucky was beginning to smell a rat in the woodpile. Still, he knew which cards he'd dealt Cerqueda. He still needed the king of hearts to fill out his flush, and Lucky was holding that card. Cerqueda had to be bluffing. The three hundred dollars in the middle of the table was all the money Lucky had. His pair would take the pot.

Lucky grinned. "Okay, amigo, let's make it interesting for both of us. I'll even add my lucky gold coin. And you throw in"—he looked around as if he were considering the wager—"you throw in the girl. Winner takes all."

"Your lucky coin?" He laughed. "I think the girl is worth more to me, señor."

"I don't think so. She's pretty pitiful-looking to me." Lucky pulled the prize from his watch pocket and tossed it on the table. The diamond, in the center of the gold coin that had given Lucky his name, caught the lamplight overhead and twinkled.

The Mexican's greedy eyes locked on the coin and he reconsidered with an exaggerated shrug. "Well, I hate to take a man's luck," Cerqueda said, "but it's your call." He turned over his cards, a straight flush to the king. The king of hearts.

Hellfire! How'd that happen? He'd dealt Cerqueda everything but the king to fill out his flush. But he'd dealt diamonds, not hearts. The king of hearts was in his own hand, not his opponent's. Cerqueda's lips curled into a grin. He dared Lucky to admit the truth. Apparently the Mexican was as adept at manipulating the cards as Lucky. He had a duplicate deck.

Once Lucky showed his cards, he was a dead man, and Louisa—Louisa was out of his reach. Lucky leaned forward as if to push the money away to lay down his hand, while he reached for the derringer he'd concealed inside his boot. "Looks like we have a small problem, amigo."

"I don't think so." Cerqueda grinned. "You got a hand to beat this? Let me have a look."

"I don't think we want trouble," Lucky said in a low voice. "So, I concede the hand, the watch. I'll even concede my lucky coin. You give me the girl and we'll call it even."

"Not until I see your cards. Hold him, boys."

The two other players came to stand beside Lucky, placing a hand on each shoulder. He might get one of them, but he'd never get them both. There was no escaping.

With a deep sigh, he laid down his cards. A seven of clubs, a queen of clubs, a two of spades, and his pair: a king of diamonds and—

"The king of hearts!" Cerqueda said in a voice straight from hell. "You can't have the king of hearts. I have the king of hearts." He stood, pulling his revolver from his leather holster. "You know what we do to cheaters?"

"I can guess."

Cerqueda laid his revolver on the table and reached for his winnings. "I never let a man get the best of me.

Bring him outside. Come along, my love. Watch me kill a cheater."

The last of the light drained from the girl's eyes. "I don't feel well," she said, and slumped forward, collapsing onto the table, upending it and the rest of the money. Lucky caught the revolver as it slid off the table, pointed it at Cerqueda and fired. A crease of red lined the gambler's earlobe and he fell backward, hitting his head on the edge of the table with a crunch. In the confusion that followed, his cronies scattered. Lucky scooped some of the pot into his hat, pulled Louisa to her feet, and headed out the door. Cerqueda's carriage was beside the building. Lucky pushed the girl inside and whipped the horses into a gallop.

"I thank you," Louisa said, "but you don't know what you've done. Cerqueda isn't just a gambler, he's an evil man—a murderer. He'll hunt us both down and kill us. He never gives up. You've signed your death sentence."

"Take this," he said, pressing the crumpled money into her hand. "We have to get you to New Orleans. Your father will be waiting for you at the St. Charles Hotel."

She looked confused. "My father is in Louisiana?"

"Yes, he sent me to find you. He'll take you to your grandparents' plantation."

"I thought he was dead," she said softly.

"He almost was."

"I can't go back to him. I'm ruined. I'm not his little girl anymore."

"You'll always be his little girl, Louisa. Your home was in Texas. It's gone. In Louisiana, nobody will know anything you don't tell them."

"But what about you?"

Lucky reached over his shoulder into the back of the buggy and pulled out Cerqueda's fur-lined coat. He placed it around Louisa's shoulders and covered her head with his own black Stetson. "From the sound of Cerqueda's head hitting the table, I think he's hurt. We should have a couple of days. I'm going to put you on the next train heading east. I'll drive this buggy west out of Santa Fe and make Cerqueda think we're going to California."

For over a week, Lucky made several stops to leave a trail. He abandoned Cerqueda's carriage, traded one of the horses to a family for some food, and rode the other one north until he reached the Rio Grande Western Railroad headed east, then caught the next train to Durango. So far, there was no indication that he was being followed. But he knew that wouldn't last forever.

Louisa's words worried him. She'd called Cerqueda an evil man who never gave up. He could believe that. He needed to put some real distance and time between him and the Mexican. For that, he needed money. A few cowboys at the end of the car were more than willing to join Lucky in a poker game and share their whiskey as well.

Lucky won a couple of hands before the train pulled into the Durango depot, where a group of Women's Christian Temperance Union crusaders were gathered, handing out pamphlets and expounding the evils of drink. They climbed on the train to warn the cowboys about what happened to men who lived ungodly lives. The example they used was of a man named Cerqueda who was injured in a barroom fight after a night of drinking and gambling. He'd killed the bartender and set out to find the gambler who'd cheated him.

Cerqueda was after him. Well, he'd expected that. But he hadn't expected the story to get out so quickly. Suddenly, the sheriff and the local newspaper editor stepped on the train—the sheriff to quell any potential disturbance, the editor looking for news.

Lucky decided quickly that he was in the wrong place at the wrong time. He gathered up his small earnings, slid out the door and into the Pullman car behind.

A change of appearance was in order. Lucky took some of the money he'd won and left it on a table in exchange for a beaver-trimmed brown coat and hat hanging on a rack by the door.

Then he heard a sound. Snoring. If the occupant of the car woke up, he'd be discovered. With the sheriff, the newspaper editor, and those women on board, Cerqueda wouldn't have to hunt him down; the spotlight would already be on him. Lucky moved out the back door toward a sidetrack, where a small mining train heading for the mountains was building up a slow head of steam.

Lucky boarded the narrow-gauge train and took a seat on the crates inside the car as it pulled out of the station—just in time to see the reporter and the sheriff exit the Rio Grande. So he wasn't going back East. Until he replenished his purse, being off the beaten track was better. Nobody knew him in the Colorado mountains.

Once the mining train had picked up speed, a dusty employee entered the car, checking the crates and kegs. He seemed surprised to find Lucky.

"Didn't see you get on, mister. This is a mining train, but you still got to have a ticket."

"Sorry." Lucky pulled out one of his last bills and handed it to the train employee, who pocketed it.

He took a good look at Lucky and grinned. "Guess you're the dude they're expecting in Silver Wind. Can't blame you. She's a real looker, she is."

"She?"

But the man had moved out the back and the car was empty.

Obviously the railroad worker had mistaken him for someone else. That was probably good. If Cerqueda asked, he'd be misled. The promise of temporary safety softened the blow of having to deplete his funds. At least he still had his lucky coin. He hoped that Louisa was on her way to her father. Pulling the brim of his stolen hat over his face, he leaned back against a crate and closed his eyes.

He'd been in tough spots before, but this time there was something in the air that disturbed him. He couldn't put his finger on it, but he would. As the little mining train wound its way up the side of the mountain, he just hoped his luck would hold out.

Inside the Silver Wind depot, Melissa Grayson waited, trying desperately to conceal her concern. What if something had happened? What if the train broke down? What if James was not on the train?

She'd planned to meet the train, connect with James, and go to the church. Once they were married, she'd have satisfied the townspeople. Beyond that, she hadn't thought of anything but the school and how James could help her build it up. Instead, she was wearing the Widow Sweeney's wedding dress, which was two sizes too large, and the Widow Cassidy was planting a panel of white lace curtain in her hair. Half the residents of Silver Wind, including every single man within riding or walking distance of the mining town, stood on the station platform waiting for the train to arrive.

"I appreciate your offering me your wedding dress, Mrs. Sweeney," Melissa had said, "but I'd really rather wear my own clothes."

"Nonsense," the widow had insisted. "This is a wedding and you ought to have a wedding dress. I only wore it once. It's still good."

"It's a lovely dress," Melissa finally said, listening for the labored sound of the train, "but it's just a little . . . large."

"I can fix that," the Widow Cassidy said, gathering up the long skirt in the back and securing it behind Melissa's bottom with a large hat pin. "Perfect. Now whatever you do, don't sit down."

Melissa resisted the impulse to grab the pin and stick it into the Widow Cassidy's ample rear. She simply smiled. Until she and James were married, she couldn't afford to offend the widows or any of the members of the Silver Wind Methodist Church Ladies' Auxiliary, all of whom were waiting on the depot platform like armed guards.

She gave a resigned nod and waited.

And waited.

When the telegraph line came to sudden life, Melissa had a bad feeling. Cob Barnett, who was both stationmaster and postmaster, bent his head over his counter to write the message, then announced, "Looks like there's been a bit of trouble with some Temperance women down at the Durango junction. At least they didn't get on the mining train to come up here. The stationmaster didn't see your man either, Miss Grayson."

Melissa's heart sank. She didn't want to think what would happen if James hadn't come.

The sound of the train whistle drew everyone's attention. Melissa felt herself being propelled by the Widow Sweeney to the depot platform. The crowd eagerly watched the engine pull into the station and come to a whining stop.

"Howdy, Cob," the engineer called out.

"Where's your fee-on-see, Miss Grayson?" somebody finally asked.

"Looks like that'd be Black Bart," one of the onlookers said gleefully as he looked around.

"Yep," Bart announced with a swagger. "Ain't no real man gonna come out here and marry a troublemaker like the teach, 'cepting me. You folks don't have to worry, I'll tame her quick enough."

"You're out of luck, Bart. Miss Grayson's intended is on the train," the engineer said. "He got on down at the junction."

Melissa let out a sigh of relief.

"Well, it don't look like he's real anxious to rescue her," Bart said. "If he's turned lily-livered, that means she picks me." Bart's hand went to his hip and he swung slowly around, daring anyone to step forward.

"Or she goes to jail," another commented.

"Yeah, it's jail or me," Bart announced with a confident grin. "There's no Eastern dandy come to save her. Let's make it legal."

Lucky, seeing the crowd, waited on the train. Another woman in trouble. He didn't know what was going on, but he knew that the bragging miner was not her first choice. Lucky sighed. He wasn't the man she expected, but he never could walk away from a woman in distress. Maybe he could get her out of her mess, whatever it was.

"Guess we'd better let the lady decide," Lucky said as he stepped down to the platform and walked toward the group of people.

Through the crowd, Melissa caught site of James and felt her heartbeat thunder. She'd never seen James, but his sister had been her roommate and she'd assumed that there would be some family resemblance. This man didn't look sickly in the least. Wearing a neat black mustache, he stood tall and slim with his feet apart and one side of the beaver-trimmed coat pulled back to reveal a gun belt that looked as though it was a comfortable part of the black trousers and frock coat he wore. But it was his eyes that stopped her—gun-metal gray eyes that radiated danger. The murmur that had begun quieted as most of the men took a step back.

"Come along, Miss Grayson," Mayor Dawson said nervously. "It seems your bridegroom is here. We've got everything ready, Mr. Pickney. Melissa, stop hiding behind the widow and greet your intended."

Mr. Pickney? Intended? Lucky felt his earlier unease hit full force. He'd stepped from the frying pan into the fire. Before he could speak, a tall tight-lipped woman stepped forward, tugging someone behind her.

She stepped aside and the most beautiful woman Lucky had ever seen was shoved against him. A gust of mountain air tousled the veil in her golden hair like a white flag in surrender. She pulled back, blue eyes wide in question, and tried to speak. Whatever she had on her mind, it wasn't surrender. Her lips formed words but no sound came. Finally, she whispered, "James? You . . . you look so different."

He didn't know what he looked like, except he must look as stunned as she did.

He finally said, "I think we may have a little problem here."

"No problem, Mr. James Harold Pickney IV," a tall man with dirty clothing and whiskers said. "Name's Black Bart. I offered for her, but the teacher chose you. One way or another, a wedding is taking place this afternoon." He touched his gun belt. "I'd just as soon the bridegroom be me."

"Is that right?" Lucky asked, his eyes still focused on the woman who was struggling to right herself. "And what will happen if a wedding doesn't take place this morning?"

"Miss Grayson will lose her school and go to jail."

"Over a wedding?"

"That is correct, Mr. Pickney," the minister said. "Miss Grayson rejected all of the local men who offered to marry her. She explained that the two of you were promised and that you were to arrive today. Are you prepared to marry her?"

The cluster of onlookers had closed in around Melissa and Lucky.

"Well," the engineer said, "sorry I can't stick around for the ceremony but I've got to get on up the mountain. They're waiting for these supplies and we're already behind schedule. I'm hoping that by the time I get back to the Durango junction those Temperance women will be gone. Else you all had better get ready for reporters and do-gooding women up here."

Do-gooding women Lucky could tolerate, but reporters he'd rather avoid. With any luck, Lucky wouldn't have to use his gun against Bart, the ringleader of this lynch mob; but the crowd seemed united in their determination to force the woman to marry or face severe punishment. Why didn't she speak up and correct them? He'd never seen her before. She had to know he wasn't her intended. Unless ... Maybe she didn't know the man she was marrying. Maybe it was some kind of arranged wedding—a mail-order groom. Or maybe she didn't care. With her looks, she must have been pretty desperate to lie to these people.

He wasn't James Harold Pickney, but he couldn't afford to admit to his real name. Until he was satisfied that Cerqueda had given up and headed back to Texas, being Pickney could be a solution to both their immediate problems. He needed a little time and a stake to get out of town. It looked as if Melissa needed a stake to stay.

Lucky considered his options. Without a horse or enough funds to buy one, he had reached the end of the line. But he still had his lucky coin. He glanced over her shoulder. Silver Wind was rough, but it looked like a prosperous enough town to have a saloon or two. Where there were a saloon and miners, there was sure to be a poker game. And Lucky Lawrence needed to get lucky—real quick.

He watched her expression turn into one of pleading. He knew he wasn't her James, even if she didn't. But all things considered, Melissa Grayson might be a temporary way out of the trap into which he'd been so neatly maneuvered. If he used a false name, the wedding ceremony wouldn't be legal, so long as it wasn't consummated.

Consummation. That and the obvious curves of the woman standing close enough to be kissed, might make that part of the solution a trial.

"Darlin'," he said, and swept the bride into his arms. When he kissed her the first time, he knew that whatever he did, he had to be careful, else he'd end up in a situation he would be reluctant to end. When he kissed her the second time, he knew he'd better find that poker table fast.

The women cheered; the men grumbled.

"Well, let's get it done, preacher," Widow Sweeney said. "Right this way, Mr. Pickney," she said, and started toward the church at the end of the street.

"Pickney?" Lucky pulled his intended close and whispered in the beauty's ear as he started to follow. "You're sure you want to marry a man named Pickney?"

"I don't understand," Melissa said, trying to jerk away. "Of course I'm sure. We've been planning this for—weeks. Why are you behaving so strangely?"

"I'm sorry, darlin'," he murmured, drawing in the sweet smell of her and forcing himself to relax. "I just wasn't expecting everything to happen so quick. I was hoping we'd get acquainted again—first."

"James, please. I can't lose the school. You know our marriage has to take place immediately." Melissa glanced around, recognized the smirks on the faces of the women and the puzzlement on the faces of the men. She planted a smile on her face and let him hold her close. "You didn't have to...kiss me like that," she hissed. "I didn't think you were well enough to..."

He grinned. "It seemed like a good idea. Would have been better if you'd kissed me back, but we can take care of that next time."

Her voice rose. "Next time?"

"Now, sweetheart," he said loud enough for the crowd to hear. "I know I'm late, but you knew I'd be here as soon as I could." Under his breath, he asked, "By the way, how come you looked so surprised when you saw me?"

Melissa started. "I didn't expect you to be ..." She whispered behind her hand, "I mean, we've only corresponded by mail."

That was what he thought. She had sent for a groom. So Lucky Lawrence could become—what was his name? Oh, yes, James Harold Pickney. That name was a mouthful he wouldn't wish on anybody.

"You're so different from what I expected," she whispered, clenching her lips into a smile. "If I didn't know you were James, I'd ask who you are."

"And I'd say, I'm the man who's going to keep you out of jail, darlin'." He leaned close to her ear. "You must have caused a real ruckus in this town."

"You're wearing a gun. And you've grown a mustache. You look more like an outlaw than a scholar and gentleman."

"Scholars and gentlemen have mustaches."

"But I don't think they look like you," she said, still trying to keep their conversation as private as possible.

"You know, that's the trouble with women; they think too much. Nice town," Lucky said, nodding to the entourage sweeping him and his bride toward the church at a determined pace. "I see you have a hotel. And a saloon," he said.

"Where's your luggage?" someone asked.

"It got stolen, along with my horse."

"The saloon is the one place you want to avoid," the

heavyset woman who'd accompanied Melissa onto the platform said.

"Why?"

"Because of Black Bart. He hangs out there. Of course, I guess Melissa told you what she tried to do to Bart."

Melissa. Her name was as feminine as her smell. "Of course, and if *my* Missy did it, I'm sure it needed doing," he said with as much pride as he thought a man ought to have when defending his woman.

"You wouldn't think so if he'd died. She's lucky the bullet just grazed Ted's arm."

That brought Lucky's forward march to a halt. "You shot a man?"

"He wasn't a man, darling," Melissa said, digging her fingertips into her intended's arm. "He was a boy. He didn't die. It was a mistake."

"You meant to kill him?"

Melissa felt a quaking inside her chest. She wasn't certain whether it came from the man who'd taken her arm or the feel of his pistol against her hip. He looked down at her with exaggerated dismay that said he wasn't a bit afraid. He had to be her James. Why else would he go along with the ruse as if he'd helped plan it? She couldn't blame him for her preconceived notions about the sickly James with whom she'd been corresponding. If she didn't figure a way out, she was about to marry a steely-eyed stranger who had singed her mouth with his kisses and her skin with his touch.

"I was simply trying to stop Bart from hurting Ted," she said. "But you're right, *James*, I didn't tell you everything and that isn't fair." She turned to face the women who had continued to form a guard unit. "Please, I need to speak with my fiancé—privately."

The men trailing along began to grumble.

"You've got the rest of your life to talk privately," one of the men said in a voice that seemed to brook no argument. "You either marry this man, or you pick another. Either way, you get married right now, or you go to jail for attempted murder. The city council and the congregation will hire a new teacher, and we'll put Mr. Pickney on the next train back East. He doesn't look much like a schoolteacher anyway."

"Not a good idea," Lucky whispered from behind her. "Looks like we'd better talk later."

In spite of his expensive coat and shiny boots, Melissa knew they were right. He didn't look like the kind of man to settle in as a schoolteacher, or the husband she was expecting. He seemed to be too hale and hardy. She was confused. If she were married, the school would be safe and she wouldn't have to deal with constant courtships. If she resisted, she'd have to pick one of these men. She had no choice.

"Are you ready, James?" she asked.

"James is ready," he said. "Let's get married." After all, she was marrying James Harold Pickney, scholar, and he was Lucky Lawrence, gambler.

"Would you like Sister Sweeney to play the organ?" Reverend Weeks asked as they entered the church.

"No," Melissa said.

"I think that would be a splendid idea," Lucky said. "Do you know a wedding song?"

Sister Sweeney plopped her plump derriere down and announced, "You betcha."

"No music," Melissa said tightly. "Let's just get married."

Lucky laughed, peering behind them at the onlookers. "My bride seems anxious, doesn't she? All right, sir, I'm ready for you to join James Harold Pickney and Miss Melissa Grayson in holy matrimony."

There were no church decorations and no rings. There was, however, a church filled with grumbling men standing between the couple and the door. For this wedding, nobody sat on the benches.

After a short prayer, the minister asked the appropriate questions, then beamed as he said, "I now pronounce you man and wife. All right, son, you can kiss the bride."

"Kiss her?" Lucky said. *Again?* This was getting a little too real for him. He could tell that Melissa was uncomfortable with the thought. But with an already skeptical audience, he couldn't see a way out. "Of course. I'm going to kiss Mrs. Pickney."

It was all for show, he told himself. The quick little peck he'd planned to deliver changed the moment his lips touched hers. The sweet sensation was considerably more enjoyable than the painful pinch she administered or the miserable smile she cast over the attendees as she turned toward the congregation.

"All right. I expect you to leave me alone," she announced to the men. "I'm a married woman now."

"For now," the tall man with the threatening look said. "But I'm willing to wait. One thing you learn when you dig for gold. Things ain't always what they seem."

3

Lucky followed his new bride down the church steps and out into the churchyard. "So, how are we traveling, wife?"

"In my wagon, and don't call me wife."

"So, what shall I call you? Mrs. Pickney? A mite formal, don't you think?"

"Listen to me, James," she said, broadening her smile as she spoke between lips frozen in place. "I'll explain all this later. For now, just do what I say."

Melissa was having a hard enough time keeping her feet from tangling in the folds of her borrowed wedding dress. Contending with a man who teased her was so different from what she'd expected. Her pulse still raced and her lips tingled as if they'd been singed. Then he took her elbow in his hand and drew her close. She felt as if she had a branding iron on her arm and a hot pot on her hip. "Let me go," she snapped and jerked away. "I told you to do what I say."

"Of course, Mrs. Pickney." In spite of her orders, he almost reached for her but caught himself in time and let her pitch forward. It was her call and he let her make it. He didn't count on the dress being caught by her knee, offering the wedding guests a tantalizing view of her undergarments and the curves they concealed. At least they fit. Where she'd gotten the garment she was wearing, he couldn't guess. Now that he was seeing the real woman, he could understand the lustful looks of the men in attendance.

With a look of sincere concern, he defied her directions by leaning over, pulling her dress down, and lifting her in his arms in one quick motion. "Sorry, darlin'," he said as he attempted to get a better grip. At that moment, a sharp object dug into his forearm. He let out a yell and dropped her legs. "You stabbed me!"

"I didn't stab you," she said under her breath. "The hat pin." She'd forgotten the widow had pinned up her skirt. She turned her back to the buggy and removed the offending item, gesturing with it. "Just get in, James. Please?"

Rubbing his arm, he swallowed a smile of his own. "That's an interesting place for a hat pin."

Melissa had the feeling her new husband was adept at masking his true feelings. His letters were proof of his spiritual nature, but in person his words were totally different. Her confusion mounted as the wicked gleam in his eyes contradicted her impression that he was a sickly, scholarly man. Melissa looked around. The townsfolk were eyeing her in disbelief, and the male saloon patrons were nudging each other and looking at Bart as if they expected him to take her away from James. Then she caught sight of Bart's pistol and made her decision. Any doubt she'd had before vanished. She was Mrs. James Harold Pickney IV. She was Melissa Pickney.

You did what you had to do to save the school, not to mention staying out of jail, Melissa Grayson. And if she'd made a mistake, it was too late now.

Taking a deep breath, she looked up at her new husband and smiled sweetly. "I'm sorry, Jamie. It's just that I am a little nervous. I mean, we haven't seen each other in sooo long and getting married—well, it is a bit scary for a woman."

"Sooo long," he repeated, choking back a laugh. Melissa might be a schoolteacher, but with her quick wit and beauty, she could have gone on the stage. His curiosity was growing by leaps and bounds. Too bad there was to be no wedding night. He had the feeling it would be very interesting.

"Now, which is your wagon, my beauty?"

She pointed toward her horse with one hand and tried to put some distance between her breast and his chest with the other. It didn't seem to matter that there was a bulky coat between them, her heart was pounding so that he surely must feel it. She shivered.

"Ah, darlin', it is a bit cool for October, isn't it? And you're not wearing a shawl." He deposited her in the wagon, slipped out of his dandy coat, and draped it over her. "Is that better?"

But his new wife didn't answer. Still holding the hat pin in her hand, she was staring at him with her mouth wide-open. What was wrong? Maybe it was the beaver hat he'd pilfered from the city slicker on the train. If he could see himself, he'd probably be just as addled. Ripping off her veil, he removed his hat and plopped it over the mass of golden hair that spilled across her shoulders, then stepped up into the wagon with her.

One of the onlookers untied the horse's reins and pitched them at Lucky. He gave the horse a tug to the right and got the vehicle back into the rutted street. "Okay, what now, Mrs. Pickney? I'm yours. Let's go home, horse."

"His name is Arthur," she said. "As in King Arthur. And he knows the way."

Lucky let Arthur have his way, while he looked more closely at the business establishments along the main street. The buildings were actually wood, not just canvas sheeting like many of the early mining towns had been. There were at least fifteen businesses spread out along the street. In the distance behind the businesses, he could see several homes with glass windows and curtains.

"Doesn't look much like Camelot," he observed.

"You know Camelot," she said with a pleased sigh. "Oh, James, I was beginning to wonder."

He could have told her that his mother had read it to his sister and he'd listened. But he kept quiet. Suddenly it seemed important that her wedding day be special, even if he wasn't her husband. "Which way, Guinevere?"

"*Where rose the mountains, there to him were friends/Where roll'd the ocean, thereon was his home,*'" she quoted. "Well, there's no ocean like Byron's, but we do have a mountain stream."

He looked at her quizzically. "Byron?" popped out before he thought.

"*Childe Harold's Pilgrimage,*" she said. "The poem

by Lord Byron, my favorite poet. Don't tease me, James. You know *Childe Harold* far better than I."

Fortunately, his reply was cut off by the approach of a horse. Black Bart rode alongside the wagon. "I'm thinking there's something wrong with all this, teacher. Can't figure it out, but I'll just be keeping an eye on you, Mr. James Harold Pickney."

"Just so long as the eye is on me and not Mrs. Pickney," Lucky said, urging the horse forward.

"You're so different from what I expected," she finally said. "I thought you'd be more..."

"More what?"

"Well I mean, you've been ill for so long. I wasn't prepared for you to look so...so healthy."

"And I thought it was the coat and hat. I wouldn't have blamed you if you'd changed your mind when you saw it."

She rubbed the fur trim on the coat collar. "I like the coat. It's very stylish. It's the...gun belt I wasn't expecting. It makes you look more like an outlaw than a scholar."

"Would that disappoint you?"

"What a strange question."

"So, give me a strange answer."

"Disappointment has nothing to do with it. I chose you because I thought we'd get on well together. After your sister told me all about you when we roomed together, and you and I corresponded for over a year, I thought I knew you."

"I don't know if a person ever knows another one," he said, conscious that he'd disappointed her somehow.

"I guess you're right. But we're married now and the

important thing is that our marriage will stop the men in town from fighting over me. I think you'll like living in Silver Wind, and with any luck, your health will improve."

"With any luck, I'll live a very long time because of our marriage," Lucky agreed. "For that I thank you."

She swallowed hard and forced herself to look at him. "I want to thank you too, James. I didn't mean to sound like such a shrew, and I really appreciate your agreeing to our marriage. Sooner or later I'd be run out of town, or sent to jail."

"Not if you married Bart. I can see why you wouldn't want that, but wasn't there another man in Silver Wind who would have served your needs? Marrying a man you've never met is a risk, isn't it?"

She blushed. "You don't understand. I never intended to marry you or anyone else. I expected to remain a spinster. I've seen what marriage does to a woman who is unhappy. And what happens to the man. I never wanted that."

"Little late for that, darlin'."

"But our marriage won't be real. We agreed that we'd be as brother and sister. You haven't forgotten that, have you?"

"Brother and sister," he repeated. "That's what we agreed to." No warm-blooded man would marry this woman and act like her brother. He was having trouble remembering that the marriage couldn't be consummated. But it had to be that way. He was helping her and she was helping him—temporarily—then he'd head back to New Orleans.

"So long as we can convince Bart," she added.

This was becoming more complicated than he'd

expected. He stole a glance at Melissa, huddled as far away as possible from him on the seat. He'd been right when he'd said she was an extraordinarily beautiful woman. She had creamy skin and blue eyes that could churn like an ocean in a storm. He knew, for he'd seen that face back at the depot when he'd kissed her.

He held the reins loosely and let Arthur find his own way, while he considered what he'd done. He had no horse and little money. He was being chased by a man whose reputation had turned out to be even worse than he'd been told. Louisa was free and he didn't regret his part in that. He just hadn't counted on Cerqueda being a man who wouldn't give up. And who wasn't the kind of man who'd be willing to negotiate. Going along with the mistaken identity had seemed like a good idea at the time.

Miss Melissa Grayson thought she was a woman who could look after herself. She decided to marry a man she obviously had never seen. By taking advantage of her situation, Lucky realized that he had put her in a precarious situation and she didn't even know it. That bothered him, and Lucky didn't like the feeling. Maybe this time he'd stepped into a situation he might not be able to talk himself out of—and he wasn't thinking only of Cerqueda.

Melissa had no choice in whether or not she got married. He could see that. And they'd gone through a ceremony. Clearly he'd made her situation worse. The dilemma was whether or not he should confess the truth. Before he decided, a few well chosen questions were in order. "Why wouldn't you agree to waiting a few days before we got married?"

"I didn't have a choice," she said, now sitting straight on the seat. "Why did you mislead me in your letters?"

He stalled. "How did I do that?"

"You said . . . you were not well enough to teach; that your asthma made it difficult for you to breathe. I thought the air out here might help you. That we might help each other, but . . ." Her voice broke off. "Never mind. I can understand why people don't always tell the truth in their letters. You never expected us to meet. This must all be a shock."

"Yes, I'd have to say it is. I mean, I didn't expect you to be so beautiful."

"And I didn't expect you to be some kind of dark stranger." *Taller and more powerful than I ever imagined. You haven't shaved, and the dark stubble on your face truly makes you look like some kind of outlaw. And I'm afraid. I'm afraid because I like it.*

"You're right, Melissa, I'm afraid I misled you."

"It doesn't matter," she said as she reached over and took the reins. "I'm the one who talked you into coming out here. This is my fault. I don't care what kind of man you are. You're my husband now and that will keep me out of jail. So long as I am married, I won't lose my school, and the rest . . . well, all you have to do is stick around long enough for the citizens of Silver Wind to see what kind of education I'm going to offer their children. I came out here to build a real school and I intend to do it. Three months, James, then you can go. By then they won't care whether I'm a widow or my husband just ran off. Promise me."

Her cheeks were flushed and her eyes filled with moisture. He couldn't fail her. Maybe he wouldn't have to. Three months, she'd said. Until the New Year. Well, that would be just about long enough to get Cerqueda off his back. Either the man would give up and go back to Texas, or if worse came to worst and Cerqueda turned up in Silver Wind—well, he'd cross that bridge when he came to it. Cerqueda might be a killer but he was also a gambler, and a real gambler would never be able to turn down the kind of challenge Lucky would offer—once he thought of one.

Lucky glanced at his bride and smiled. Right now he had nothing to do that he couldn't put off. Why not stay and help Melissa? As James Harold Pickney IV, he'd be safe from Cerqueda until he could replenish his empty coffers, and Miss Melissa Grayson would save herself and her school.

He didn't feel good about it, but his feelings didn't count.

Melissa drove Arthur at a fast clip. With James suddenly silent, they left Silver Wind behind and headed toward the San Juan Mountains ahead. She hoped James would understand her father's vision for his school. He'd written, *Dearest Melissa, I'm so sorry that your mother didn't live to see it, but Grayson Academy will be the finest school in the West.* Well, it might be, if she could stop the local people from fighting her every time she tried to broaden the horizons of her students.

"I don't know much about how you do things out here," James said, "but isn't the school a long way out of town?"

"He built the school on land he already owned. It was originally his mining claim."

"His claim?" Lucky's voice sounded skeptical.

"It turned out that there never was a mine. He panned just enough gold from the stream to build a school and the dormitories. He finished the small house I live in. Then before he could send for me, he got sick."

"From what I've heard, mining is a hard life. I thought about trying it, but book learning seems a lot easier."

Melissa glanced at him sharply. "James, you never mentioned that you were interested in mining."

He gave a weak laugh. "I was once. Now I'm more into filling—" He almost said his "pockets with gold", then at the last minute changed it to, "filling minds, than shovels."

The kind of answer she expected from her James, she decided. He continued to surprise her by being different in person than in his letters. And then he'd say something that touched her. She hadn't expected anything to be easy, but their response to each other was not only intellectually but physically unsettling. And Melissa didn't like being unsettled. She'd spent the last year of her life planning her future. When her father died, she'd learned that being successful meant having goals and working toward them. Now she was worried. Her Jamie hadn't been a threat on paper, but this James just wouldn't conform. The fine coat and hat he'd been wearing had been what she'd expected. But once he'd removed the coat and revealed the gun belt, the black frock coat, and trousers beneath, she'd been stunned. This James was too big and wicked-looking. His irreverent way of grinning threw her into a state of confusion that made her feel like a kite in a strong wind. If she was going to make this arrangement work, she had to get past her reaction to him as a man.

She tried desperately to shake off the high edge of

stimulation Jamie, the man, cast and turn her thoughts to the gentle teacher he'd claimed to be. "Out here, children are accustomed to traveling long distances to school. But sometimes the weather is too bad. That's why I'd hoped to take in boarding students."

"Wouldn't it be easier to just build a new school back in town?"

"Not unless you are willing to invest in the construction."

She'd surprised herself with her reply. Until now, she hadn't dared hope that James would be willing to contribute financially to Grayson Academy. In fact, no mention had been made of money at all. She'd simply assumed that because James's sister was boarding at the exclusive school where Melissa had been teaching, they were wealthy. That and the fact that James had never been well enough to work. But maybe she'd been wrong. Since money hadn't been the object, she hadn't thought of their marriage in those terms.

"Sorry," Lucky confessed, "I'm strapped. Eh, did I tell you I had money?"

"Well, no," she confessed. "In fact, we never discussed money, did we?"

They were approaching the Academy. Melissa tried to see it from James's point of view. He'd come from New York City where, according to him, every kind of building and every nationality in the world were pressed together. Still, what he was seeing had to be a disappointment. It had been to her the first time she'd seen it. The school building was attractive, though even Melissa questioned its location at the very edge of a stream gushing from an outcropping of rock at the base of the mountains. In the spring, the water had come dangerously close to the school. The nearby dormitories were made up of wings built on either side of her tiny house; one for the boys and one for the girls. They were crude but serviceable.

All this was hers, and when the sun came up over the rocky mountaintops, she felt as if she were breathing in the sheer beauty of the morning. She might fault her father for his choice of location, but in spite of the abandoned mining shacks marring the mountainside, she could never fault him the peace and hope Colorado promised.

And she forgave him. After all, he was a scholar like her new husband. She glanced quickly at James, expecting to see dismay. Instead, she found interest. Maybe their venture was salvageable. But something about James still bothered her. She just couldn't figure out what it was.

As they drew nearer, a large lop-eared black dog with camel-sized feet came racing toward them, barking wildly.

"What in hell is that?" Lucky asked.

"That's Mac, my dog. Quiet, Mac!"

"I'd have sworn it was a small horse," Lucky said, as Arthur ignored the dog and headed toward a lean-to that was attached to the end of one of the dormitories.

"Put Arthur in the corral," Melissa said as she gathered up the massive skirt of the awful dress she was wearing, and shimmied down.

"Corral?" Lucky lifted an eyebrow and followed. With Mac dancing about his feet, he unharnessed the horse and gave him a pat on his haunches, sending him off to the corral.

"Fine construction work," he said, eyeing the barbed wire from the building to the rocks and back.

"My fingers are still nicked from the barbs," Melissa said, "but I did it. I've done a lot of things that I'd never done before I left Philadelphia."

The look James gave her was one of admiration. She felt an unwelcome shiver run down the back of her legs. Her breathing took a sudden lurch, and she knew that her plans to keep her distance were in jeopardy.

She'd had visions of her and James being able to teach their students about music and art and poetry, along with basic reading and writing. Perhaps they'd work in elocution and debate. She'd planned for history and geography to be interwoven with the study of the classics. But now she was worried. "I know it doesn't look like much, James, and I'm sorry if you think I got you out here under false pretenses. I was desperate. So"—she took a deep breath—"if you want to call off our arrangement after three months, I'll certainly understand."

"And how would you explain my sudden disappearance?" he asked, taking the bridle and harness into the lean-to and reappearing without it.

"Out here, men ride off every day to prospect, to find lost cows, to hunt. And many of them never come home again. It wouldn't be unusual for a woman to be left behind. I need help but I can do this by myself."

He looked at her for a long, silent moment. She was a proud one, she was. And determined, like his sister had been once. But she'd been forced to make her own way when he hadn't returned. He couldn't do that to another woman left alone.

"You're right, Mrs. Pickney, you could do this by yourself. But you need help. I may not be the man you expected, but I won't leave until you're ready for me to go. You asked for three months, you got 'em. Now, where's your room?"

"My room?" The shiver in the back of her knees froze, and she had to hold on to the wagon to keep from tumbling to the ground.

"Yeah. Where do you sleep?"

"Sleep?" she echoed. "Why?"

"I think it's time you got out of that...whatever it is you're wearing."

"It's the Widow Sweeney's wedding dress, and believe me, wearing it wasn't my idea. None of this was my idea. Come with me, Mac, leave Mr. ...James alone."

To her surprise, the dog obeyed, falling in step between them as if he were guarding her—or James.

"So, you didn't want to get married."

She came to a stop. "No, I didn't. But it became clear that I had no choice. It wasn't just my shooting Ted. There aren't many single women out here. Men just wouldn't leave me alone. Eventually...well, I had no choice but to take a husband to end the last situation. I don't expect you to be responsible for me...but I appreciate your agreeing to the marriage."

He could look at her and understand the problem. The men would be after her if there were a dozen available women in town. But it was Bart who brought the situation to a head.

She nodded. "If it weren't for Bart, I wouldn't have bought a gun. If I hadn't pulled the trigger, I wouldn't have wounded the mayor's son. People in Colorado seem to think women can't live without a man. I can. I did—I still can."

His gaze moved slowly across the school and the small rough house and dormitories close by. He didn't miss the meager stack of wood or the crude lean-to and fence corralling the horse. Everything had a temporary but functional look about it, as if the builder hadn't planned his work to be what it had become.

"I don't know, Melissa, but from the looks of this place, I'd say you need some help—desperately. And it looks as if it's going to be me."

Him? Of course it would be him. Oh, she hadn't thought that far ahead, but she'd imagined having James around; she just hadn't counted on the man she married. In spite of their conversation, her heart was racing and the weakness in her knees made her tremble. James was still a dark stranger. She'd brought home a man she didn't know. Pure frustration made her want to jerk that pistol out of his gun belt and shoot James Harold Pickney IV.

"I know this isn't New York, James, but if you'll give it a chance, I think you'll learn to love it as I have," she said, heading to the house. "If not, I'll say the Comanches carried you off. If I have to, I'll even marry Black Bart."

Lucky swallowed a laugh and followed. The dog hadn't taken his eyes off Melissa. His adoration was all over his goofy face. Lucky looked at the mountains. He was certain that when he looked at Melissa, his expression was pretty goofy too. In the face of disaster, she still had a sassy attitude.

"Mrs. Black Bart Jamison. That does have a ring to it. If he were the real thing, you might get on well. The

Black Bart written about in the dime novels was really a well-to-do man of San Francisco who robbed Wells Fargo stagecoaches primarily. He'd disappear for months, then reappear and rob a stagecoach and vanish again. Apparently he became an outlaw to settle old scores with the California establishment and left them little notes at the scene of his crime. But he was never a very successful robber."

"There's nothing well-to-do about Bart. He's just a miner who never struck it rich. He works in Colonel Curtis's silver mine over the other side of the mountain."

They reached the house, where she opened the door, lifting it so that its corner wouldn't scrape the floor as she pushed. Just as Lucky reached the door, she turned. "I know it will sound silly, but I'd rather you stay in the dormitory, James. We agreed that we'd be as brother and sister. Remember?"

"Of course," he replied seriously. "I'll just take Arthur, ride back into town, and get a room at the hotel."

The door opened. "You'll do nothing of the kind. What would people say?"

"They'd probably laugh at me, but I've been laughed at before. Relax, Melissa. I'm not going to attack you. You're safe with me."

"It's the dormitory or the lean-to with Arthur," she ventured, "for three months."

He leaned his shoulder against the building. "The dormitory, it is. I'm a man of my word. But what happens if I like the idea of being married?"

Liked the idea of being married? She quelled a shudder that she didn't want to identify and let out a deep sigh. He was right. She was stuck in a mess of her own making. James wasn't what she'd expected, but maybe she'd misrepresented herself to him. She was full of sass and grit, not tea parties and museums as she'd written. And she'd embellished their future together.

She supposed her letters were a wish list. Grayson Academy wasn't the kind of school she'd led him to believe. It would be someday, or it could be if she had some help, a little time, and—she admitted—more money. But James had misrepresented himself to her as well. She'd expected Lord Byron and she'd gotten a smooth-talking, handsome devil who looked like he was more experienced with a gun than a McGuffey Reader.

It made no sense. Everyone in her life had left her. Now that she wanted to be alone, she'd married a man with a streak of conscience who apparently was not the leaving kind. And she didn't want him to leave. That thought swept through her like the jolt of the first taste of hot, strong coffee in the morning. Maybe she should just use that concern to her own advantage. For whatever reason, James seemed agreeable to staying—temporarily. Fine. He was her husband, but she didn't have to be his wife. She'd stated her position on that clearly. They'd be as brother and sister.

"All right, James," she said. "You want to stay. Fine. I'll give you a quilt and a pillow. The boys' dormitory is the building between the house and the school."

He gave her a hangdog look and an exaggerated sigh. "All right, but couldn't we eat first? It's been a long time since I've been sent to bed without my supper."

"Eat?" she echoed.

"Eat. You can cook, can't you?"

"I'm a very good cook. But there's no fire in the stove

and I didn't prepare anything before I left." The truth was she'd been in a state of agitation with tons of questions running through her mind. Had she done the right thing? Would James be on the train? What would happen if he wasn't? She'd been too preoccupied to think of food. Then she'd seen James and he'd been the only thing she'd thought of since.

She looked up and caught him watching her. Her father had always said that a person could read her mind by looking at her eyes; they flashed from blue to green and back again as she worked her way through a problem. She had the uncomfortable feeling that James was doing just that.

"You're right. Today was your wedding day. We should have celebrated by having a meal in town."

"Doesn't matter," she snapped.

"Look," he said, "I'll build a fire, while you go into your bedroom and take off that dress."

"But..." she stammered, trying desperately to find an excuse to keep wearing the dress. The thought of removing her clothing while a stranger was in the next room was daunting.

"On the other hand," he nodded, "we are married, so if you need some help with your buttons, I'll be glad to oblige."

Melissa scurried into the next room, closed the door behind her, and removed his fur-trimmed jacket and hat, while trying to unwind the peculiar knot of sensation in her lower body. She shimmied out of the dress without unfastening the buttons. Moments later she was dressed in a simple green day dress.

With a quick check in the tiny mirror that had been a present from her father on her tenth birthday, she straightened her unruly hair, then chastised herself for having such a concern. Pacing back and forth, she tried to plan her next move. Unfortunately, all she could think about was the feel of her new husband's lips, about his flashing white teeth and the black mustache that bunched in skepticism every time she answered one of his questions. Finally, she realized she'd better get back to James. No telling what he'd do if she delayed. Straightening her back, she strode purposefully into the main living area. A fire had been started but the room was empty.

Her husband was gone. And, she discovered when she looked out the door, so was Arthur.

4

October 5, 1888
St. Louis, Missouri

James Harold Pickney IV gave a labored gasp, struggled to sit up, then fell back, more disappointed than he'd ever been. For a year he and his younger sister's former roommate, Melissa, had corresponded. They'd both poured out their dreams and expectations to each other as strangers, never expecting to meet.

He knew all about her father and her determination to make a success of his school. But when she arrived in Silver Wind, she found that her father had misled her. His school was in a little mining town with few students, and so far as James could tell, there was little hope for more. James hadn't mentioned his idea to Melissa yet, but if the mountain air helped his lungs, it was his thought to change the focus of the school to that of a place where students with problems like his own could board, receiving both instructions and a chance to regain their health. If only he could stay well enough to get there.

The truth was, he'd done the same thing to Melissa as her father. He hadn't lied to her; he'd told her of his health problems. But he had exaggerated his accomplishments. And if he'd given his best friend's physical description instead of his own, it was a harmless gesture to a woman he'd never meet. Long ago, he'd learned that his illness had sapped him of his full growth. In a family of tall men who bore their position and authority well, he'd been thin and frail. James—Jamie, the scholar—had never taken part in the family banking business. He'd never sailed or ridden horses at their summer home in the Hampshires and he'd never been with a woman.

Then her proposal of marriage had come, and he knew he'd never have such an opportunity again. Poor Jamie Pickney, who'd longed desperately for a grand adventure, was being offered more than he'd ever dreamed of. Without discussing his decision with his family, he'd agreed to the marriage, loaded up a year's supply of medications, and headed for Colorado. He might not survive. She might even reject him when he arrived, but Melissa Grayson had opened a whole new world, and he'd thrown caution, and a lifetime of being careful, to the wind. James Pickney was going out West. James Pickney was going to take a wife.

And it had been a grand adventure until he'd reached St. Louis and collapsed. The damp weather settled in his chest and his weakened lungs didn't want to breathe. The climate in the West might be beneficial, but there was a possibility that he might never get there to find out. The only thing he could do was hope that Melissa would get the telegram he'd paid one of the hospital employees to send. For a moment, he'd been tempted to contact his father, then changed his mind. If he were ever going to stand on his own two feet, now was the time. Either he'd recover or he wouldn't.

Beyond the curtain of his meager hospital room he heard voices.

"You gonna send it?"

"Nah. Waste of good money. He ain't gonna make it. And if he does, what woman's gonna want a dried-up weakling like him. If she's looking for a husband, she'd better pick herself out a healthy one. Be better if she thinks he changed his mind."

Maybe the voice was right, Jamie thought. He'd struggled for so long. It wasn't that he didn't like books and education; he did. It was all he'd ever known. Secretly, he'd read every dime novel he could find. Pretending to be a reckless, gun-toting sheriff wasn't just a game for boys. But it was a game. He'd come so close to living out his fantasy. He closed his eyes and drifted off into a world that was more than sleep and less than death.

Melissa stared at the empty corral and swore. Arthur was gone. Married one day and her new husband was gone. He was a low-down, lying, horse-stealing thief. She should have known it the moment she'd caught sight of James Harold Pickney IV. Big and dark and wicked-looking, he'd stunned her. After that, everything had moved too quickly. Mr. Shakespeare's three weird sisters couldn't have conjured up the kind of spell she'd been under.

Jamie had described himself as being a very ordinary man with dark hair. The man she'd married matched that description. But he was taller than she'd anticipated, and rather than thin, she'd call him lanky. His arms were strong and his chest was hard, much more solid than she'd have expected of a man who'd suffered from a breathing problem all his life. He was no outdoorsman; after all, he'd been confined to his bed for much of the time. Still, Jamie had the look of a man who'd spent some time in the sun. There were little lines radiating away from his eyes, as if he'd squinted a lot. And she couldn't forget his gray eyes—dancing, wicked eyes that matched his wicked grin.

None of this made sense to Melissa. His actions made no sense. Her reaction made no sense. She suddenly thought of Sir Walter Scott's words: *O what a tangled web we weave/When first we practice to deceive!* Now that she could believe.

Well, it was done, whatever *it* was. If he didn't want to eat, so be it. She had to get ready to teach her students tomorrow—if she had any students tomorrow. Moments later, she was entering the schoolroom, where she allowed a sigh of pride to escape. No matter what her father might have done in the planning of his school, he hadn't skimped on its interior. There were neat wooden benches and desks, inkwells and pens, a large slate on the wall behind an unusual platform on which the teacher's desk and chair were placed. In one corner was an iron potbellied stove. Two windows with real glass and shutters covered the wall facing the mountains. But more than that, there was a division within the room whereby the younger students occupied one side and the older students the other. It might not be as finished as the academy in Philadelphia, but it was a fine schoolroom.

And it was hers, as were the new dormitory sleeping quarters and the tiny two-room house her father had built for the two of them. With the new school year ready to begin in earnest, she'd hoped to have boarding students. Maybe now she would.

From the corner of her desk she picked up a piece of chalk and wrote on the board. *My name is Miss Grayson.* But that wasn't true. She was married now. She wiped the board clean and once again, she started to write, *My name is Mrs. Pickney.*

And my husband is gone.

Lucky rode Arthur up the draw. Mac loped along beside the big horse. Lucky told himself he was going after a fat rabbit for their supper. What he'd really done was get out of the small house so he could think. What had he gotten himself into? When Louisa had told him that Cerqueda wouldn't give up on finding him, he'd scoffed. Leaving a false trail would give Louisa time to get to her father and safety. But the Temperance League women back in Durango said Cerqueda killed the bartender and was looking for a gambler. That forced him to take Cerqueda more seriously. Now it wasn't just him anymore. Rescuing Louisa could put Melissa in danger and she would have no idea of it. Suppose Cerqueda found him? What would happen to his new wife?

He ought to be putting as much distance between himself and Melissa as possible. Instead, he was stalling, telling himself that he needed to find a way to buy a horse and refill his purse. Lucky had always lived by his wits, and some of the things he'd done in his life hadn't been exactly legal. But after he'd lost his sister, all his actions had been to benefit someone else, and he'd considered them morally correct.

Until now.

Until now, he'd never gone so far as marriage to rescue anyone before, though technically Lucky Lawrence wasn't married. James Harold Pickney had married Melissa Grayson.

Arthur picked his way across the creek and into the foothills. It was clear that this was new territory to him and he moved slowly. In the distance Lucky could hear a muted sound. Explosions, perhaps from a mine somewhere up there. He'd heard the San Juans were the highest mountains in Colorado, maybe even anywhere. Snow came early and stayed late, so providing dormitories to take in boarding students made sense—providing she could find firewood and keep enough food on hand.

With his revolver in hand, Lucky kept his eyes peeled, waiting until Mac finally scared up a pair of rabbits and took off after them. He missed the first one, but his bullet found the second. It crumpled in a heap. Lucky captured his prize and headed back to the school. He wasn't a hunter but he knew enough to skin his prey and dress it. He returned Arthur to his corral, fed him some oats he had found in a barrel under the lean-to, and made his way back to Melissa Grayson's house. She met him at the door.

"I thought you'd decided to leave," she said.

Her face was smeared white with flour, and behind her he could see a pan half-full of biscuits ready to bake. The smell of perking coffee tortured his empty stomach. It was clear to Lucky that she might have believed he was gone, but that she hadn't been sure.

"I considered it," he admitted.

"Why didn't you?"

"I was hungry. I thought we ought to have our wedding dinner." He held out his rabbit.

"You killed a rabbit?"

"No, the little critter jumped out from behind a rock and said, 'I give up.' Of course I shot it."

She was still stuck on his words. *Wedding dinner.* She took the rabbit and stepped back, allowing him to come inside. "Thank you, James."

"Did you really shoot the mayor's son?"

"Not intentionally. He was trying to stop a fight."

Lucky grinned. "You were in a fight?"

"No, not me. Bart tried to . . . well, he took my arm and wouldn't let go. Young Ted hit Bart but he was no match for that brute. I had to stop Bart from hurting him. I fired in the air but my bullet hit the church bell and ricocheted off and hit Ted. The bell fell and broke."

"What's wrong with the people in this town? They ought to appreciate what you did. A beating could have been a lot worse for the boy. A bell can be replaced."

Melissa made her way to the corner of the room and laid the rabbit on the cook table. She filled her frying pan with grease and set it on the stove to melt while she cut up the rabbit. By the time she'd rolled the pieces in flour, the grease was bubbling. The sweet potatoes she'd baked the day before were returned to the oven to heat while the biscuits baked and the rabbit fried.

She turned the meat in the grease and when it was done, removed it and sprinkled flour in the pan to brown, added a little water from the bucket by the door, and the gravy thickened. She hadn't looked at James but she was constantly aware of him, and that made her feel awkward. Now, she lifted her gaze. He was sitting in her rocking chair in front of the hearth, watching.

"You do that well," he said. "I would have thought a lady like you wouldn't be at home in the kitchen."

"I taught in a boarding school for young women. Since I had no family to go home to and I needed to earn my keep, I helped out in the kitchen. It was the warmest place in the house." *You know that*, she wanted to say. But he appeared not to remember. Maybe he didn't.

Maybe it was time to find out the truth.

She put two plates and cutlery on the table, along with two coffee cups, then brought the meat and gravy. With the tail of her skirt, she opened the hot oven and removed the biscuits and potatoes. Finally, she poured the coffee and took her seat on the bench. "I hope you washed your hands, Mr. Pickney," she said, indicating that he was to join her.

"I did," he said as he slid his long legs under the table. "In the creek when I dressed the rabbit—and isn't Mr. Pickney a little formal? My name is—James," he said.

"Is it?" she asked, giving him a long look. "I don't think so. I don't think you're James at all. Who are you?"

The moment of truth. He owed it to her for her own protection. "Does it matter who I am?" he asked. "Let's just say I'm the husband you married, even if I'm not the one you expected."

"But you're not a scholar. Tell me the truth, please. You're not James Pickney, are you?"

"I'm not James Pickney."

She'd known from the beginning. She just hadn't wanted to face the truth. Clasping her hands, she took a deep breath and asked the inevitable question. "If you're not James, who are you?"

"Folks call me Lucky. Lucky Lawrence. I'm a gambler."

It made sense now; his appearance, his teasing. He didn't remember what she'd written to James because he was someone else. "Why did you pretend to be James? Where is he?"

"I don't know. I've never laid eyes on James Harold Pickney IV."

"You're a thief," she accused. "You stepped off that train and stole Jamie's identity. Why?"

"It seemed like you were in a fix. You needed a husband and I . . . well, let's just say I needed a place to stay for a while. Seemed like a fair exchange. I see now that it was a mistake."

"A mistake?" She stood and walked over to the window. "James is missing. He could even be dead. And I'm Mrs. Lucky Lawrence, wife of a gambler."

"The preacher married you to Mr. Pickney. I'm thinking that for the time being it's just as well if we leave it that way until we figure out what to do. I don't want to have to explain the mistake to Bart."

She didn't answer but he could feel her confusion.

He stood and walked over to her, standing close enough to hear her tight breathing. "I caused the problem, Melissa, and I'll figure out a way to fix it. For the next three months, I'm James and you're—my wife. For now, James is hungry."

5

It was midnight when Melissa heard Mac barking, not in alarm but excitement. Normally she would have charged it off to his cornering a rabbit. But tonight was different. There was a man sleeping in the dormitory. She sat up, listening. If Mac followed his normal pattern, the animal would outsmart him and get away. But tonight that didn't seem to be happening.

Where was her gambler husband, Lucky? No, James—she had to continue calling him James. A mistake would invite suspicion, which she couldn't afford. Melissa pulled on her wrapper, slipped her feet in her shoes, and padded into the living area. No sound of any movement that her new husband was coming to help keep her safe. With a silent swear, Melissa lifted her father's shotgun from its place by the door and crept out onto the porch.

She'd wanted someone who wouldn't interfere in her life, but what kind of man wouldn't get up and check on an obvious problem? Unless . . . maybe there was something wrong.

Hugging the shadows alongside the house, she hurried to the outside entrance to the dormitory where Lucky was sleeping. The door was open. Quietly, she crept inside. "James? Are you in here, James?"

There was no answer. She waited. Between Mac's barks, the silence told her that Lucky wasn't there. Retracing her steps, she returned to the yard.

Like a giant burning candle, the moon threw a finger of brightness down the draw through which the stream flowed. Mac was dancing along the bank, lunging forward, then pulling back.

Taking a deep breath, Melissa stepped out into the moonlight and started toward the dog, her heart in her throat. When she got closer, there was a ripple of water and a dark shape rose and headed toward the bank, hugging the shadows.

"Don't move!" she called out, took aim, and hoped shooting the shotgun was just a matter of pulling the trigger.

"Murdering your husband with a shotgun on your wedding night isn't a smart idea," Lucky said, reaching forward. "You could drown me and no one would know."

At that moment, Mac grabbed something and ran off dragging his prize behind.

"Mac! Get back here!" Lucky shouted.

Mac started a new round of barking.

"Hush, Mac! Get back on the porch. You, Mr. Lawrence—I mean, James, what are you doing?"

"I w-w-was taking a-a-a bath. Don't suppose you have an extra blanket, do you? Mac seems to have run off with my clothes." He was hugging his chest and moving about in the water.

That was when she realized that he was totally nude.

"What are you doing now?" she asked, realizing how foolish her words sounded even as she was speaking them.

"At the moment, I'm f-f-freezing to death. You're going to have to give me something to wrap myself up in, or turn your back. I'm coming out."

Whirling around, she ran back into the house, leaned the shotgun against the wall, and grabbed a quilt. She reached back and held it out through the crack in the door. She heard the sound of his bare feet on the wooden floor of the porch, and the quilt was claimed.

"I suggest in the future you take one with you, or heat water and use the tub inside, as I do." She turned and scurried into her bedroom, listening as he entered the kitchen.

"Hot water and a tub? Sounds good. I'll try it next time. Mac, you're supposed to be on guard duty, not retrieval, though I think a prairie dog might be more fierce."

"Mac can be fierce," she snapped. "I don't suppose you've read Shakespeare, but Mac's full name is Macbeth, an evil character in one of Mr. Shakespeare's plays."

"No, I haven't," Lucky replied, huddling near the stove. He could have told her that he'd seen the play once in California, or a traveling show's version of it. Macbeth, tired from his romp with Lucky's clothes, was now snoring loudly in the corner. "It would take a good imagination to see Mac as evil."

"Macbeth is a warrior name. It was meant to inspire

him to be more aggressive. I just call him Mac." She leaned against the door frame, forcing herself to breathe deeply. "I'll admit my father had an unusual imagination. He said that people and animals live up to their names. What about your name? Are you lucky?"

"At cards? Yes. Otherwise, not always. I like your father's thinking. Imagination is an interesting thing. Sometimes it sets a man on edge when he least expects it."

Now he was standing just outside her bedroom door—too close. "Mr. Lawrence, since you're not a scholar, I don't expect you to try and prove yourself to be one."

"I reckon I don't have to be a scholar for my imagination to stir my senses. For me, a beautiful woman in a nightgown carrying a shotgun will do it every time. What does it take to stir yours?"

"Certainly not a nude man!" she snapped.

"And I didn't think you noticed," he said with a laugh.

She'd noticed.

"Sweet dreams, Missy. Mac, let's find my clothes."

"I don't dream," she answered.

Melissa left her bedroom and slammed the front door behind him. The wall shook. The shotgun crashed to the floor and discharged, spattering the opposite wall with buckshot. Mac went into a tirade and the front door opened with a crash, admitting the quilt-covered Lucky Lawrence.

"Melissa! Are you all right? Where are you?"

"I'm here," she said in a shaky voice.

Moments later he was pulling her to him, holding her close. His concern surprised her.

"What happened?"

"The gun fell. It went off."

He was dry but he was cold.

"You could have been killed," he growled.

The warmth of his breath feathered her cheek in the darkness, sending a shiver scissoring down her spine. She swallowed hard and let out a deep sigh as she pushed him away. "Thank you for your concern. But I wasn't hurt. You need to go to bed. If you want to sleep by the stove, I'll get more quilts. You can find your clothes tomorrow."

"How many times have you shot that gun?" he asked from the darkness.

"Once, in the air. It was my father's."

"Tomorrow I'll teach you."

"Tomorrow I have to teach my students," she said.

"Afterward, then. You can't stay here alone without being able to protect yourself."

Alone? He didn't have to remind her that she— they—were alone. Every inch of her skin prickled in awareness. As her eyes grew accustomed to the darkness, she realized that her white gown and wrapper stood out. Worse, a total stranger was in her living quarters, and he wasn't wearing any clothing. And as far as the world was concerned, they were married.

"I've been here alone for two years," she argued. "And I have Mac."

"Some protection he is," Lucky said. "He's already asleep."

She couldn't argue. He was right. "Please, Lucky, it's very late and classes begin tomorrow. You're cold. I'll get more bedding."

She retrieved her father's bedding from the chest

and returned to the room to find Lucky adding firewood to the stove. She laid out the blankets and quilts,
then returned the shotgun to its rack. "My students will
expect you to help in the classroom. I know you're not a
teacher, but could you start a fire in the schoolhouse
stove while I prepare our breakfast?"

"I can handle building a fire, but help in the classroom? I plan to ride into town in the morning. There is
something I have to take care of."

"Fine," she said, realizing that she was chattering
nervously. "And when you return, you can help with the
little ones. I'll teach the older children. Good night."
She couldn't bring herself to call him James and swallowed "Lucky," as she moved into her bedroom and
closed the door. There was no lock. She slid the trunk
against it, then acknowledged the futility of that move.
If Lucky Lawrence wanted to make this their wedding
night, she couldn't stop him.

She stood listening to him move around; then there
was silence. But the moon had set when she finally went
to sleep.

James Harold Pickney IV sat up, slowly forcing himself
to slide his feet over the side of the hospital bed. He'd
lost track of time, but the doctor who was treating him
said he'd been ill for over a week, little of which he remembered. His lungs were almost clear but he was very
weak.

For several moments he simply sat, allowing his body
to adjust to being upright. Then he caught the head-
board of the bed and let his feet touch the floor. His
legs were so weak that he swayed. Lord Byron couldn't

have felt any more spent after swimming in the Aegean Sea. But he wasn't Lord Byron. He wasn't even Melissa's knight in shining armor. He'd missed his own wedding. He didn't want to imagine what had happened to his dear friend. Had he sent a telegram or simply dreamed it? He could only get to Colorado and hope he was in time to save her from whatever horrible fate she'd feared.

"Mr. Pickney! What are you doing?" Agnes, the spinster nurse who'd bullied him into eating for the last three days, was standing in the doorway like a bulldog eyeing a bone.

"I'm going to walk around my room. Tomorrow, I'm going to put on my clothes and walk outside. Then I'm going down to the train station, where I'm going to buy myself a ticket to Colorado."

"But you're not well enough," she protested. "It'll take you at least two more weeks to regain your strength. You must wait until you're stronger."

"That's the trouble. I've been waiting all my life. If I wait until I'm well, I'll never get there." He straightened his back and took a step. Then another and another. He was very weak but he had to do this. For the first time in his life someone needed him, and he didn't intend to let her down—if he hadn't already. That's when he fainted.

The bright morning light woke Melissa. She lay for a moment, the memory of what had happened last night washing over her. Then she heard a sound in the room beyond. Her *husband* was still out there.

She crept quietly out of bed, shoved the chest aside,

and opened her door, peering through the crack. All she could see was the back side of a man wearing black trousers and a towel across his shoulders. He was leaning forward, his front half out of sight.

Apparently, he'd found his clothing. But what was he doing?

Curious, she pushed open the door.

"Come on in," he called out. "Fire's built in the schoolhouse, though I don't think you're going to need it. Looks like we're going to have a warm day."

He straightened up.

She didn't answer. Didn't the man believe in wearing clothes? At least only his chest was bare this time. She could see a strip of flesh between the towel he'd thrown across his shoulders and his water-spotted trousers, thanks no doubt to Mac's dragging them through the brush.

"Coffee's made, but I didn't know what you'd want for breakfast."

"What are you doing?" she finally asked.

"I'm getting ready to ride into town. What time does school start?"

"Eight o'clock."

He turned.

She gasped. He was shaving. Somehow he'd found her father's razor, heated some water, and removed most of the stubble on his chin. And his mustache. He'd shaved off his mustache. Somehow, without it, he looked as naked as he had the night before when he'd stood in the moonlight.

"I hope you don't mind my using these things," he said. "I thought you seemed a little disturbed about the way I look."

"Why...no," she stammered. If she'd been Pinocchio, her nose would be growing. "You didn't have to do that."

"Trust me, Melissa. I shaved because I *had* to. I wouldn't want to frighten the children." He turned back to the mirror he'd propped on the shelf over the sink and took a final sweep, then leaned forward to wash his face in the pan, wiped it, and turned back toward her. "What do you think?"

"You look...very different."

"And you're looking lovely this morning."

She glanced down at her nightgown, turned, and scurried back into her bedroom. While she performed her morning ablutions and pulled on a freshly laundered blue dress, she thought about what he'd said. He'd changed the way he looked because he had to. Why? And why was he going into town?

"Mr. Lawrence...Lucky?" she called out as she re-entered the kitchen area.

With Mac at his feet, Lucky tucked in his shirt and slipped his jacket on, buttoning it so that the streaks of dirt didn't show. He turned as she entered. "Yes, ma'am?"

"Why are you going into town?"

"I want to check with the sheriff, find out if he's heard anything from the real James."

She hadn't thought of that. She'd been more concerned with why he was willing to pretend to be James. "Are you a criminal?" she asked.

He lifted his eyebrows and seemed to think about his answer. "If you mean, am I wanted by the law? No, I'm not."

"But someone is after you?"

There was no reason to alarm her yet. But he couldn't lie to her. Somehow that seemed wrong. Instead, he said, "Let's say my last good deed didn't please everyone. Don't worry, dear wife," he cupped her chin in his hand and held her as he kissed her on the forehead, "you'll be safe with me." He moved out into the yard. "Oh, I'm taking Arthur. And you'd better call me James even when we're alone. Safer for both of us."

Safer? Why did that worry her? She stood in the doorway and watched as he saddled Arthur and climbed on. "Anything you want from town?" he asked, as if this morning was a normal occurrence.

"We could use more flour," she answered. "Will you be gone long?"

"Not long," he said. "After all, we're newlyweds."

Before she could respond, the sound of young voices and a wagon approaching, caught her attention.

"Students," she whispered. "They've come."

Lucky passed the wagon, gave Ted a nod, and let out a sigh of relief. It looked as if the people in town were living up to their word. Melissa Grayson had taken a husband, earning their support for the school. The four students in the wagon weren't enough, but it was a new beginning.

He rubbed his upper lip. Shaving his mustache was a new beginning as well. He could only hope that his outcome would be as successful as his bride's—or James's bride. Too bad he wasn't of a mind to be a married man. Melissa would be a favorable candidate. She was smart. She was determined and she was beautiful. He smiled as he recalled her standing in the doorway in her white nightgown, looking every inch the virginal bride. She followed him into the kitchen and he'd kissed her, a perfectly normal thing for a man to do if he were leaving. But he didn't want to leave her.

Lucky gave Arthur a tap with the reins and felt him break into a trot. At the top of the hill Lucky looked out over the valley in which the town had grown up. The sun draped over the mountains like golden syrup, waking the blue jays, who squawked as they darted across the sky in a flash of blue on blue. Yellow leaves trembled on the aspen tree, then fluttered to the ground. Here and there, between the spruce trees, water dripped from the rocks and gurgled out of angry spots where some prospector had dug into the ridges hoping his pick would hit gold. Lucky took in a deep breath of clear air. He felt like the first man to have ever drawn it into his lungs.

Going into town the morning after his marriage might seem strange to the citizens of Silver Wind, but Lucky knew he wouldn't be satisfied until he checked out the town saloon. He might be hiding out, but he had to find a way to pick up some money. Neither mining nor school teaching offered him a livelihood. Gambling was the only thing he knew. He patted his pocket, feeling the few coins he had left, and hoped they'd be enough for the flour Melissa needed. The flour would be his excuse for coming to town.

The valley widened into a flat space split by the narrow-gauge railroad track on one side of the mountain and Melissa's valley with the creek on the other. Between the mountains and the town, Victorian houses with yards and fresh paint bespoke the fortunes of the miners who'd struck it rich. Silver Wind was apparently the stopping-off spot between Durango and the mining farther north. The depot and the tracks were laid out behind the line of stores along the main street. Though small, the town seemed prosperous. He paid closer attention to The Dawson Banking Company, an assayer's office, several boardinghouses with signs that advertised baths and clean clothes, and Sweeney's Dressmaking and Millinery shop.

That explained the wedding dress Melissa had been wearing.

Behind the businesses were crudely built shacks that bespoke the fortunes of the prospectors and the families of those who hadn't been so fortunate.

Lucky rode past the businesses, giving a smile and a nod to the curious who stopped to stare at him. When he came to the general store he glanced up at the sign proclaiming Sizemore's General Store. Fortunately, it was next to the saloon, which he could then look at without being obvious.

He dismounted and tied Arthur to the rail in front of the store. As he headed inside, he heard angry voices coming from the saloon.

"Now look, I told you to go home! You better get on back to the mine before you end up in jail."

"You ain't throwing me out! I paid my tab like I always do."

"Miners," the store owner said, stepping out onto the wooden-planked sidewalk in front of his store. "Work like crazy, then go drink it all up and end up in jail. Go get the sheriff, Cob," he directed the man who followed him.

"Lot of good that'll do, but I'll get him," the second man said as he passed Lucky, shouting, "Sheriff, you'd better get up here!"

"Morning, Mr. Pickney," Sizemore said. "You're out pretty early, aren't you?"

Before Lucky could answer, Bart came plunging through the saloon doors, dragging a pretty woman with tightly coiled curls with him. "You been cozying up to me for weeks, sweet thing. I think I'll just take you up the mountain with me. If I can't have the teacher for a wife, you'll do."

She tried to pull away, yelling, "Let go of me, you crazy man. I wouldn't marry you if you asked me."

Bart picked her up, and holding on to both her hands with one of his, deposited her on his horse.

Lucky looked around. The customers in the saloon had come outside and stood watching. Cob Barnett was heading back toward the fracas, followed by Sheriff Vance, who was pulling suspenders over his shoulders. The sheriff stopped and turned back.

"Where you going?" Cob called out.

"Gotta get my gun."

"Oh, for heaven's sake," Sizemore said. "He'd do just as well without it. The old fool can't see, so all he does is fire it in the air."

The woman kicked out at Bart as he climbed on the horse behind her.

Lucky let out an oath. Avoiding trouble wasn't going to happen. He stepped into the street. "Morning, Bart," he said.

Bart looked down in surprise. "Well, well. Honeymoon over so soon? Maybe what the teacher needed was a real man?"

Lucky pulled back his coat and rested his hand on his revolver. "She's got one. But your party's over."

"My party? Ain't had no party—yet."

"Let the lady go, Bart."

"What? You want her too? Forget it, fella, she ain't no lady. Now get out of my way!"

"I don't think so."

At that moment a series of shots were fired from the street behind Lucky. Bart's horse reared up, and Lucky knocked the startled Bart to the street. As the sheriff reached the saloon, Lucky pulled the woman down and stood her on the sidewalk in front of the saloon.

"Thank you, but you made things worse for your wife. Bart is crazy over losing her. My name's Sable. The saloon belongs to me. Drop in and I'll give you a drink," she said as she reached up and kissed his cheek.

"Bart," Sheriff Vance said, brandishing his pistol, "how many times have I told you to leave Sable alone? Ain't none of the girls going nowhere with you, specially Miss Sable. Now climb up on your horse and get out of town."

Bart reclaimed his reins and mounted, his gaze focused on Lucky with such intensity that Lucky knew the woman was right. If marrying Melissa hadn't made Bart his enemy, this incident had. "Watch your back, Pickney," he said, and rode by.

Sizemore walked out into the street, followed by several women who'd been in the store. "That was a pretty slick move, Pickney," he said. "Sheriff, we're going to have to do something about Bart."

"I got here as quick as I could," the sheriff said. "You know he don't mean no harm. He's just disappointed that he didn't get the teacher. Sorry, Pickney. No offense intended."

"None taken," Lucky said. "Ought to turn those Temperance League women loose on Bart. They'd take care of him. Or, say, maybe that man they were talking about . . . that Cerqueda. Any word on him?"

The woman who'd dragged Melissa onto the depot platform had left her shop and joined the group. "Now why would a man like that come up here? Come to think of it, Mr. Pickney, what are you doing in town? I thought you were going to help your wife in the school."

Everyone was looking at him. Checking out the saloon for a poker game was going to be harder than he thought. "I am," he finally said. "Mrs. Pickney sent me for flour. I'd better get it and head back."

Moments later, Sizemore placed a sack of flour on the counter. "Bart usually manages to cause some sort of fuss every time he comes into town. Last month it was my store he tore up. He's broke now, so we won't see him for a while."

Lucky pulled out the change from his pocket. "How much?"

"I'll just put it on Melissa's . . . Mrs. Pickney's tab. She always settles up at the end of the month," the shopkeeper said. "Anything else?"

Lucky glanced around, his eyes settling on a shelf of hats. He'd passed up wearing the beaver hat he'd taken off the train. "I need a hat," he said, lifting a fine-looking black Stetson from the shelf and testing it for size. "This one will do. Now how about some work clothes?"

The store owner pulled out a gingham shirt and a pair of denim trousers with yellow thread along the seams. "These do?"

"Fine. Oh, and what about some canned peaches and a wedge of that hoop cheese there?"

"Certainly." Sizemore cut a slice of cheese, added it and the two cans to the counter, then wrote up the additional items in his ledger. "Appreciate your stepping in out there. Sheriff Vance is . . . well, let's just hope that outlaw Cerqueda doesn't decide to come here. We'd be in big trouble."

Lucky didn't reply. He left the shop, fastened his parcels on Arthur, and headed back to the school. With Vance as the sheriff, he'd be in big trouble too.

By eight o'clock Melissa had only four students: Ted Dawson, who claimed his wound was practically healed, Russ Pilcher, and the Sizemore twins, who made certain that everyone knew about the riot set off by the women of the Temperance League down in Durango. Eight-year-old Lucy and Mary Lee already understood the value of gossip, even imparting that the town was abuzz with talk of Miss Grayson's new husband. Their giggles continued to break out until Melissa threatened to send them to the woodpile. They quieted, but it was obvious that the first day of school was going to be a challenge.

By eleven o'clock she heard the whistle of the mining train heading back down the mountain beyond her canyon, carrying ore to Durango. The fire inside the schoolhouse had burned down but they didn't need it anymore. She suddenly recalled Lucky had said he'd made coffee, which had probably already boiled dry. She set Ted and Russ to work on their arithmetic and gave the twins chalk to practice writing their letters on the blackboard, while she ran back to the kitchen to check on the coffee. She'd arrived just in time. There were only a couple of spoonsful of liquid left.

Leaving the house, she glanced down the canyon.

A granite cliff jutted out into the valley, blocking her view of Silver Wind. If there'd been a rider, she wouldn't have been able to see him. What had Lucky really needed to check on?

Melissa felt a shiver of dread sweep over her.

Suppose this time he'd really left?

6

On the way back from town, Lucky found himself noticing things about the canyon, things he would not normally see. The small valley was separated into corridors by a series of rocky cliffs. To the left he could see the narrow-gauge railroad circling upward and out of sight. Though he couldn't see it, he knew that Grayson Academy, hidden by a cliff, lay to the right.

Though the morning sunlight warmed the valley, the towering San Juan Mountains were white-capped with snow. The layout of the rock formation trapped the wind, and when the sun went down, the temperature dropped. Where other streams were polluted by miners, the water from the melting snow above Melissa's school was clear. He could hear the water splashing against the rocks, then rolling away. The leaves of the white-trunked aspens skipped like children across the flat canyon where Silver Wind had sprung up.

Rounding the rocky abutment that jutted out into

the trail, he caught sight of a hawk sweeping across the sky. The bird seemed to rise and fall with the current before disappearing into a stand of spruce on a far mountain ledge. He'd heard a man say once that being in the mountains alone was as close to God as anyone ever got. Up to now, his close brushes with God had most often come when he was looking down the barrel of a gun. He'd spent his adult life on the move, leaving one place, heading for another, always searching.

He envied people who found where they belonged. He'd honored his mother by attending school long past the time he was interested. But afterward, he became a wild kid on the New Orleans dock, directing travelers to his mother's boardinghouse and learning to gamble for his own money. His school days had ended when he stowed away on a boat headed for the gold fields of California. He'd planned to hit it big, then come back for his younger sister and his mother. Instead, he'd ended up shanghaied and on a ship headed for the South Seas, which kept him away for over a year. By then, his mother was dead and his sister was gone.

After that, Lucky's life had taken him into the darkness of the world of a gambler, where men lured innocent young women like his sister into a false exciting life. During the day he'd either slept or traveled to the next town, always looking, never finding, forever wrapped in the lingering gray guilt of not being there to take care of his sister. New Orleans was home, but New Orleans was dark and painful. New Orleans was a secret. Here in the sunlight of the San Juan Mountains, there was a kind of stark truth.

Melissa, with her golden hair and sense of purpose, had found her place. And she was prepared to do whatever was necessary to keep it. He admired that. It was her father he didn't understand. Why choose such a spot to build a school? Their valley was just outside of town, yet hidden peacefully in the flat area surrounded on both sides by trees and sheer cliffs. Along the rocky precipices there were piles of rock, the abandoned attempts of earlier prospectors. The little mounds looked as if they'd been left by some prehistoric flying creatures who'd dug holes into the mountainside to lay their eggs.

The valley was rugged, yet there was something peaceful about the scene. The air, tinged with ice and the promise of snow to come, seemed cleaner, the sunlight brighter.

Arthur picked up the pace.

The school and Melissa's dormitories came into view. The students' wagon was still outside the corral, the horse inside. One wagon. One horse. Melissa stepped out of her living quarters and walked across the yard to the school. She walked with her head down. There was no spring in her step. Mac followed her slowly, as if he sensed that there was something wrong. Where was the courage that had brought her running from the cabin with a shotgun?

Suddenly, Mac broke into an excited bark and rushed out to welcome Lucky and Arthur. Arthur came to a stop. That silly dog made Lucky feel like he belonged. He sat studying the rough little school with the elegant name—Grayson Academy. Their marriage might have saved Melissa's school, but he hadn't truly considered what that meant. Her reputation was still on shaky ground. His original plan had been to hide out long enough for Cerqueda to give up and go back to

Texas—a week at the most. That would give him enough time to make some money, buy a new horse, and rest a little. Good plan. Everyone would benefit.

But now he couldn't do that.

It was made clear to him back in town that he wouldn't be able to walk into the saloon and ply his trade without doing damage to Melissa's school. But he was neither a teacher nor a miner. All he could do was gamble, and he couldn't gamble without harming Melissa. He had to stay—for now.

No matter how confident Melissa was about explaining his leaving, this time Lucky wasn't sure his conscience would let him ride away. He'd done that once, and he'd lost his sister.

He rode Arthur into the yard, dismounted, and unsaddled the horse. Removing the bridle, Lucky turned him into the makeshift corral with the other horse. He could fix the corral. That wouldn't replenish his coffers, but he'd at least earn his keep. Once the saddle and bridle had been put away, he took the flour and the cheese into the house. He'd bought the peaches on impulse. Now that seemed foolish. Maybe he'd hide them until later. He stored the cans under his bunk, then changed into his new clothes. It was time he headed for the school. Whatever Melissa had expected of Pickney had become his task. He just hoped he remembered enough of the schooling his mother had forced on him and his sister to avoid embarrassing Melissa. As he reached the door, he heard her speaking.

"Today I want to read to you from the poem *Childe Harold's Pilgrimage*, by Lord Byron. People said

Harold was Byron. That could be true, for Byron left England and went on the same journey as did Childe Harold. I don't know what Lord Byron intended, but I believe this is the story about a man who sets out looking for knowledge and a place to belong. This recounting of his journeys turned out to be some of his most famous work. It is Mr. Pickney's favorite."

Lucky had been about to enter the classroom. *Mr. Pickney's* favorite? Pickney's maybe, but not his. He not only had never read *Childe Harold's Pilgrimage,* he didn't want to. He could see trouble coming. He began to back away.

"Come in, Mr. Pickney," Melissa called out. "I'm about to read from *Childe Harold's Pilgrimage.*"

There was a collective groan from the students.

Caught. She'd known he was there. Taking a deep breath, he stepped inside, giving her a frown that announced his disapproval. He felt like a little boy with his finger caught in the jam jar. He was being punished for leaving her to go into town.

Melissa looked up with a twinkle in her eye, a twinkle that quickly changed into a frown. She stared at him for a moment, then pursed her lips and looked away. What had just happened?

"Unless *you'd* rather read it, Mr. Pickney?" she said.

He bit back a quick refusal. In front of the students, he had to be Pickney. "No, I'll let you read it. You're the expert in literature and poetry. I'm more into..." he groped for a moment. A framed print hung over her desk, a photograph of a man playing a fiddle, and finished, "I'm more into music."

There was a second chorus of groans.

"Oh? Perhaps you'll play for us, James?"

"No. I . . . don't play. I . . . sing."

"Good." Melissa clapped. "Would you like to hear him, children?"

The children began to clap. "Sing us a song," one called out. "Yes!" the others echoed.

A song? Lucky groaned silently. What kind of song did he know that was respectable enough for children to hear? None. The only music he'd heard in the last ten years was sung by saloon girls. He knew he was frowning. And he knew without looking at her, that Melissa was smiling. And she was waiting. They were at some strange impasse. There would be no help from her. She was enjoying his discomfort too much.

"All right, here goes," he said, and burst into a lively chorus of *"Jimmy Crack Corn and I don't care. Jimmy Crack Corn and I don't care. Jimmy Crack Corn and I don't care. The . . . teacher's gone away."*

The boys clapped. Lucky pulled one of the twins up and danced her around the room until she collapsed in a giggling fit. The second girl refused to be left out, and as he continued singing the only four lines he could remember, they bounced out the door into the yard, followed by the others. Finally, Lucky let her go and turned to Melissa. "Your turn, Mrs. Pickney," he said, determined to punish her for whatever had just happened between them. He pulled the protesting teacher into his arms, enjoying her discomfort this time.

She was stiff at first, trying to hold herself away, but soon he felt that rigid stance melt and she started to keep step with the beat. Her hair pins fell as she bounced around the yard, allowing strands of blonde curls to join in the merrymaking. The sun caught the gold in her hair and the blue in her eyes. She was the most desirable woman he'd ever seen. And he was her husband.

No. Lucky. Don't even think about that. She's made it plain that you're temporary. But his mental directions fell on deaf ears. His imagination had been fired from the beginning, and feeling her breasts brush against him as he whirled her about was a constant reminder of how long it had been since he'd been with a woman— how long since he'd even thought about it. For the last day and a half, he'd thought of little else.

They were whirling around the yard when Mac interrupted their dance by barking. Melissa saw the man on horseback first. He was a big man, with a thick white mustache. She knew who he was, though they'd never been introduced. Colonel John Curtis, retired U.S. Cavalry officer, the owner of one of the largest mines in Southwest Colorado and a successful breeder of horses. His wife was dead, leaving behind a daughter named Ellen.

"Quiet, Mac. Welcome, Colonel Curtis," she said, dropping Lucky's hand and moving toward their visitor. "What can we do for you?"

He dismounted and studied the breathless group with a stern eye. "You're the teacher?"

"I'm Melissa Grayson...Pickney," she corrected. "This is my husband, James, and these are my pupils."

"These are your only pupils?"

"Yes. The term is just beginning. Today is our first day. Students, go on into the schoolhouse. You may study your Readers while I talk to Colonel Curtis."

Ted and Russ led the way inside, reluctantly. The two girls followed.

"Are you a good teacher?" Colonel Curtis asked.

"I am."

"What about you, Pickney? I'm told you're a teacher too."

"That's not...entirely correct, Colonel. I've never actually taught—children." He hoped they wouldn't pin him down any further. He'd represented himself as James Pickney without realizing that he would be forced to lie about his abilities. Teaching sailors to play poker was teaching; it just didn't have anything to do with a proper education.

"What about a seventeen-year-old young woman?" Colonel Curtis asked. "Any reason you couldn't teach her?"

Melissa lowered her voice so the children wouldn't hear. "Has she ever had any schooling?"

"Of course she has!" he barked. "She knows reading and writing and history. Her mama hired a tutor for a while. Back before...before she got sick, she even learned a little Latin."

"What, exactly, would you expect from me?" Melissa asked, mentally thinking about what it would mean to have the colonel's daughter in her school. Aside from the saloon, a barbershop, the hotel, and a church, the rest of the town was growing. A second general store was being built. A restaurant and a boardinghouse had opened. And the Widow Cassidy was talking of opening a bakery. New people were moving in, people who weren't prospectors. If the colonel's daughter enrolled in Grayson Academy, others would follow.

"I heard that you're into poetry and art. My Ellen likes to write and draw. I thought you might give her some lessons."

Draw? Of all the things Melissa had been trained to do, painting was her greatest failure. Still, she'd had lessons. Somehow she'd manage. "I'm sure we will be able to instruct Ellen in all phases of the arts."

"That's fine. As long as the weather holds, I'll get her here. What's it gonna cost me?"

Melissa considered her answer. She needed students, but she also knew that the colonel had a reputation for having high expectations. "Would she be a day student, or would she board?"

"Board? You mean stay here? Didn't know you had boarders."

"I don't have any yet, but I expect to. You can see my father constructed a dormitory."

The colonel directed a skeptical eye on the facilities. "For now, Ellen will be a day student. What about a dollar a day? Would that cover it?"

"Make it a dollar and a quarter and throw in some firewood," Lucky said, "and it's a deal."

"A dollar and a quarter and some firewood?" He nodded in agreement. "You got yourself a smart husband, Mrs. Pickney."

"I think so too," Melissa said in a strained voice.

The colonel nodded and held out his hand, which Lucky shook. Then he tipped his hat to Melissa and turned his horse back toward the road. "Ellen will be here tomorrow."

"Good."

"One thing you should know. I guess I ought to warn you, my Ellen is used to getting her way. I suppose you know that she can't walk. You'll have to help her get about, Pickney. I'm counting on you to make this schooling thing work. From what I've heard, so's the town. Just so you know, Pickney, I'm known as a hand-shake man, and we just shook hands."

Before Lucky could respond, the colonel galloped away. Lucky knew he'd been politely warned not to leave town. He had to avoid Cerqueda, keep Melissa out of jail, and now the most powerful man in Silver Wind had threatened him.

Melissa turned away from the school and said in a low, soft voice, "I appreciate your pretending to be James, but in the future I'll make my own financial arrangements. You could have ruined it, asking for more. Why would you do that?"

"If a man like the colonel doesn't have to pay for the thing he wants, he's liable to wonder if it's worth having. Besides, I intend to help you make this place a success."

"How?"

"For starters, I intend to see that Miss Ellen Curtis learns how to draw."

"I didn't know you were an artist."

"There are a lot of things you don't know about me, Mrs. Pickney."

She had that same odd expression on her face again. He had the feeling that she was about to pin his ears back as his mother used to do. Maybe now was the time to leave. He started backing up.

"You're right, Mr. Pickney, and I have one more big question." She started toward him, her hands on her hips, matching every backward step he made, with a forward one of her own. "I do appreciate your help. I'll admit, you have a fine singing voice, but what do you know about teaching art?"

"Not a thing, but I think the colonel is the kind of

man you have to have an understanding with, unless you want him and his daughter to run all over you. By the way, what are the other students paying?"

"They pay three dollars a month for one child and five dollars for two."

"So, for five days a week, the colonel is paying twenty-five dollars and furnishing firewood. I'd say you're already ahead. Doesn't that satisfy you?"

They were almost back to the house when she stopped. "No. What would satisfy me is knowing what kind of business you had in town that would bring you home with lip color on your cheek."

Lip color on his cheek? The woman back in town he'd saved from Bart. She'd thanked him with a kiss. He hadn't thought another minute about that. Now he understood Melissa's odd expression. Lucky grinned. "Obviously my bride has a jealous streak."

"I do not!" She whirled around and marched in double time back to the school.

But she did.

And he liked that.

After the children went home, Melissa straightened up the school and tried to think about Ellen, but the thought of the lip prints on Lucky's cheek kept intruding. He'd offered no explanation and he hadn't returned to the school. She didn't know where he was.

Finally, unable to put off confronting him, she started back to the house, noticing that a new stack of kindling wood was piled by the door and a fire had been rekindled in the stove. But there was no Lucky. She paced back and forth, the events of the day tossing around in her mind. Technically, Lucky was only pretending to be her husband. But she'd seen the lip color on his cheek when he returned from town. He simply couldn't go around kissing other women. It would reflect badly on her, she told herself, and she couldn't afford that.

Melissa decided to start supper. She made biscuits, rolled them out, and placed them in the greased pan. Next, she cut up two mountain trout Russ had brought as a gift from his father, who was employed as a cook at the Silver Wind Hotel.

Melissa had learned to cook when she helped in the kitchen back at school. She'd liked the cooks and enjoyed their acceptance. But she'd never planned a meal for a man before—except her father—and it surprised her to find that she was nervous about the evening. She glanced around the small living/kitchen area and allowed herself to feel pride over the feminine touches she'd added. There were checked-gingham curtains at the windows and a cloth on the eating table. An oil lamp sat on the mantel and another one on the table. Her father had built the tiny house, but now it belonged to her.

Her mother had always been melancholy, and she'd taught herself early on to take what came and make it work. Never one to remain out of sorts, she soon found herself humming as she rolled the fish in cornmeal. When she realized the song was *Jimmy Crack Corn,* she blushed. What was wrong with her?

Lucky's impromptu dance had not been a good idea, but it had happened, and she'd felt—for that moment—happy. Even now, as she waited for the grease to get hot, she struggled with her confusion.

Through the window she watched Lucky head across the yard toward the creek, his dirt-streaked shirt in one hand and the bar of soap she'd left by his dormitory bed in the other. Apparently he'd decided to do his own laundry.

For now, they seemed to have an agreement to continue the marriage ruse. The truth be known, her bravery had been the biggest ruse of all. She'd been afraid of everything when she'd first come out here. Her father had written about the school and his plans and she'd believed him. Then he was gone, and all she had left of him was his school and his dreams. When she arrived to find such crude facilities, she'd been overwhelmed. Then angry. Then determined.

If it hadn't been for James's letters of advice and confidence, she might have given up. James understood her. He had the same background, the same moral values, the same dreams. But out here, life was different. Being pursued by every bachelor and even a few of the married men in town, soon made her position even more difficult, and threatened her reputation. She hadn't known how to stop them.

Until James had agreed to marry her.

But this man heading confidently toward the creek wasn't her Jamie. He was big and dark and animal-like, a predator accustomed to making his own way. If she'd had any doubt in the matter, the lip paint on his cheek told her the truth.

Why had he really agreed to stay? What was his real secret? For she was certain he had one. He didn't seem afraid, but nothing else made any sense. He could have his pick of any woman he wanted. Apparently he'd found one in town the day after their wedding. Why had he married her? Then she reminded herself, he hadn't really married her. He was Lucky Lawrence. The minister had married her to James Pickney.

In his black frock coat and trousers he'd looked every inch the gambler he'd confessed to being. He hadn't confessed to being a ladies' man, but Melissa had seen the way the women in town eyed him when he'd stepped off the train. Now, wearing a new black Stetson and new store-bought clothes, he looked like a dark, weathered cowboy. Who was the real man and what was she going to do? She needed him to be her husband, but she knew he'd be leaving. Once he acquired a horse, he'd have the means to be on his way, and she was worried.

Between the end of the dorm and the school, she watched as Lucky knelt at the stream and submerged his white shirt, wetting it thoroughly before rubbing the bar of lye soap briskly across both sides of the garment. Then he rinsed it and turned to hang it on a bush on the bank. As he turned, the slick bar of soap shot out of his hand and plopped like a fish into the center of the stream. He poked at it with a stick for a moment, then stood, stripped off his pants and boots, and wearing only his long johns, stepped out onto a rock, then another, until he reached the spot where the soap had fallen. She could have called out that she had more, but she didn't. He reached forward, slipped on a slick rock, and followed the course of the soap into the stream. The cold water covered him up to his shoulders.

To make matters worse, the water tugged at the shirtsleeve hanging from the bank and threatened to carry it into the current. Lucky, searching for the soap, was unaware that his shirt was escaping.

Melissa pulled the pan filled with the melting grease from the stove, put it on the cook table, and headed out the door. As she reached the stream, she saw that the shirt had temporarily caught on a tree limb downstream.

A startled Lucky looked up just as she caught her toe on a vine and fell headlong into the water. She'd collected buckets of creek water and she'd sat on the bank and dangled her feet in the stream, but this was the first time she'd had to fight the cold and a current so swift that she couldn't stand. She knew that the water came from the snow melting up in the mountains, but she'd never been soaked, clothes and all, in ice. Planting her foot against a rock, she learned firsthand how slippery they were. In moments she was plopping along like some fat frog leaping across the water, until she was grabbed by the same tree that had snagged Lucky's shirt.

"Melissa!" Lucky yelled and charged after her. "Hold on!" Once he reached the tree, he lifted her under one arm and rescued his shirt with the other. Melissa's eyes were directed downward; but this time, downward from Lucky's waist was exactly where she didn't want to be looking.

She closed her eyes and wondered how she'd turned into a fish. She couldn't even swim.

Lucky marched back across the yard with Melissa in his arms and into the house. "Of all the fool things. What did you think you were doing?"

"I-I-I-I gues-s-s I wasn't thinking." Her teeth were chattering. "Just put me down!"

"Be still, woman."

As she struggled, the sleeve of his shirt got tangled

with his feet and he stumbled, dropping her on the floor and falling with one knee on either side of her. He swore. She let out a cry of anguish.

"Melissa, if you're hurt, say so. I don't intend to become a widower."

"If-f-f y-y-you d-d-don't l-let me g-g-go, you're g-g-going to be," she said, forcefully ramming her head directly into his chest, pushing him backward. He reached out to steady himself by grabbing her shoulders. When they'd both stopped, she was on top, her wet dress covering them both like a frozen blanket. Her nose was directly over the red lip marks.

"You c-c-could have washed your face," she said and struggled to stand, falling once more. "Oh, for pity's s-sake. Help me up."

"Melissa, be still. Help was what got us into this. You just saved the life of my shirt. That was no small thing for a woman who doesn't seem to be able to swim. My shirt thanks you and so do I."

His stern voice had the desired effect. She stopped struggling. For two years she'd lived out here, facing the skepticism and suspicion of the townsfolk, the unwanted attention of the men, and the loneliness of her private life after her students had been dismissed for the day. She hadn't thought she needed anyone. Now she was lying intimately on top of a man and he was holding her.

With the sudden knowledge that he could overpower her at any moment and have his way with her, she ought to be frightened but she wasn't. His breath warmed her forehead. His scent was becoming familiar and pleasant. His strong male body caused an intriguing reaction. She'd never been so close to a man before. He moved and she tried to push herself upright. But in order to balance herself on her hands and push upward, she ended up pressing against the lower part of his body. She felt it change.

Lucky groaned.

Her heart raced and she couldn't breathe.

A strange shimmer swirled through her. "Please?" she whispered, not sure what she was pleading for. With one finger he pushed her wet hair from her cheek. She stiffened, trying to conceal the shudders from his touch.

"Don't be afraid," he said softly. "I won't hurt you." Taking her shoulders in his hands he suddenly rolled them over, intending to stand up and pull her with him.

The road to hell was paved with good intentions.

He couldn't. He wouldn't. He did. He lowered his head and kissed her. The kiss was hard at first, then turned gentle, exploring, and for a moment, he lost himself in the wonder of her lips. He felt her soften. The tension seemed to flow out of her body.

Then a soft moan of protest hit his ear and he pulled back. He expected her to struggle. She didn't. She was so small, this woman who could have drowned trying to save his shirt. What was he doing? He'd just told her she didn't have to be afraid. Now she was completely still.

He didn't know why he was so drawn to her. She was the kind of woman who'd be gentle, who'd charm her students into doing her bidding at the same time she issued firm instructions. She was the kind of teacher he'd once had, except his teacher had been only a few years older than he had been. Miss Hawthorne had taught him about other worlds, about polish and manners, and he'd fallen head over heels in love with her. Then one day after school, she'd kissed him. It was plain bad luck that another student happened in and saw them together. The next day Miss Hawthorne's father sent for Lucky and suggested that it might be a good idea for Lucky to leave town if he wanted his mother's boardinghouse to remain open.

Lucky hadn't understood. There'd only been the one kiss. But his explanation fell on deaf ears. Miss Hawthorne was an only child and Lucky was not in her league. She had resigned from the school and Lucky decided that looking for gold in California seemed like a good idea. He felt sorry for Miss Hawthorne and offered to take her along, but her papa had roared that no decent person would ever want him—or his sister. He swore that he'd see to that. And he had. Mr. Hawthorne bought his mother's mortgage and foreclosed. That was when his sister had left with a musician on one of the riverboats.

Now Lucky was holding another properly bred young woman. Suddenly he was fourteen again. Only trouble could come of this.

She whimpered. "Please, Lucky. I'm ... cold."

Of course she was. Darkness had fallen and she was wet. What the hell was he doing? He was cold too, but spending a year on the deck of a ship taught a man to fight the elements. Controlling his shivers, he got to his feet and pulled her up.

"Turn around, Melissa. We have to get you out of this wet dress and warm you up."

"I'll do it," she said between lips that trembled so that she could hardly speak.

"I don't think so. Now stand still. It's too dark for you to be modest."

It wasn't modesty that was bothering her, it was the knowledge that her trembling came as much from his touch as the cold. Even as she had been protesting, he'd been unbuttoning the hooks. Now he peeled the dress from her curved body. "Step out."

But she couldn't move.

Forgoing gentleness, he jerked the dress and her underclothing down her hips and off her body. She crossed her arms across her chest and looked up at him, glad that the darkness concealed her turmoil.

He pulled back the quilts on her bed, lifted her once more and laid her down, then covered her gently. "Do you have more quilts?"

She managed to nod, inclining her head toward a chest. Plundering through the drawers in the darkness, he pulled out another quilt and a tattered spread. "I'll warm these. Just stay there."

The stove in the kitchen was still hot. He opened the oven door, then stuffed the quilt inside. Beside the stove he found two fabric-covered bricks and added them to the oven to heat, rubbing his hands briskly to bring back the feeling in his own hands.

The smell of hot cloth told him the quilt was ready. It burned his fingers as he pulled it from the stove and hurried to Melissa's bed. He wrapped her quickly in the heat, watching for a moment as the chattering lessened. Once the bricks were hot, he shoved them under the covers to rest against the two icy chunks that were Melissa's feet. Hot coffee was next.

First he put the biscuits in the oven to bake, then pulled the frying pan back to the eye. As it heated, he built up the fire in the stove, then filled the pot with water and spooned in ground coffee. When the grease was

ready, he added the fish. As they fried, he went back to
the bedroom. Melissa's eyes were closed. He glanced
around. There was a fireplace in the main room, a potbellied iron stove in the schoolroom and in the dormitory, but Melissa's room had no heat.

But it would have. He would see to it.

She needed to stay warm, not catch a chill. He was realizing more and more that he couldn't just walk away.
He'd build a fireplace in her bedroom. Then there was
wood to be chopped for the winter and food to be laid in.

And there was Black Bart.

October 15, 1888

MISTRESS MELISSA GRAYSON
GRAYSON ACADEMY
SILVER WIND, COLORADO

MY DEAREST MELISSA,
*I send my deepest regrets over missing my
arrival on the third Sunday, last. Unfortunately,
I was taken ill in St. Louis and have been
incapacitated until now. I hope this doesn't
inconvenience you too much. I will arrive within
ten days.*

Your future husband,
James Harold Pickney IV

James sealed the envelope and addressed it. This time,
to deliver it, he picked the one person he knew he could
trust, the nurse who'd forced him to eat when he didn't
have the strength. "Be sure this gets to the postal clerk,

Agnes. My friend's life depends on it. And buy me a train ticket to Durango."

"Why would you want to go to Durango, Mr. Pickney? There's nothing there except a railroad and the ovens that crush the gold ore."

"Oh, I'm not staying in Durango," he said. "I'm going north into the San Juan Mountains to a beautiful little town called Silver Wind."

"And why would you want to do that?" the nurse asked.

"I'm going to be a teacher."

"What do you know about living out there? You're a . . . a gentleman."

James smiled. She wasn't asking him anything he hadn't asked himself. But he had an answer. "Because I've read the California newspapers and Horace Greeley's columns. I've read every novel published about the West," he said. "I know about the outlaws, about the miners, about the Indians and the settlers. Please, will you do as I ask?"

"You know I will, but I'm not sure those books tell the truth, Mr. Pickney. Lots of people going West meet failure and come through here on their way back home. They say they've met the elephant. I wouldn't want you to be disappointed."

"Home? Oh, Agnes, I've already met failure and disappointment at home. Don't you ever just want to run away and do something completely impractical?"

"Yes," she said wistfully. "But I'm a woman alone. The only place I go is home."

"Not me. I'm going to Colorado."

"I hope you know what you're doing."

"I do. I'm getting married."

7

Lucky removed his wet long johns, hung his wet clothes over a bench near the stove, and pulled on his dry denim pants, socks, and the train dandy's coat. After days of travel, he'd taken an icy water bath last night, but hadn't planned on another so soon.

His heart seemed to have stopped when he saw Melissa in the rushing current, slamming into the limb and being held there. Only when she was safe in his arms did it begin again, beating in double time. He told himself she was only chilled. She'd be fine. But he couldn't be still. His movements were charged by the knowledge that the woman he'd falsely married was so close... so desirable... so untouchable.

He should never have kissed her. He'd crossed the line, changing their relationship. He was sorry he'd done it. Yet even now he wanted to kiss her, but he wouldn't. After all, she might just get out of her bed and use him for target practice with that shotgun. Melissa

Grayson *Pickney,* he added reluctantly, was a woman with her eyes clearly on the future. At some point he'd have to find another way to leave.

He pulled the coffeepot to the back of the stove and went to check on Melissa. She was still. He lit the lamp beside her bed and lifted it as he glanced around until he caught sight of her nightgown and robe hanging on the back of the door. He lifted them and came to the bed.

Melissa looked at him and giggled.

Lucky smiled. "I know, it's the coat. I look like some dandy, but at least it's warm and dry. Maybe I ought to give it to you."

"Oh, no." Melissa pulled the covers up to her neck and blushed. "You keep it. I'll be warm soon."

"You look like a little girl all wrapped up in her blanket. All you need is a stuffed animal."

"I never had a stuffed animal," she said. "My mother always promised me one, but then I got too old...."

"I'll get you one," he promised. "Every girl ought to have something to hug when she's cold and wet." He thought about his sister; he should have been there to comfort and protect her.

"Thank you," she said, unable to control the nervous chatter of her teeth.

"You're still cold. Let me get you another quilt. We can't have you catching pneumonia."

"Pneumonia?" She gasped. "No. My father died of pneumonia."

"I'm sorry, Melissa. I never knew what killed my mother, only that she died." He paused a long time, then turned. "I'm going to put your quilt back in the oven to warm. While I'm gone, I want you to put on this gown and robe."

She nodded, knowing that much of her shaking came from being so close to Lucky. Now they shared a different kind of connection.

He yanked the quilt off the bed, picked up her wet dress, and left the room. The sound of bed covers rustling behind him let him know she was following his directions. The quilt went into the oven. Her dress could be hung out tomorrow. Until then, she had more clothes. He was pouring coffee when he heard the floor creak behind him. He turned.

"Thank you for taking care of me, Lucky," she said. "First you saved my school, and you don't know it but you've saved my life too."

He dragged the rocking chair close to the stove. "You wouldn't have drowned."

She didn't move. "I don't know how to swim."

"The water isn't that deep."

"But—the current. I couldn't stand up. I panicked."

"I know," he said, and held out his hand. "Please, sit down."

Her hair was hanging in wet tendrils, framing a face laced with uncertainty. It was all he could do to stop himself from clasping her in his arms.

"Please, come and sit by the stove. I'll wrap you in the quilt."

Slowly, as if she were sleepwalking, she put her cold hand in his. He touched her cheek; it was ice-cold. "Come close to the heat."

She followed him.

"Stand here for a moment."

He took the quilt from the oven and wrapped her in it, then lowered her into the rocking chair and bent down on one knee to tuck the quilt under her bare feet. "Better?"

She nodded.

He didn't know or understand what was happening. Desire rocked him. And she was looking at him with wide eyes that said she felt it too.

He stood up and looked away from her and turned to their supper. The fish were done. He removed them from the pan and laid them on a tin plate. Then he took a cloth from the table by the stove and moved behind her.

"What are you doing?"

"I'm going to dry your hair."

"You ought to dry yourself." *And wipe that lip rouge off your face*, she added to herself. The mark was a barrier, a reminder that he really wasn't hers. He caught the wet strands of her hair between the corners of the towel and rubbed them. Over and over, one strand, then the next. There was silence, except for the crackle of the fire.

She'd been holding herself as stiff as an icicle. But the slow rhythm of the cloth and his gentleness relaxed her. "My mother used to dry my hair," she said. "Before she got sick."

"I dried my little sister's hair when she was small," he answered.

"Tell me about your sister," Melissa said. "What's her name?"

He stilled his drying for a long moment. "Her name was Loraine. I called her Rainey. She was so beautiful, so full of life."

"Where is she now?"

Lucky's hands were patting the sides of her head. They paused just above her ears. "I don't know."

Melissa froze. "I'm sorry. Forgive me. I had no right to pry."

"My sister disappeared. My mother ran a boarding-house, but Loraine didn't want that kind of life. The boardinghouse fell on hard times and Rainey started to work in a saloon. I was . . . away when my mother died. After that, Rainey left with . . . a riverboat entertainer. I've been looking for her for six years."

"I'm sorry, Lucky. I know what it means to be left be-hind. At least your sister is still alive."

"I can only hope she is."

He changed one cloth for a dry one and slowed his actions. He wasn't touching her face, but he might have been. Her skin tingled as if he were caressing her cheeks. Melissa closed her eyes and let out a deep sigh as he lifted a strand of hair from her forehead and dried it. It would have been easier if he had touched her, since the anticipation was far worse than reality.

The room seemed suddenly warmer—more intimate. Melissa had never seen her father—the only other man she'd ever lived with—behave with such compassion.

The silence strung out between them like the fine, brittle thread of sugar candy.

"Are you sorry," he finally asked, "about what hap-pened?"

"Sorry we both got wet? Yes."

"No." He stopped his wiping. "Sorry I kissed you."

No, she'd wanted him to but she couldn't say that. "Yes," she finally said. "I think it would have been eas-ier if you hadn't. You were my husband in name only before, a piece of my plan. Now...now you're more. You're a man and I don't have any experience with men."

He knew that and he didn't know what to say. This was not part of his plan, but it had happened. "I know it doesn't mean much, Melissa, but I promise you I won't kiss you again, or do anything else unless you want me to."

"You'll give me your word?"

"I give you my word."

"Why doesn't that give me comfort? You're a gambler. I think you may play with words like you play with cards, Lucky Lawrence. I think you always win."

"I win when I need to."

The tension grew, as did the intimacy in the room. All of it—the heat from the fire seeping into her bones; Mac lying by the stove snoring like a hibernating bear; Lucky drying her hair—drew a cocoon of warmth around them. He tucked a tendril of hair behind her ear, gently rimming the outer edge until his fingers rested against her neck.

"Lucky," she said, resisting the urge to lean her cheek against his hand, "I thank you for drying my hair, but it's too...too overpowering. I don't know how to handle all this."

He touched her cheek. "All this?"

She pulled away, ending the connection. For that brief moment, they'd shared something that went deeper than the kiss. For whatever reason, he'd come into her life when she needed him. And just for the night, he seemed to need her. "I think it's time we eat before our food gets as cold as I am," she lied. If she got any warmer, she'd begin to sizzle.

"All right," he said, and brought the food to the table. He'd started to sit, when she held up her hand to stop him. "Lucky, wait, there's something I have to do. Come around here, close your eyes, and lean over," she said.

He looked at her warily. "Why?"

"Just do it, Lucky Lawrence."

He moved in front of her and bent forward. With the corner of her quilt, she wiped his cheek. He opened his eyes and she showed him the red smudge. "Just so you know, I won't have your actions put my school in jeopardy. The next time you come back from town with red lip color on your cheek, I'm going to show you that I can use that shotgun."

Southwest of Durango, in the mountains north of Santa Fe, the old man cowered before the dark, angry *vaquero* rolling the black cigar back and forth in his mouth.

"The man, he traded one horse to me for supplies. The other, he rode away."

"You fool. You don't own anything worth what either one of those horses was worth. Where did the man go?"

"I don't know señor. It was dark and I was busy with the horse."

"I don't believe you," the man on horseback said. "Get the horse, Manuel."

"Please, no. I need the horse, señor. Maybe... maybe. Wait, I remember. He asked how far to the railroad going west."

"The railroad?"

"*Sí, sí.*"

"And what did you tell him?"

"I told him it was two days' ride over the next ridge."

"You should have remembered sooner. Take the animal, Manuel."

The old man looked into the Mexican's eyes and knew he'd just escaped death. He hoped the stranger who'd traded him the horse a week ago would be so lucky.

October 17, 1888
St. Louis, Missouri

Finally, after almost two weeks, James declared that he was leaving St. Louis, ready or not. Agnes, his nurse, protested vigorously. "You're not strong enough to make the journey yet, Mr. Pickney."

"I'm not walking, Agnes. I can sit on a train as well as I can sit here on this hospital bed. Besides, my future wife is waiting for me."

"At least you have a future," Agnes said wistfully. "If you had me to look after you, you might have a chance of getting there."

Jamie smiled and said with excitement, "Then why don't you come along too? I'll bet there's a big demand for a good nurse in a mining town. You've told me how you hate your life here. Think of the adventure. Think of the gold you'll get paid for your services. Take a chance, Agnes. Go West with me."

Agnes thought—for about five minutes. Then smiled.

"I'll do it," she said, then resigned her job and went home to pack. The next morning, James Harold Pickney and Agnes Fulbright were on the Union Pacific heading for Wyoming. By the time they'd reached

Cheyenne, James's strength was wavering. Agnes insisted that James spend a couple of days resting before heading south to Durango. This time he didn't argue.

Lucky fingered his lucky coin and watched from the dormitory as a buggy driven by a slightly-built young woman with pale skin and red hair, rumbled into the yard. She looked around for a moment, then lifted a cowbell from under her seat and rang it vigorously.

"Hello! Someone attend me!"

Lucky walked out to the buggy. "Yes, ma'am?"

"Unload my chair and get me down!"

"You'd be the colonel's daughter?"

"Yes. I'm Ellen Curtis."

"He lets you drive around by yourself?"

She looked irritated at being questioned. "I go where I please. And I believe I asked you to get me down."

"No," Lucky said in a low voice. "You told me. Now you're asking, I'll be glad to assist you."

He led the horse to the corral and tied the horse's reins to the wire, then moved to the other side of the buggy and took out a chair with wheels.

"Please hurry," she said.

"Please?" Lucky responded. "That's better. We like please and thank you. Manners are important here at Grayson Academy."

At that moment Melissa came out of the schoolhouse with a bright smile. "Good morning, Miss Curtis. We're glad you're joining us."

"I'm not glad," she said, "but my father insists."

"I don't understand. He said you wanted to learn to

paint and draw," Melissa said, obviously surprised by the attitude of her new student.

"And who's going to teach me out here?" Ellen asked skeptically.

Lucky lifted her in his arms and plopped her unceremoniously into her rolling chair. "I am."

The mountains were already growing cold at night. As the miners changed shifts, they collapsed into their bedding and tried to stay warm. Bart removed his boots and emptied the small fragments of black rock onto the fire he'd built. He was too tired to gather wood. They'd long since used up any wood close to the camp.

He was angry with himself. When he'd come out West, he'd had visions of striking it rich, just like every other prospector—to be somebody. He'd failed. Just as he'd failed at being a cowhand and a storekeeper. There seemed to be nothing he was good at, and finally, he'd hired himself out, first to Mr. Grayson, then to Colonel Curtis. Mining wasn't a bad life. It was the loneliness that ate away at him. Why was it so wrong to want a woman? If he'd been given a chance, he would have made that schoolteacher understand that after her father died he'd waited for her. He'd take care of her. He'd be willing to stay away from the saloon. But she'd looked down on him. And she'd done it publicly, in front of the other men. They'd laughed at him. He couldn't let her get away with that. She'd have to be punished.

The sound of a coyote cut through the night. He was calling for his mate. A short time later came an answering yip. Bart swore. Even the wild critters had partners.

He wiped his face on his sleeve, setting off a cloud of black dust. Finding the silver at first had been easy, but now they'd hit a pocket of black rock that was worthless. Sooner or later the colonel would close off this mine, and he might not even have a job.

Then he noticed his fire. The small particles of rock he'd emptied from his boots had begun to glow around the edges. It would burn. Bart leaned over and blew on the coals: the glow intensified. He didn't have far to reach to pick up more of the small rocks and some larger ones. Adding one at a time, he watched them begin to turn orange, then powdery around the edges. The heat reached out and curled around him. Bart capped the bottle he'd been drinking from. For the first time in days, he didn't need whiskey to keep him warm.

The next morning, when one of the other miners asked him how he'd managed to keep his fire burning, Bart realized he might have found a way to change his fate. Instead of heading for town and Saturday breakfast at the hotel, he ate at the cook tent, then went to call on the colonel. He'd never been to his ranch, but he knew where it was.

By noon he was riding into the courtyard.

He hadn't dismounted when he was met by two men with drawn pistols.

"Whoa there, fella," one of them said. "What do you want?"

"I want to see the colonel."

"About what?"

"That's for me to know," Bart said, "and for Colonel Curtis to find out. He here?"

"He might be. What's your name?"

"Name's Jamison, Black Bart Jamison, and I work for him. I'm a miner."

One of the cowboys took a long leering look at Bart and laughed. "That's not hard to figure out. If you have a problem at the mine, you take it up with the man in charge. Colonel Curtis don't bother with the details."

"Colonel Curtis will when he finds out I know a way he can double the money the mine's bringing in."

"I don't think so." The guard gave Bart a sneer. "Now get out of here. The colonel don't take time to talk to the likes of you."

Bart trembled in rage. He'd lost his job, the woman he wanted, and now, when he was in a position to help the colonel, they wouldn't even give him the time of day. He rode away with the sounds of the men jeering behind him, echoing in his ears. He'd been ridiculed again. It dug at him like a thorn in his flesh. The farther he rode, the madder he got.

He might as well head for town. In fact, since it was on the way, he'd just stop by the school and remind the teacher that he was keeping watch.

Something about Mr. James Harold Pickney bothered him. He didn't look like a teacher, and he didn't look like the marrying kind. 'Course, he couldn't blame Pickney. He hadn't been the marrying kind either, not until he saw Melissa Grayson's picture. He'd come to call, to offer his protection. He'd tried to do the honorable thing, and she'd pulled out her gun. She'd be sorry about that.

As the schoolhouse came into view, he reined the horse to a stop. He couldn't see her but he could see Pickney. He was stringing wire between the lean-to and the trees behind it. That surprised him. He would have guessed that the dandy would be inside reading poetry with his new bride. But the figure he watched stretching the wire didn't look like a dandy. Maybe he'd wait until later before he stopped for a visit.

Maybe on the way back.

8

Once the residents of Silver Wind learned that Ellen Curtis had enrolled in Grayson Academy, they'd enrolled their children. When the number reached twenty-two, Melissa began to worry. In the last two weeks, Lucky had made two more trips into town, and each time, his face was clear of lip color on his return. He spent part of his time enlarging the lean-to and stringing wire to make the corral a proper restraint for the horses being ridden to school by the children. Some of his time he spent observing his wife teach. When called upon, he was surprisingly adept at teaching the younger students who were having difficulties in arithmetic. It bothered her that he insisted on taking them into the dormitory instead of remaining in the schoolhouse. But it seemed reasonable when he explained that he felt uncomfortable with her looking over his shoulder. And he was getting good results.

Until the morning she needed something from the house, and paused outside the dormitory door to listen.

"See the hearts on this card. Let's count them."

"One, two, three, four, five, six, seven," chirped Willie Cotten.

"Now you pick a card, Aaron," Lucky instructed. "Good, another heart. How many does that make? Count them."

"One, two, three, four, five," Willie said.

"Now, Minnie Lee, in playing blackjack, you know you can't go over twenty-one. So, how many hearts do you have?"

"That would be twelve," Minnie Lee said proudly.

"Right. Now, let's practice our subtraction. How many more hearts can you draw without going over twenty-one?"

"Nine," the three children shouted out together.

"All right, Minnie, you draw."

There was a groan.

"Sorry, folks," Lucky's voice said. "You drew a ten and that's too many. If you were gambling, you'd lose. But, if this was your arithmetic paper, you'd make a hundred."

"I'd rather play blackjack," Willie said.

"Then when you're doing your sums, pretend they're hearts and diamonds."

Minnie whined, "But I don't want to play cards."

"No, problem, darlin', you just pretend they're cookies."

Lucky was teaching the children how to count by teaching them how to play blackjack. What in the world would their parents say? This had to be stopped. She knocked and stepped into the dormitory. "Children, please return to the schoolhouse and practice your letters. I need to speak with Mr. Pickney."

As soon as they'd left, she set her chin and took a deep breath. "What do you think you're doing?"

"I'm teaching the little ones how to count and tally figures."

"By playing blackjack? No wonder you wanted to leave the schoolhouse."

He could have told her that he'd left the schoolhouse because it was becoming uncomfortable to be so close to her. Being scrutinized was part of his profession. But he knew how to play cards. He told himself he was out of his depth, but it wasn't his mind that was taxed, it was his imagination. It was all he could do to keep from reaching out to touch her. When she'd laugh he'd completely lose his train of thought. When she'd hug one of the children and compliment her on her recitation, he'd think of what a loving mother she'd make. She was never out of sorts with them, but she'd become more and more impatient with him. "Counting cards by playing blackjack is interesting and infinitely more profitable than using sticks," he finally said. "But more than that, it works, and that's what you wanted, isn't it?"

"Not if it turns them into gamblers. What do you intend to teach them next, how to measure liquids by the shot glass?"

His smile disappeared, as if she'd stuck a knife in his chest.

"I hadn't thought about it, Mrs. Pickney, but that's an idea," he said. "I do have more experience in measuring whiskey than other liquids, low-class person that I am."

She emitted an audible gasp. "I'm sorry, Lucky. I can't blame you if I ask you to do more than you're qualified to do. All you've done is help me and all I've done is be rude."

"You're right. I shouldn't have been using the playing cards," he said, then hesitated, wondering why he felt as if he'd let her down. She was right. He might be masquerading as James Harold Pickney IV, but he was no teacher. "I won't do that again," he said, pushing past her into the courtyard. Whistling to Mac, he walked up the creek bank toward the mountains.

For the next few days they avoided each other. He'd started making the breakfast coffee and pancakes, eating quickly, and leaving the rest for Melissa. But every night, as soon as dinner was over, he immediately left the house and retired to the dormitory. During the day, he did enough hunting and fishing to provide food and filled a flour sack with small, flat rocks that would skim the water. He'd figured out another way to teach the children to count. Skimming the water was a plus. Sinking was a minus. That was a life lesson as well. Problem was—he felt like he was sinking.

A lesson he'd learned well. Rescuing Louisa Hidalgo had been a success. Not being able to find his sister was a failure. Marrying Melissa? Well, he wasn't at all certain whether that rock had skimmed the water or plunged to the bottom.

For Melissa, the situation was a little rocky too. She didn't know how to change the awkwardness between them. She'd thought that time would make things easier, but it simply made her more anxious. She didn't see him take any more baths, and the shaving equipment had disappeared to the dormitory. He was doing just what she wanted him to do: act as if they were married around her pupils, and as if they were strangers when they were alone.

But she wasn't alone anymore.

And she'd never felt more lonely.

So far, Melissa had spent part of every day showing the students pictures of paintings by the masters. They'd discussed the life and times of the artists and what the critics said about their work. Clearly, that wasn't what Ellen Curtis wanted and she made it known. But Melissa tried to ignore Ellen's rudeness and her selfish demands for all the attention.

Ellen was used to getting her way, and she was responsible for bringing in enough students to ease Melissa's concerns for the future. She tried to make allowances, but Ellen's attitude was in direct contrast with her delicate appearance. She could have been a model for some of the expensive porcelain dolls sold in exclusive toy shops. They always looked a little startled, and like Ellen, they never smiled. Her demands were queenly and she expected immediate attention. When she didn't get it, she pouted. The other students avoided her, refusing to give in to her demands. Melissa was seriously considering telling the colonel to remove his daughter from the school. She'd refund his money and release him from his promise to help her get ready for winter, even if it did mean losing some of her other students.

It all came to a head the day Ellen interrupted the history lesson and called once more for attention. "Bring me some cold water," she demanded of Lucky, who was walking past. "This room is much too hot."

"You're absolutely right," Lucky agreed in a suspiciously pleasant voice.

"And when you're finished, I expect you to begin my art instruction. My daddy paid for it and if you don't do it, he's going to want to know why."

"You're right about that too. Why don't you and I go outside? I've been waiting for Mrs. Pickney to get the students settled into a routine. I think it's time to start."

"Good!" she said, tossing her head toward Melissa as if to say, "I'm the boss, not you." "You'll have to push my chair, Mr. Pickney," she said.

"Nope, you push your chair. I'll carry your sketchbook and your charcoal pencils."

"But I can't make my chair move on grass," she snapped. "It's too hard. And I'll need a blanket to keep my legs warm."

"Then you'd better get one from your buggy. I'll go and find us a good, level spot," Lucky said, and headed through the door.

"Mr. Pickney! You come back here right this minute, or I'll have my father speak to Mrs. Pickney!"

The children giggled.

"Shush!" Melissa said. "It's impolite to laugh at a person who has an affliction."

"What's an affliction?" one of the children asked.

"It's a physical problem that prevents your living the same kind of life that others live," Melissa explained.

"I'd trade with her," the first child said. "She gets everything she wants. My daddy got an affliction too; he got blowed up in the mine."

Melissa knelt down by the child. "What kind of an affliction?"

"He's blind. He helps my mama do laundry all day, and we all have to help."

"Mrs. Pickney!" Ellen was still in the doorway. "Have

someone push me outside. I can't move this chair on grass."

Melissa walked over to her. "Don't you ever go outside?"

"What for?"

"To see the flowers. To smell the sweet scent of spring. To touch the snow."

"Not alone," she said. "My father always sends someone with me."

"But you come here or so you said..."

Ellen blushed. "I don't come alone. Brady accompanies me and follows me home."

Melissa was startled. "Someone comes with you every day. Where is he?"

"I don't know where he goes. All I know is that he rides with me until I can see the school, and comes back to meet me in the afternoon. I suppose from now on I'll have to have him stay here so that he can push me around, since Mr. Pickney refuses to help."

"I only help those who try to help themselves, Ellen," Lucky said from where he stood on the bank of the stream, his back to her. "You can do it, Ellen. Please get yourself out here or I'm going to start without you."

He'd placed her sketchbook on a newly constructed easel just about the right height for a person sitting down. After a moment, he leaned over and began making firm, dark strokes on the paper.

"I believe that's my sketchbook," Ellen said. "I didn't give you permission to draw on it."

He ignored her.

"I'm telling you to stop," she said.

"And I told you to come out here," he responded. "And I said *please*."

Ellen took a deep breath, let out a sigh, and pushed against the wheels.

Melissa had listened to their conversation. She hoped Lucky knew what he was doing. She wasn't at all certain that Ellen could move the chair. It was obvious that she'd never done it before, at least not outside. But she didn't interfere. Something had to change. She'd already considered the possibility that she would lose her best-paying pupil. If this did it, so be it.

Finally, with a flourish that bordered on tears, Ellen forced the chair to move, propelling the wheels forward, a few inches at a time. Finally, halfway to where Lucky was standing, she came to a stop and whispered, "Will you please help me?"

"I'll be glad to," he said, laying his charcoal on the keg and coming around behind her. "I thought we'd start off with simple drawings. Let's get your chair in a position where you can reach the paper." He handed her the charcoal.

"Where did you get the easel?"

"I made it."

Her eyes widened. "You made this for me?"

"Not just for you, for the school."

"Oh!"

"You don't have to use it," he said, "if you'd rather hold the pad in your lap." He reached for it.

"No. I'd like to use it."

"Fine. Can you see that rock across the creek, the way the light hits it and makes it change color?"

"Yes," she answered, with the first enthusiasm Melissa had heard since Ellen had entered the school.

"Why don't you try and sketch the scene. Not in detail, just place what you see on the paper. Then ..."

Melissa turned back to the class. She didn't know what to make of what she'd just seen. A gambler, a man with a secret who apparently never stayed in one place, had the makings of a real teacher.

"Class, let's work on our reading. I know you younger students won't be able to read this, but you can listen. Our minds learn words without our being aware of the process. Look out the window at the mountains as you listen. Ted, would you like to read this poem?"

She handed him the open book and he began to read.

THE BALLAD OF THE DARK LADIE
by Samuel Taylor Coleridge

Beneath yon birch with silver bark,
And boughs so pendulous and fair,
The brook falls scatter'd down the rock:
And all is mossy there!

After the students left that afternoon, Melissa wandered over to the easel, where Ellen's sketch was displayed. It was hesitant but good. The scene was readily identified, down to the branch where Lucky's shirt had been caught. But the sheet beneath it was Lucky's work. His bold black lines portrayed the same scene, but there was the suggestion of a figure in the water, a figure reaching out toward the branch.

The figure had to be her. James—no, not James—Lucky could actually draw. And he'd drawn her. Somehow the sketch was intimate, and she felt a hushed flutter of response. She didn't want that. She didn't want to form any kind of relationship with a man who had a mission, a man who'd leave her. She put it back where she'd found it and tried to put it out of her mind.

Melissa swept and mopped the schoolhouse, wishing her father had not built a platform for her desk. It did give her a vantage point to see all the students, but she feared that it might be intimidating to the younger ones. She'd never seen such a layout, except at the university.

Afterward, she made a list of the supplies she needed. Feeding Lucky was depleting her pantry at an alarming rate. Everything in the mining town of Silver Wind cost twice as much as it would have in Philadelphia. Her money didn't go as far. Though her students would not be paying their fees for another week, the registration had increased enough to justify buying on credit at Sizemore's. Maybe she could work out an exchange of services with Ida Sizemore, teaching her daughters in exchange for goods. Tomorrow she'd go into town and talk to her.

Later, as she stirred the pot of beans cooking on the stove, she became more confident about her plan. At least now she could go into town without worrying about causing trouble, that is, if Lucky would go with her.

James. Mr. and Mrs. James Harold Pickney. The more she tried to put him out of her mind, the more he filled it. After she'd fallen into the water and he'd kissed her, everything changed. She'd known then that it wasn't James who had kissed her; her racing heart had been caused by Lucky, who seemed to be invading every corner of her world. Now there was the picture that made it more real. She wondered if he knew what he was doing to her peace of mind? She wondered how she'd stand it once he'd gone.

"Please try and act like a husband," Melissa said as she climbed into the buggy. "For now, the town needs to think that this marriage is real."

"Indeed I will," Lucky said and nodded, "if you'll tell me what the rules are. I wouldn't want to embarrass you." He took the reins and urged Arthur into a trot. For a time, Mac loped down the rutted road beside them, but once they reached the abutment, he turned back.

"Well, I suppose that we should carry on a conversation."

"Of course. If you'll select the topic of conversation. It can't be literature, because I don't have James's scholarship. It can't be politics, because I know nothing about government. It can't be gambling, for obvious reasons. I can't even talk about New York City, because I've never been there."

"Lucky, you're a very smart man. You know a great deal more than you want to let on. But if you'd rather, I'll make the small talk. You just follow my lead."

The carriage hit a rut and flung Melissa against him. She jerked away, holding awkwardly to the side of the seat to keep their arms from touching.

It was obvious to Lucky that Arthur was bent on following his lead. The stubborn horse was determined to hit every rut. Lucky started to apologize to Melissa, but when he turned his attention on her, he lost his words. This afternoon she was wearing a cream-and-blue-striped dress with a perky little blue hat pinned to one side at an angle. Her cream-colored gloves matched the stripe in her dress. A blue shawl lay across her knees, waved with a thread of cream, like the ocean along the Gulf of Mexico. This afternoon, she was honey and blue sky.

He liked that. But he liked the white sleeping clothes she wore better.

It surprised him that he liked the silence too. He could hear her breathing. He was certain that she could hear the beat of his heart, pounding like an Indian drum in his ears. "This is beautiful country," Lucky finally said, breaking the tension that was building steadily.

Melissa let out a deep breath. "I like it too. Sometimes the snow comes in October and closes everything down. It drapes the mountain like a white fur cape. The prospectors mark their claims and disappear until spring. Most of the ones you see in town work in Colonel Curtis's mine."

"He doesn't close down until the spring?"

"No. They say that the tunnels are hot year round."

"What does the colonel mine?"

"It started with gold, but the mine kept filling up with this gray-colored mud. It took them a long time to figure out that the mud was filled with silver."

"Both gold and silver in the same mine?"

"Yes. My father wrote me about it. Said it almost never happens, mining gold and silver from the same shaft. He said that whatever kind of upheaval caused these mountains left all kinds of mixed elements," Melissa said. "Out here men look at what's under the ground. I just look at the purity of the mountains. The snow makes the world new."

Lucky had seen snow in Alaska. But he'd been shanghaied and thrown on a ship sailing south before he'd learned to appreciate the kind of white, silent world she was describing.

"It's beautiful but it can be treacherous. I never would have thought a woman like you would come to a place like this and stay. Surely there were teaching positions back home that offered a friendlier environment," he said.

"But this is already mine. Nobody can take it away from me, because it's something *I* can do," she said. "I don't have to work for someone else and help out in the kitchen between terms. Here, I don't have to depend on anyone else."

But she did, Lucky thought. He had no doubt she could run her school, but whether she'd admit it or not, she was being forced to depend on him. He'd never stayed in one place long enough to take on such responsibility. He'd known the town forced her to marry, but he hadn't truly appreciated what was at stake for her. It was more than just satisfying them, it was proving something to herself. His plan to hide until he was sure Cerqueda had given up, had changed. He'd become a married man who wasn't married and had to act as if he were. He had to be there for a woman who thought she didn't need him. It was harder and harder to keep his hands off her, because more and more he wanted to act like a married man.

How the hell had he gotten himself into this, and where was the real James Harold Pickney IV?

* * *

On Saturday afternoon, Silver Wind was a busy place. The saloons were noisy. The wooden sidewalks in front of the businesses were filled with women shoppers, and children chased each other around the posts, into the street, and back again.

Like a window shade being pulled down, silence descended on the town as Lucky drove the buggy down the street. The women shoppers gave Melissa a watchful eye and Lucky a curious one. Melissa felt like a bug under one of those microscopes that the scientific world was using. This was going to be harder than she'd thought. Back in her house, they'd formed a strained truce, both refusing to admit the mutual desire that flared between them. He'd kissed her at the wedding, then again after he'd snagged her from the water. But here . . .

Though she'd feared what those kisses would lead to, nothing had happened. Why? The fear that he'd want more had slowly dissipated as she realized he didn't. As a gambler, he was experienced with more worldly women, something she certainly wasn't. But she'd thought he'd felt something for her. Now she was very confused.

"Looks like we're the center of attraction," Lucky observed and tipped his hat in an exaggerated gesture to the Widow Sweeney, who stepped outside her shop.

"Stop that," Melissa snapped. "You're not following my lead."

"Oops, sorry," he whispered in her ear. "Hadn't considered that saying hello would break your rules. I won't do that again."

"Morning, folks," the widow called out. "Come in for the church box supper, did you?"

"No," Melissa answered. "With the opening of school and...everything, I'm afraid I forgot about it. I didn't bring a box."

The widow gave Lucky a long look and smiled. "Hmm. If I were in your place, I'd have forgotten too. No matter. You're here, and I want at least one dance with that husband of yours. Bertha Cassidy and I will just prepare an extra box for you, Melissa. It'll be a kind of wedding present for you."

"Mighty kind of you. It will give me a chance to show the town how happy I've made my blushing bride. We'll be there," Lucky replied and gave the widow a wink.

"How dare you!" Melissa said under her breath. "We are *not* going to any box supper."

"Certainly we are. You wanted me to act like a husband, and that's what I'm going to do. Smile, darling."

"You were flirting with her. Everyone in Silver Wind will know you winked at her."

"You're jealous. Don't worry, wife, I'm yours for at least three months. Now, be nice. Don't want the townsfolk to think we're having a tiff."

"We are having a tiff!"

"Well, I guess we'll have to kiss and make up."

Before she realized what he'd said, he'd caught her chin in his hand and kissed her.

Applause broke out on the sidewalk, along with a voice that called, "Hoo-eee!"

Melissa took a deep breath, then another, forcing herself to gather her senses. She'd badgered Lucky into playing his role convincingly, but he had no call to go that far. "Husbands don't kiss their wives in the middle of Main Street on a Saturday afternoon."

"Well, they ought to. Besides, Bart was watching," he lied.

"Oh. Well, don't let it happen again." It was more than all right. It was . . . she couldn't put a name on what it was or why she'd been unable to catch her breath afterward.

"Where're we going, sweetheart?" he asked.

"To Sizemore's General Store," she answered. "I have business with Ida."

"And what would you like me to do?"

"Whatever . . . no. You'd better come with me."

"Of course I will, darlin'."

"And stop calling me that!"

"You said I should act like a husband. I've never been a husband, you'll have to help me out here."

"Just do exactly what I say."

"Yes, ma'am." Lucky reined Arthur to a stop in front of the general store, and started around to help Melissa from the buggy. But she was already out and heading for the door.

"Melissa?" Lucky called out. "Dear!"

She came to a stop. "What do you want?"

Lucky held out his elbow and waited until she walked back to him and hooked her arm inside his. "That's better, dear. Now smile. We're newlyweds, remember?"

"But . . ."

"Everyone's watching. You're doing this for the reputation of Grayson Academy."

She squeezed his arm, looked up at him, and gave him a smile that he felt in his toes. The minx. "You're right, dear," she said. Then she whispered, "Lucky?" When he leaned down to hear, she smiled again and planted a saucy kiss on his cheek. His toes curled and the motion sent sharp streaks of heat up the back of his knees.

"You're right. Come along, sweetheart!" she said. She turned and did her best to sashay into the store. "Bart's watching."

9

Cerqueda was not a man to give up. He was a man who got what he wanted. But locating the man who'd taken Louisa and stolen his horses and carriage was proving to be a failure that preyed on his mind. Every mile he rode west fed the fury. When there was no trace of the gambler, Cerqueda realized that not only had he been hurt, but the man who made him look bad hadn't gone toward California. By now, he'd wasted so much time there was no telling where he was.

"Can we go home now, *patrón*?" one of his men asked.

"You want to go home, do you?"

"*Sí*. My wife, she is expecting a little one and the time is near."

"And what about you?" Cerqueda asked the other one in a casual voice that should have made them think.

"Me too. Winter is coming, and the snow. I heard

that last year it was so bad that the cattle all died. I don't think we will find the man-in-black. He's too smart."

Cerqueda drew his pistol and shot the second man in the heart, then glanced back at the first. "No *hombre* is too smart for Cerqueda! I say when it is time to go home."

Cerqueda pushed the dead man's body down an embankment, gathered the horse's reins, and handed them to his helper. "I will go to the railroad station and take the train east. You will take these two horses and return to Texas and your wife. But you will never question me again. *Comprende*?"

The white-faced man nodded, letting out a deep breath. He took the reins, turned his horse and galloped quickly away.

Cerqueda narrowed his eyes. He should have killed them both, but a wife and a baby made him soft. Just as his feelings for Louisa had made him soft. The poker games with her father had been carefully plotted and played out, one loss at a time, until her foolish father had been willing to risk everything on one last hand. He'd planned to make her his wife, but she'd refused him repeatedly, until at last he'd stripped her of any spirit. His spurned affections turned to rage and finally he'd raped her, then taken her dignity by forcing her to accompany him everywhere, as if she were his slave.

Until this gambler had come along—a gambler as adept at dealing from the bottom of the deck as he. Looking back, he came to the conclusion that Louisa had been the object of the man-in-black's mission, not money. And he'd accomplished his task, then disappeared. Cerqueda removed his hat, ran his fingers through his hair, and felt the scar across the back of his head where the edge of the table had sliced into it. The scar would forever remind him of the only man who'd ever bested him. The man he intended to find. His guess was that a poker game would be his means of locating Louisa and her gallant rescuer. That and a lucky gold coin with a diamond in the center.

Colonel Curtis was sitting behind his mahogany desk in his study when he was told about Bart's request for an interview. "So, what did he want?" he asked his ranch foreman.

"Said it was for him to know and you to find out" was the answer. "Said he knew how you could double your money at the mine."

"Who is the man?"

"You know him. He calls himself Black Bart. He's the one who set his sights on that teacher and caused all that trouble for her."

The colonel turned his head quickly, frowning at his ranch foreman. "Mrs. Pickney?"

"Well, she wasn't Mrs. Pickney then. She was Miss Grayson, until Bart approached her one time too many and a fight broke out. She's the one who shot the mayor's son. That's when the town told the teacher to pick a husband or go to jail."

"I met her husband," the colonel said. "And he doesn't look like a miner."

"No, I heard she sent for a dandy from back East."

His bushy eyebrows rose in question. "I don't think he's a dandy, either."

"So what do you want to do about Bart Jamison?"

Always conscious of presenting a picture of power

and success, Colonel Curtis took a draw on his cigar and thought about it for a moment. "Just let it go for now. I'll talk to Davis over at the mine. I can't think what Jamison would have to say that would interest me. But if you hear anything about him bothering that teacher, you let me know."

"Daddy," his daughter's demanding voice came from the veranda. "Mrs. Pickney has ordered more paper and paints. Mr. Pickney is going to teach me how to use watercolors next."

"Mr. Pickney?"

"He's really quite knowledgeable and very sophisticated," she said. "I think he likes me."

Something about that didn't sound right to the colonel. Something about the man didn't seem right either. Without a mother, Ellen had always been a handful. Maybe he ought to have a little talk with Mr. James Harold Pickney. A horse was to be part of their arrangement for Ellen's schooling. He'd just pick one out and take it over next week.

"They're holding a fund-raiser in town to replace the church bell. Would you like to ride in with me?"

"And have everyone there stare at me as if I am some kind of freak? No, thank you."

Colonel Curtis didn't argue. It made him sad that Ellen had turned into such a recluse. The doctors had said that with determination, she might walk again someday. Only the promise of art lessons had drawn her to the school. Since then, she'd talked of Pickney constantly. He was worried. Her obvious attraction to Pickney was a problem that needed to be nipped in the bud. He wasn't surprised. Ellen was a young woman of an age to be interested in boys. Nothing would suit him any better than to have Ellen married to someone who could care for her and take over his holdings when the time came. But Ellen was a girl. And this James Pickney was no boy. There just weren't any prospects in Silver Wind.

Not to mention Mr. Pickney was married. And Melissa's school depended on that marriage. So Ellen's wishes had nowhere to go. Just to be sure, maybe he'd send out some inquiries. He was a man who liked to know what was going on. Silver Wind didn't belong to him, but it suited him to control its residents. Authority and wealth equaled power; he learned that at West Point. Successful officers married well. Ellen's mother had position and wealth; she just didn't have the stamina for childbearing. She'd produced only a daughter, a daughter who came down with a sickness that took away her ability to walk. Up to now, nothing had inclined her to try. If it took using Pickney to convince Ellen to get out of that chair, he'd leave things alone for now.

They'd come into town this afternoon like any other couple. Lucky looked around at the number of businesses, evidence of Silver Wind's financial success. As they entered the general store, Melissa attempted to pull her arm from Lucky's. "Ida, may I have a word with you—in the back?"

Lucky smiled and held tight. "Yes, we want to speak with you."

"I don't think so," Melissa said sweetly, continuing to try and pull away. "Why don't you just wander around while I talk with Ida?" Melissa said, and pinched Lucky's arm.

Ida looked at the two of them with a confused expression, but pulled open the curtain strung across the doorway separating the store from their living quarters, and motioned for Melissa to enter.

"Certainly, Mrs. Pickney," Lucky said, and let go her arm. His hand slid casually down Melissa's back, reached under her shawl, and gave her an unexpected tweak in approximately the same spot where she'd had her wedding dress pinned up.

She let out a startled gasp and took a quick step forward into Ida's back room.

Lucky walked away, glancing at the shelves filled with yard goods and cans of food. The peaches he'd bought were still hidden under his bunk. The time hadn't seemed right to bring them out yet. He didn't know what Melissa would say if Mrs. Sizemore asked her how she liked them.

Once he'd made his way around the store, he took a cigar from a jar on the counter, left a coin, and stepped outside. It wouldn't hurt to check around and see if there was any word of Cerqueda. About that time, he saw Cob Barnett heading up the walk. When he noticed Lucky, he grinned and stopped. "Glad I caught you, Pickney. Got a letter here for the wife. She in the store?"

"Ah, yes." He didn't think Melissa would want Barnett walking in on whatever private conversation she was having with Ida. "But," he added, "she's in the back . . . trying on a dress. I'll give the letter to her."

"Reckon it's all right, seeing it's from you. Don't

know why it took so long to get here. The train mail service is faster, but I still like the Pony Express."

"The Pony Express was fine as long as the rider didn't get waylaid by Indians," Lucky agreed. He took the letter, glanced at the envelope, and slipped it inside his coat. The address on the back was a shock. It had come from James Harold Pickney, St. Louis. Barnett waited, standing, as if he wanted to talk. Lucky, still stunned by the letter, grasped at something to say. "Say, Barnett, the day I came in there were some Temperance Leaguers down in Durango. They were really giving a Mexican gambler named Cerqueda a hard time. You heard anything about him?"

"Don't know anything about any Cerqueda, but I heard the women tormented some men in a saloon up in Durango. Who's Cerqueda?"

"Cerqueda? Just a man I've heard bad things about. He's supposed to be a killer. Wouldn't want a man like that in Silver Wind."

"Why would he come up here? All the gold and silver from here goes to the mills in Durango. Easier to just rob the train."

"Somebody on the train said Cerqueda was looking for a man, another gambler. Wouldn't want to be him."

"Ain't no real gamblers in Silver Wind, just the miners and a few cowhands."

Lucky decided he'd pushed his questions far enough. When he saw the Widow Cassidy headed his way, Lucky looked past the telegraph operator, nodded his head and tipped his hat as she passed by. "Afternoon, ma'am."

Barnett took one look at the widow and headed the other way. Lucky wished he could go with him.

"Mr. Pickney," she trilled. "I hear you're coming to

the supper social. We're certain to raise money to buy a new bell."

"Oh, yes," Lucky said with a grin. "Wouldn't miss it since a new bell will be a kind of memorial to my new wife."

The widow tucked in her chin. "Tsk, tsk, tsk. Melissa didn't intend to cause the bell to fall. Just like Obie said, 'It was God's will.'"

Lucky hoped God was going to make a contribution to the new bell fund, because he had only a few coins left from his winnings and at the rate he was going, he was more likely to have an audience with the man upstairs than he was to get into a poker game. Why hadn't he pretended to be a prospector? At least he would have had an excuse to visit the saloon and he wouldn't feel responsible for Melissa.

At that moment, Melissa exited the store and called out to him. He turned, caught sight of her and his lips curved into a smile. His question was answered. "Where to now, Mrs. Pickney?" he asked and offered his arm.

"Well, since you've obligated us to stay for the social, you'd better take Arthur to the livery stable. He'll need water and some feed."

"Yes, ma'am. By the way, what exactly is a social supper?"

Melissa planted a smile on her face and looped her arm in Lucky's. "A woman prepares supper for herself and someone else, either her beau or her husband. In this case, it's mostly husbands. Then the men bid on the boxes. They get to have supper with the woman the box belongs to if she's unmarried or they just get the supper if she has a husband."

"And the husbands go along with that?"

"Well, it's understood that the wives come prepared to feed more than one. It's all in fun."

Lucky winked. "So I bid on your box of food and we share it—privately?"

He made it sound like some intimate, secretive venture. She couldn't help but blush as she nodded. "That's the idea."

"There's only one problem, wife, I don't have the funds to bid for you."

"Then I guess I'll share my box with someone else."

About that time Lucky looked up and caught sight of the men standing outside the Lucky Chance, a name that was wasted on the one man who needed one. One figure was tall and thin—Bart Jamison. He gave Lucky a dark, swarthy scowl. "Having men fight over you is what got us into this pretend marriage, my dear. I don't think starting it up again is a smart idea, even if it is for a good cause."

Melissa started. He was right. Ida had agreed to allow her to trade out the twins' schooling for her food bill, but this pretend relationship was not working out the way she'd planned.

"I wouldn't worry, Lucky," she said. "Everybody knows you're my husband now; they won't bid against you. It's only the single women who are available."

"And just how many single women are there?" Lucky asked.

"Well, there's..." Melissa couldn't think of a single one except Ellen, and she'd never seen her in Silver Wind. Unless...there was the woman who wore red lip paint. "I think we'd better go home," she said and turned back toward the wagon, then stopped. "No.

Refusing to take part in replacing the bell that I helped destroy wouldn't be smart. The town needs to know that our marriage is a success."

"And how do we show them?"

"We'll figure out a way, I'm sure." She was sure—well, reasonably sure.

After two days of rest in Cheyenne, James, with a bossy Agnes in tow and fussing over him, climbed on the Rio Grande Railroad heading for Denver and on to Durango.

"Oh, Mr. Pickney, I've never seen such mountains," Agnes kept repeating.

"They are spectacular," he admitted. "Historians say that volcanoes formed the mountains and ice glaciers slid down between them to polish the granite walls. *'High mountains are a feeling, but the hum/Of human cities torture: I can see/Nothing to loathe in nature...'*"

"My, my, you are a wonder with words."

"Those aren't my words, Agnes, they're from *Childe Harold's Pilgrimage*, written by a very famous poet, Lord Byron."

Agnes twisted her handkerchief. "Me, I'm afraid the only reading I've done is my medical book, *Godey's Lady's Book*, and"—she ducked her head and said shyly—"now and then one of those dime novels about the West. They sometimes get left in the hospital, you know."

James grinned. "Me too. I've read them all. My favorites are the stories about the lawmen and the gamblers. One of the writers, Ned Buntline, wrote a play staring W.F. Cody. I saw it in New York."

"Cody? You mean Buffalo Bill?"

"Yes, it started Cody on his stage career."

"Just think, we're going to a real mining town. Do you suppose it's as wild as they say?"

"From what my fiancée said, Silver Wind is pretty wild. When gold is discovered, the prospectors swoop in, and then come the trading posts, the saloons, hotels, banks. You name it. But it takes a while for a mining town to settle in and become civilized, even today."

"Mr. Pickney, I know I'm a bit older than you and only came along to act as your nurse, but do you suppose your fiancée is going to be upset that we . . . traveled together?"

James blinked. It had been his distinct impression that Agnes was as eager for adventure as he. But if she chose to mask that need with duty, he could understand. "Well, I never thought about that. Can't see why she would, seeing that I've not been well and you're a nurse. I'm more worried about what happened when I didn't arrive on time."

James was used to having his health interfere with his plans, and he'd learned to accept disappointment. He'd been more concerned about arriving at all than he had about being late. Now, suddenly, he was worried. Melissa had plainly stated her dire circumstances, and their marriage was to save her and her school. He'd failed her. Suppose she was in jail—or worse. Suppose she'd been forced to choose someone else. He wouldn't want to frighten Agnes or embarrass Melissa. On arrival, it would behoove him to keep his identity confidential until he'd spoken with Miss Grayson.

Growing quiet, he looked out the window. The jerky little train spit soot and sparks as it meandered through the foothills into Durango. They'd find a couple of rooms and spend the night in Durango and catch the mining train to Silver Wind. Now that he was so close to meeting this woman whom he'd corresponded with for over a year, his concern grew for his ability to fulfill his obligations. Could he really be a teacher? Would she still want to marry him? Was he too late?

Durango was an anthill of activity. The pounding of mills crushing the ore for shipment was constant. Curls of black smoke poured from the stacks, then was caught by the mountain breeze that swept down the valleys and lifted the haze away. A line of mules, each carrying two timbers, one attached to each side of a kind of saddle, was headed toward the mountains. Braces for a mine, James decided. There were buggies, horses, and people; there were people everywhere. People who gave off an energy that fed James's excitement. Stepping off the train, he drew in a deep breath of air.

James Harold Pickney IV was in Colorado. He'd almost made it.

In Silver Wind, the Saturday social was almost setting off as much activity as in Durango.

Instead of taking Arthur to the livery stable, Lucky unhitched him and moved him to a patch of grass behind the hotel, where he could graze during the festivities. "So," Lucky said as he and Melissa walked along, "what do we do this afternoon until the bidding begins?"

"We go to the churchyard, where I will spend my time sticking a needle in my fingers and bleeding all over someone's quilt."

"And what do I do?"

"You will help the men shuck corn."

"Why?"

"Because that's what they do in the afternoon before the supper."

"But why are the men shucking corn?"

"We'll eat it later."

"And do I have to buy it too?"

Melissa shook her head. "No. The local farmers donate some of their crop for the social. I understand everyone shares the boiled corn and lemonade."

"You understand? Haven't you been to a social before?"

"Only one. That's when my trouble with suitors started. They wouldn't leave me alone, fighting and drinking and fighting some more. Eventually I had to hide under a quilt. I left before the dancing even started. Haven't been to another one since."

"You didn't stay for the dance?"

"No, and I really don't think we need to stay either. We'll eat our supper and go."

Lucky grinned. "Maybe. But I doubt that the Widows Sweeney and Cassidy are going to let that happen. They've already penciled my name on their dance cards."

"I expect Black Bart and his friends won't let it happen, either. They're going to want to dance with *me*." She shuddered. "I'd hoped all that was behind me."

"Out of curiosity, how'd you keep them from bothering you at your school?"

"I told you I know how to use my shotgun. I found out that you don't even have to be good with it."

"What about the sheriff?"

"Well, he did have a talk with them. It took a while, but we eventually figured out that they'd rather drink and gamble their wages than spend the money to pay fines—or worse—work it off."

"I'll take care of Bart and his friends," Lucky said. "In the meantime, let's play husband and wife."

Melissa was surprised at how comfortable it was to walk through town with her arm folded around Lucky's. In every doorway, someone called out a greeting. Lucky responded to their welcome as if he were actually enjoying himself. When they reached the end of the street, they entered the churchyard, where a wooden quilt frame was already set up. Some of the women were tucking the quilt and the batting between the wooden pieces of the frame and pulling it taut. Others were draping tablecloths across boards laid over barrels. Children were gathering wood and tossing it beneath a large iron pot next to a mound of green ears of corn.

"I know it's convenient, but just out of curiosity," Lucky asked, "why did they build the church next to a saloon?"

"I guess you could say the saloon built the church. It started off as a jail. Then the townsfolk got the idea of charging tolls, like on a road. Every miner heading for the saloons made a contribution toward the church. When they got too drunk or caused trouble, they were arrested, and those who couldn't pay their fines had to pay it with labor. Thanks to Colonel Curtis, who provided a steeple and the organ, the jail was enlarged and soon turned into the church. Then it was easy to build another jail."

Lucky opened the gate. "How long has Silver Wind been here?"

"Like it is now? About three years, ever since the colonel found gold, and later silver. Things get done quickly out here. Towns spring up. Farmers and ranchers move into the valleys. Then the mines play out and most of the town dies."

"What will you do if that happens here?"

"I don't know," she admitted. "I really don't know. Become a dance-hall girl, maybe."

He stopped. "If you become a dance-hall girl, I'll go back to gambling. I think we might make a very good team."

She didn't answer. She couldn't admit that she was beginning to believe the same thing. Not that she'd become a dance-hall girl, but they did seem to be well matched, even if he didn't know anything about poetry.

Still, there was a nagging worry in the back of her mind. What had happened to the real James Harold Pickney IV?

10

The men used brooms, shovels, and boards to smooth out the hard earth at the end of the street so that the dancers wouldn't trip on the ruts. Sheriff Vance tuned his fiddle while a man Melissa didn't recognize played a bouncy tune on his harmonica.

Melissa watched as Lucky shucked the corn with such good-natured enthusiasm that the men soon stopped teasing him. He looked up at her, gave her a wink and a smile. Melissa swallowed hard, and true to her word, pricked her finger on the needle she was using to stitch the quilt. Glancing around at the other women, she wondered if they shared private moments with their husbands, moments in which no words were necessary. She'd never seen such examples of togetherness between her mother and father. For that, she felt a strong sense of regret—not for herself, but for them. If a man and woman married, it seemed to Melissa that at some point they surely must share some kind of private communication that indicated a commitment, even if it wasn't forever. Perhaps they had—once. After all, they'd produced a child together.

After her second stick and subsequent groan, Lucy Dawson, the mayor's wife, said, "You'd better quit looking at that handsome husband of yours, or borrow one of my thimbles."

Melissa blushed, accepted the thimble, and placed it over her injured finger. "Thank you. I'm afraid I'm not too good at this."

"Don't blame you for being more interested in your man than making stitches," another of the quilters called Hattie said with a giggle. "I saw Mr. Pickney in town the other day. Had a little run-in with Black Bart. Feel kinda sorry for Bart. He started off okay when he came out here from the Carolinas. Ran out of money and never found any gold. When he's sober, he's a good enough carpenter. It's when he gets too much to drink that he gets crazy."

Lucy knotted her thread and reached for the scissors. "Folks don't trust him anymore. Even your daddy fired him before he died."

Lucy's statement caught Melissa's attention. "My daddy fired him?"

"Didn't you know?" Lucy asked. "He helped your father build that school. Thought he might be straightening himself out, but once Mr. Grayson told him to hit the road, Bart went right back to drinking and over to the colonel's mine."

Mary nodded. "Guess he thought you'd be his friend like your pa was, but then he wanted to be your suitor. When you refused him, he went a little crazy again."

Ida Sizemore took her seat, nodding to the others. "If I had a choice between Bart and Mr. Pickney, I'd choose Mr. Pickney too. The twins seem to think highly of him. They say he's a good dancer, and he sings too. I hope that's not part of your schooling, is it?"

"Not usually. James was just trying to make the students relax, it being the first day of school."

"Maybe he could give Ted a few pointers on dancing," Lucy said. "He seems to have two left feet."

"I am thinking of expanding the curriculum to include elocution and debate," Melissa said. "The academies back East offer many options, but dancing wasn't one I was considering."

Ida snorted. "Dancing? I should think not. Cooking and sewing would be more sensible." She glanced at Melissa's work and pursed her lips. "Come to think of it, maybe you'd better leave the sewing to me."

"And the cooking to me," Widow Cassidy said, holding up two very large boxes tied with bright yarn. "Your box supper, Mrs. Pickney."

"Thank you, Mrs. Cassidy."

Melissa was grateful when darkness put an end to the quilting. They were disassembling the frame and folding the squares for another day, when one of the corn shuckers let out a yell.

"Lookie what the teacher found! A red ear. It just ain't fair. He's already got the girl, he don't need no permission."

Lucky was turning the oddly colored ear of corn over and over. "What's wrong with it?"

"Red kernels are just one of nature's quirks," the sheriff said. "Any man who finds a red ear gets to dance with the lady of his choice. 'Course we know who that will be, Pickney being a newlywed. Don't know why you let him into the shucking anyway."

"Ah, Vance, you wouldn't recognize a red one if you found it," Widow Cassidy said. "Why don't you forget about the dancing while we bid on these boxes? You don't need to worry, I've bought enough for you and me."

The sheriff growled. "Who said I'd want to eat with you?"

"Don't act like an old fool. You know I brought everything you like."

Blankets and quilts were being spread on the ground. The Widows Cassidy and Sweeney offered Melissa one of theirs, then brought two of the church benches out and sat down.

The tinny sound of the piano inside the Lucky Chance rippled out into the night air. It took Lucky a moment to figure out that the sound carried because so many of the drinkers were standing outside the saloon watching the goings-on in the churchyard. He could sense trouble coming. One by one, the boxes were auctioned off; the mayor ignored the bids made from the sidewalk outside the saloon, until Melissa's box was offered.

"The last box is that of Mrs. James Pickney, our teacher. Any bids?"

He looked at Lucky. But before Lucky could answer, Bart called out, "I bid $50.00."

Lucky should have seen it coming. Now Bart, followed by his cronies, was heading toward the churchyard. Lucky thought fast. He could refuse to let Melissa share her supper with Bart or he could allow it. Catching sight of her face, he decided to find a way to avoid a confrontation. Bart had to learn to leave Melissa alone now that she had a husband. Even if he were only temporary.

"Just a minute," Lucky said, coming to his feet. "I have an idea. I was told that you miners provided most of the money for this church, and I know you wouldn't want to be left out of the chance to contribute to the new bell. So, Bart, let's you and I step inside the Lucky Chance and talk."

"Don't want to talk," Bart growled. "I'm ready to eat."

"Good idea," Lucky agreed. "Eat first, and then we'll dance with the ladies. But before that, we need to move the piano. Come on, boys."

Bart's companions looked around in confusion as Lucky pushed through them and into the saloon. "Come on, Bart." The few men left inside went silent. "Excuse me, sir," Lucky addressed the musician, who turned to look at the intruder in amazement, "we need some dancing music. Would you donate your services to the town's fund-raiser to buy a new church bell?"

"Well . . ." He looked befuddled. "I don't know."

"Sure he will," said the woman who'd kissed Lucky in gratitude for being saved from Bart. "Let's roll it outside."

Moments later, the piano was outside the saloon. The townspeople were watching in shock. The mayor was still holding Melissa's box and Melissa was charging toward Lucky, ready to spit fire.

"Come along, Bart; you too, Miss Sable." He reached back for the woman's hand.

"What do you think you're doing, Pickney?" she asked, as he pulled her along.

"Bart and my wife are about to share their supper with you and me. Aren't you, Melissa, darling."

"We are . . ." She took a look at the men around Bart and swallowed the *not* she was about to say, changing it instead to, "We certainly are. Come along, Miss Sable. We have a quilt over here."

Bart, caught by surprise, didn't know what to say. This was not going the way he planned. Every time he crossed paths with James Pickney, Pickney got the best of him. Any other time, he would have stood him down, but spending time in jail for starting a disturbance didn't appeal to him. Maybe he'd go along with the dude. Maybe he could figure a way to wrangle a dance with the teacher. She didn't know it, but after her father died, he'd swiped a picture of her. He'd carried it around until it began to fade, then hid it inside his bedroll.

"Well, Bart?" Lucky prompted.

"Why sure, but fifty dollars for a supper I have to split four ways don't seem fair, Pickney."

"He's right, darling," Melissa agreed "I'd say twenty-five dollars is enough. I think you ought to pay the rest. Come along." She took a look at Sable's revealing dress, pulled off her own shawl, and said, "You must be cool out here without a wrap. Take mine." She threw it around Sable's shoulders and walked beside her to the churchyard.

Moments later, Sable and Bart and Lucky and Melissa were sharing the huge supper the widow had provided. They ate fried rabbit, sweet potato biscuits, corn on the cob, boiled potatoes, and washed it down with the lemonade punch the women had mixed.

Melissa glanced at the crowd, who had their eyes planted on them in astonishment. Colonel Curtis was talking to the mayor and the sheriff with a serious look on his face. At that point, Cob Barnett walked up and listened to the colonel, then nodded and left. Melissa could only conclude that they didn't approve of Sable and Bart's being included in the activities—an invitation that made her just as uncomfortable. Her new husband had a strange way of handling differences, but they seemed to work. She knew that Sable must feel out of place and she'd been taught to make everyone comfortable. Pulling her attention away from the colonel's frown, she asked. "Where are you from, Sable?"

"Everywhere and nowhere, Mrs. Pickney."

"I'm originally from Philadelphia," Melissa confided. "My husband is most recently from New York, but he was reared in the South."

"My mama was from Virginia," Sable said, "but she died on the way out West. My aunt and uncle had too many mouths to feed, so I've been on the move ever since."

Torches were lit, throwing fingers of light into the shadows. Everyone clapped when the mayor announced they'd raised enough money to buy the new bell. The musicians set up on the walk in front of the saloon and the music began. When the Widow Sweeney claimed the first dance with Lucky, Sable caught Bart's arm and pulled him into the street. "Come on, Bart. Tonight you're a gentleman and I'm a lady."

Suddenly, Melissa was standing and watching everyone else dancing. A few weeks ago, every man in Silver Wind would have been standing in line to be her partner; now nobody came close. Lucky was swapping partners with Bart and swinging Sable around the street. He kept looking back at Melissa with an odd expression on his face. Was he sorry for her? The pain in her chest was so intense that she could hardly breathe. She didn't want Lucky's arms around Sable. He was her husband. They ought to be around her.

No, he wasn't truly her husband. No one there would believe her if she told them that they'd never shared a bed. No one would believe that every night he walked away, sleeping in the dormitory. He'd kissed her, and since the night he'd dried her hair, she'd sensed that he wanted to touch her. And she'd waited, rehearsing how she'd refuse. But he hadn't even tried. She was beginning to believe there was something wrong with her. Every other man there wanted her. Why not Lucky? She couldn't allow it, of course, but rejection smarted.

She turned away, making her way to the punch bowl where several of the miners were gathered. She filled her glass nervously, emptied it and refilled it, ignoring their smirks. Finding a place in the shadows under a tree, she drank the liquid without even being aware of the taste.

"What are you doing hiding over here?" Bertha Cassidy asked.

"I'm not hiding," Melissa said. "I'm thirsty. This lemonade is really very good. I believe I'll have some more."

"Ah . . . Think I'll have a taste of that." The Widow Cassidy followed Melissa back to the punch bowl. Melissa refilled her cup. The widow took a sip, then shook her head. "That's what I thought. All right, you boys. Who messed with our punch?" But the men around the table had disappeared into the darkness. "You'd better not have any more of that, Missy," she said. "I think I'd better fetch James."

"Never mind," Melissa said. "He's my husband, *I'll* fetch him." She finished her fourth glass of lemonade and handed Bertha the cup. The music came to a stop, then started up again. Sable was standing beside Lucky, laughing brightly. *The witch!* It was time she showed the dance-hall girl that *James* belonged to her.

"Hello, darling," she said, and stumbled slightly as she slid her arm around Lucky's waist. "Sable, you ought to get some punch. It's delicious. Lucky...eh, James, I think it's time you danced with your wife."

Lucky didn't know quite what Melissa was up to. But if he didn't know better, he'd think she'd been in the cooking sherry. Still, when she threw back her head and put the other arm around his neck, he followed her directions, pulling her close and dancing her across the street.

"You're very different tonight, wife. I didn't know I'd married a wild woman."

"You would if you only took a little time to find out." She snuggled closer.

His feet stepped lively, his pulse kept time with the music, teasing his masculinity into announcing its need. This was a new and exciting Melissa. A dangerous one who was heading down a road of no return as fast as her freed emotions could fly, and he was going with her.

Finally, the music slowed to a waltz that lulled their activity to a dreamy state of being together. She fit his arms perfectly. Her golden hair had become mussed with their movement, and she was unbuttoning the top of her dress.

Bart watched Melissa melt against her husband. If James Harold Pickney weren't here, it would be him holding Melissa. She should have been his. He had been a gentleman once. He could be again. Somehow, she'd have to understand. He'd have to find a way to make her.

"Oh, Lucky," Melissa said, oblivious to being watched, "I'm a little dizzy." She pulled him out of the street and around the church into the shadows. She laughed, let go of his hand and whirled around. "I'm feeling strangely warm and tingly. What about you?"

"Oh, Melissa, I'm feeling strangely warm myself. I know what caused my problem. What caused yours?"

"I think you'd better hold me or I'm going to melt into a puddle." She flung her arms around his neck.

"Melissa, don't do this. Tomorrow you're going to be sorry."

"Maybe," she whispered, planting little kisses along his neck and chin, "but if I'm going to be sorry, it ought to be for something I've done, not something I haven't."

"Come on, Melissa," Lucky said. "Let's go home."

"Home? But I want to dance with my husband."

He put his arm around her, and pulling her close, started back to the wagon, where he lifted her up to the seat. "Now sit still while I hitch up Arthur."

"You're so good to me, Lucky. You agreed to stay with me when you didn't have to do it. You've helped me with the children, particularly with Ellen. You put a stove in my room. You may be a wicked, roving gambler, Lucky, but you care about me. I never thought I would, but I care about you."

"Shush! Someone is going to hear you." He climbed into the wagon and headed Arthur out of town at a fast clip. He didn't have to look back to know that the whole town must be watching. Melissa slid across the seat and scooted her head under his arm. He was sunk before they got out of Silver Wind. He tried. God knew he tried. But he couldn't push her away. When her lips found his, he couldn't say no.

She was right. Arthur knew the way home. He was also content to wait patiently by the lean-to while Lucky lifted Melissa and took her inside. Mac followed until they reached the doorway, then lay down as if to ward off intruders. Lucky intended to lay Melissa in her bed and make a quick exit. Apparently she knew that, for by the time he got her into her bedroom, she'd unbuttoned her blouse and his shirt. Her full round breasts were pressed against his bare chest.

"What are you doing, Melissa? You belong to James."

"But you're James. Take off your boots," she said as she reached for the top button of his trousers.

Both were gone before his mind fought for some semblance of control. "Melissa," he growled, "you don't want to do this. You're not yourself."

"Oh, yes, I am. I've never been more myself. And tonight, you're my husband."

11

"You told me, the next time, I had to ask for what I want," she said, as she ripped off her gown and shift. "So, I'm asking. Kiss me, Lucky."

"Melissa..." he protested. "Are you sure? I feel like we're standing on thin ice without skates."

"We have skates. I feel the blade," she whispered, "and it's poking against me."

"That's not a skate you feel, darlin'. It's part of me and if you don't stop, it's going somewhere you don't want me to go. Think about what you're doing."

"I have. You're my husband. If you don't want to kiss me, I'll kiss you." She stood on her tiptoes, put her hands around his neck and forced him down so that she could nibble on his chin.

He moaned and forced himself to pull away. "You don't know what you're doing. This is not a good idea."

"There are a lot of things I don't know. I don't know why you didn't dance with me first? I'm your wife."

"Have you ever tried to change the Widow Sweeney's mind?"

In the back recesses of her mind, Melissa remembered the incident of the wedding dress. "Yes. But then you danced with Sable. Was she the one who kissed you that day in town? She is. I know it."

Her kisses were growing more insistent. "Yes," Lucky managed to say, "but she only kissed me on the cheek. It was to thank me."

"Thank you for what?"

"Saving her from Bart."

"So, dancing with her was your way of saying 'you're welcome'?" She worked her away across Lucky's mouth, tugging at his upper lip. "She wasn't passionate? You didn't feel lust for her?"

"No. I didn't feel lust for her." He was having a hard time resisting her. "Melissa, why are you doing this?"

"I can't say for sure that what I feel is passion. Maybe I'm just overheated. I think you'd better do something."

"Melissa, I think you've had too much *lemonade*. Obviously something alcoholic was added. You don't know what you're doing."

"Oh, but I do. I really, really do. Why don't you want me, Lucky? I thought strong, worldly men like you went after any available woman. I'm available. Is there something wrong with me?"

Not want her? There was no way she could possibly understand how much he wanted her. He ached with want. He was amazed by her honesty. No woman had been so open with him. "No," he whispered, "there's nothing wrong with you, nothing at all, except brothers and sisters don't act like this."

"But we're not brother and sister, are we?" she asked, as she slid one hand between them and touched the part of him that took over his mind, the part of him that felt as if it would explode, the part of him that refused to take directions.

"Is it always like this?" she asked as she clasped him tightly, wanting to be closer, wanting to quell the insistent twitching between her legs. Wanting? She didn't know what, only that if she didn't get it, she would die. "Swollen, I mean. I mean, I would have noticed if it poked against your trousers or when you were in the creek, wouldn't I? Does it hurt?"

"Yes!" he said, groaning, lowering his mouth to her breast, rimming the nipple with his tongue, feeling it bead up against his lips. "But it's the best kind of hurt a man can feel."

"Oh! What you're doing...I mean, it hurts, but it hurts good. Is that what it feels like for me to touch you?"

His groan deepened.

She stumbled back against the bed and fell onto it, pulling him across her. Suddenly there was a sharp pain and he was inside her, his thighs against hers, his chest against her breasts, his chin in her hair. He froze.

"Oh!" she said. "Did it hurt you too?"

"Please don't move about. If you don't stay still, I'll—" But it was too late. As he felt the rush of his release, she lifted herself against him and he was lost. Two unchecked thrusts and he was over the top, exploding inside her, releasing all the pent-up desire and frustration he'd felt from the first time he'd seen her on the platform at the depot. At last, spent, he collapsed against her, reality crashing over him. What the hell had he done? He should have stopped himself. She had been innocent, untouched, and he'd ruined her—even if she had initiated it, she couldn't have known what she was doing.

"Is that all?" Melissa asked, continuing to squirm beneath him. "I'm on fire. I feel as if I want to go running into the night and plunge into the stream. But I'd boil the water and the fish would die. What have you done to me?"

He groaned again. The horse was out of the barn now. It was too late to close the door. Still, he couldn't quell the elation that rushed through him to know that she responded to the demands of her body, that she was a woman who didn't look on lying with a man as her duty. If only...

"Melissa, my love," he whispered, withdrawing himself and pulling them forward on the bed so that they could lie side by side. "Lie still and listen."

"I don't want to listen," she said crossly. "I just want ... I don't know what I want. I was on fire ... and then ... nothing. Is that all there is to lying with a man? 'It's your duty,' my mama said. She was wrong; it's pure frustration."

"Your mother *was* wrong," Lucky said, pulling her into the curve of his arm and rubbing the side of her cheek. "When a man and woman lie together and it's *right,* they both feel something wonderful." That's what he'd always heard. Now, to his surprise, he realized it was true. "It's like a Chinese firecracker bursting into waves of heat that rock your body and leave you feeling warm and happy."

"Then why am I still twitching like some kind of racehorse chomping at the bit? Does that mean it isn't right between us? You seem all warm and happy. What's wrong with me?"

Not only had he done the unspeakable, but as her voice rose, he realized that the intensity of her feelings was out of control. She was fighting back tears. He'd left her caught by her passion, with no outlet for her predicament and no understanding of what was happening to her. If he were to take the blame for ruining Melissa for another man, he was obligated to finish what he'd started, else she'd be forever wrong about what it meant for two people to love each other.

Love each other? Where had that come from?

"There's nothing wrong with you, darlin'. What's wrong is with me. I've wanted you from the first moment I saw you. It's almost driven me mad. Then tonight, my wanting you became so physically overwhelming that I could no longer control myself. I confess, I'm a weak man."

"This isn't about you," she snapped. "You seem to be over your condition. How did you accomplish that? What can I do to keep myself from jumping out of this bed?"

"You can't do it alone. I have to do it for you."

"Then do it!"

"You're certain?"

"I'm certain," she whispered, closing out all the demon voices that shouted warnings. This was her house, her school, her husband, her body. "You promised to do exactly what I said. Tonight, you're my husband. Teach me what I should know."

This road to hell wasn't a road, it was an avalanche; a steep, polished cliff heated by some inner fire that could neither be put out nor controlled. How could he have expected otherwise. This woman had come to the West alone, determined to control her life, run her school, and protect what was hers. Now he'd introduced her to physical need and desire without giving her the way to find the glow of her release. He couldn't leave her this way. As she'd said, he might as well show her the way; his fate was sealed anyway.

Lucky sucked in an agonizing breath. "Hush, my lusty lady. I'll take you to the place you want to go. Then you'll understand."

"Describe this place to me," she said.

"I'd rather show you."

He raised himself up on one elbow and touched her cheek with his fingertips, rubbing the pad of his thumb around the corner of her lips. "The journey usually begins with a kiss." He lowered his face, his lips nibbling at her mouth. He kissed her eyelids, her earlobes, the place on her neck where he could feel her heart beating. His fingertips ranged lower, swirling around the fullness of her breasts. Her immediate response brought her arms around his neck as she tried to burrow under him.

"Not yet," he said. "Men can take their pleasure almost instantly but women need longer."

"Longer for what?"

"Be patient, Melissa, I'll show you." As his hand ranged lower, she went still. His fire had only been banked. It came quickly back to life as his fingers moved lower. She began to squirm when he found the curly mat of hair between her legs.

"Please, please hurry," she gasped. "I once saw someone shake a bottle of champagne. It fizzed and fizzed until the top popped off and the bubbles erupted like a geyser into the air. I think my body is making bubbles. If they aren't let go, I will soon explode and die."

"Explode? Yes. Die? Not unless it's from pleasure." He reached down and touched her most private place, hesitantly rubbing the little nub of sensation. He'd never taken such a slow approach to seducing a woman before. But Melissa had been untouched. She was his to teach, to bring to the height of ecstasy. "Shall I continue?"

She lifted her hips, unable to control her breathlessness enough to answer.

"It means that you'll be forever changed," he said, knowing that she was already changed. As he slid his finger into the moist warmth of her body, she moaned and began to thrash back and forth. "Please, please," she was saying over and over. "I feel as if I'm going to... Oh, I feel..."

God help him, he pulled himself over her and plunged inside her. She instinctively wrapped her legs around him and lifted herself up to meet him. He was filling her, sliding in and out of her as if they were perfectly matched, as if she'd been created just for him. Then he felt the stirring, the intense contractions that said she was trying to hold back, yet couldn't stop. And then she screamed in pleasure, holding herself to him as his own intense spasm overwhelmed him.

For a long moment she stared up at him, confusion and wonder stealing her voice. "I didn't know," she said finally. "I never dreamed. Why on earth would my mother refuse to lie with my father?"

Lucky turned over, pulling Melissa half across him. "It isn't always like this for the women," he explained.

"They hold back, don't let their bodies respond to being stimulated."

She felt a wetness dribble from inside her body onto his knee. "Oh, I'm sorry." Embarrassment tightened her voice. "I appear to be . . . leaking."

"Don't be, sweetheart. That's a lot of me and a little of you. It's normal. It makes us able to do what we just did."

"That makes sense. I've read enough to understand the mechanics, but this kind of detail isn't described in the books I've read."

"There's something we need to talk about. You do know this fluid is what gives a woman a child?" There, he'd said it, voiced the unspeakable.

A *child?* "Of course," she responded, glossing over his suggestion. No, she hadn't considered that, but it was obviously the possible outcome of such a mating. Having Lucky's child? She'd read about reproduction, but having a child was beyond her comprehension. All she could think about now was being together, lying with this man who was not her husband.

"The touching makes you warm," he said. "You respond by making moisture that allows you to—I mean, when a man is swollen, penetration for the woman would be very painful, wouldn't it?"

"How long does it stay like that?"

She reached down and touched him, sending a sharp eddy of sensation from the tip of his male organ to his backbone. "Oh, it's all gone," she said in disappointment.

"It won't be gone long if you keep touching me like that."

"Does it work the same for me? I mean..." She reached over, took his hand, and placed it on the nub that had garnered such a wild response earlier. "I think it does."

"Wait," he said, pulling back his hand to catch her fingertips. Once entwined, he held them close to his stomach, rubbing the pad of his thumb up and down hers. "I think we should stop."

"Stop?"

"For now. You're going to be very sore."

"Fine. When I'm sore, we'll quit."

He grinned. "I've awakened Sleeping Beauty."

She returned his smile. "And I've kissed my frog."

"I'm not certain that frog is the right word. Toad might be more accurate," he said, enjoying the exchange.

"Aren't they the same thing?"

"Of course not, Melissa. A toad is a swarthy, knotted little thing."

"Well, then," she said with a lilt in her voice, "they're not the same at all. There's nothing small about you." She blushed. "A frog is a big handsome fellow. Every woman knows he's a prince in disguise."

Lucky groaned.

"Well, this prince has worked up an appetite. What do we have to eat?"

"Oh, dear. I'm not sure. I'll have to see." She made a move to get up, winced, and fell back.

"See, I told you that you'd be sore. You stay put. I'll find something for both of us."

She nodded. "Good idea. I do feel a bit weak. I might need to restore my strength. Do we have any lemonade?"

"More lemonade? That's the last thing you need. You just stay put. I'll be back in a minute." He rose from their bed. She heard the rustle of clothing and the sound of his footsteps leaving the living area. She forced herself to her feet and lit the lamp. The stain on the bed covers made her gasp. Quickly she ripped the soiled muslin sheet from the bed and replaced it with another—at least, as quickly as she could manage. Lucky had been right. She was sore and sticky and suddenly aware of the potential consequences of what she'd done. She washed the sticky residue from her body and donned her nightgown. Lucky would return shortly. What could she say? How could she explain that she'd never before acted so wildly? She'd never known a man's touch or the intensity of a woman's response. Then came the sound of pounding from the kitchen.

What was Lucky doing?

As the floor creaked, signaling his return to the bedroom, Melissa dived into bed and pulled up the covers. He lit a lamp in the other room. A thin wedge of light revealed his bare chest as he entered the bedroom. She closed her eyes.

"Sit up, sweetheart," he said. "I have a surprise for you."

"I'd rather not."

"Why?"

"Because." *Because I'm wearing my nightgown. Because I've just behaved in a way I never expected. Because I've become someone else.* "I don't know."

He understood. Time and the emotional energy spent had erased the aftereffects of whatever alcohol had been added to the lemonade. Now she was facing what she'd openly asked for.

Holding the open can of peaches in one hand and a fork in the other, Lucky sat down on the edge of the bed, nudging her over to make room. "Melissa, you don't have to be uncomfortable. You don't have to look at me. All you have to do is trust me. I won't harm you. Open your mouth."

She didn't have to answer to know that he was asking for more than just an open mouth. He was telling her that he understood. That he wouldn't hurt her. But what he didn't understand was that she was no longer Melissa Grayson. Nor was she Mrs. James Harold Pickney IV. She didn't know who she was.

"Trust me, Melissa."

She did. Letting out a deep sigh, she parted her lips.

Moments later, a sweet substance hit her taste buds. "Peaches?" She sat up, eyes wide in astonishment. "Where did you get peaches?"

"In town. From Ida Sizemore."

"When?"

He speared another section of the plump, sweet fruit and started toward her mouth, dripping the juice across her chest. "That first day I went to town alone."

"The day Sable kissed you? You thought of me?"

He nodded, realizing that even then he'd thought of pleasing Melissa, the woman. "I thought of you. I bought the peaches and kept them for a special occasion."

He fed her another chunk.

"Aren't you going to have some?"

"Yes. I think I will." He leaned forward and kissed her, drawing the sweetness into his mouth. He pulled back, slowly licked his lips and said, "Thank you. Best peaches I ever tasted."

* * *

For Lucky, recriminations came with the morning. What the hell had he done? He'd consummated the marriage. No, he'd consummated James Harold Pickney IV's marriage. Did that make it legal? Did it matter? He'd made love to Melissa for most of the night, and now, in the late morning light, he already wanted her again.

Suddenly Mac began to bark. Lucky slid out of bed and pulled on his pants. Melissa's eyes flew open. "Someone's coming," she said, as she reached for her gown and drew the covers up to her neck.

"Either that or Mac is chasing a very confused rabbit around the yard," Lucky said, heading for the door.

"What if someone catches us like this?"

"*Everyone* thinks we're married, Melissa," he barked, wondering the same thing.

There was a rap on the door.

Lucky looked back at the bedroom, conscious that Melissa was pulling on her nightgown and wrapper.

Ruefully, he opened the door to find a small wren-like woman with red hair. Behind her a slightly built man, wearing a tailor-made suit and a bowler hat, huddled beneath a blanket in one of the buggies from the livery stable.

"What can we do for you, ma'am," Lucky asked.

"If this is the home of Miss Melissa Grayson," the little woman said, "you can help me get her fiancé into the house. He isn't well and we've come a long way."

Lucky swore under his breath. The *real* James Harold Pickney IV had arrived. He'd just spent most of the night making love to the woman who was supposed to be Pickney's wife, the woman who still smelled of their lovemaking. Their house of cards was falling down around them. He was going to have to do some quick thinking.

"Melissa," he called out in steely resignation, "I believe James is here."

Melissa, entering the room, saw the woman and came to a sudden stop. "James is here?"

Agnes held out her hand. "I'm Miss Agnes Fulbright, Mr. Pickney's nurse."

Melissa looked stunned for a moment, then shook Agnes's hand quickly. She gave Lucky a helpless look and said, "Let's get James inside."

Lucky went to the buggy where James was already climbing out. "Come in, Mr. Pickney. The name's Lawrence and I think we have some talking to do."

Miss Fulbright went back for her medical satchel and scurried into the house. Lucky helped James inside, his mind grasping for a way out of this situation that would protect Melissa. He was surprised that the town fathers weren't coming up the trail already. They would be if they knew the truth. What had James told them back in town?

What had he done out here? He'd consummated the marriage of Melissa and James the night before the real James had arrived.

Lucky stuck a case under each arm, took one in each hand, and pushed the door open with his foot.

Melissa spoke. "I'm sorry, James. I . . . I thought you'd changed your mind."

"Didn't you get my telegram?" James asked. "I paid one of the hospital employees to send it, but I wasn't sure I could trust him."

Melissa shook her head.

"What about my letter? Agnes took it to the postmaster. Surely you got that."

Lucky let the cases hit the floor. "Letter. Oh, God!" He walked past Melissa, picked up his jacket, and walked back into the living area, pulling the letter from his pocket. "Here, Melissa. This came for you yesterday, and in all the excitement . . . I forgot to give it to you."

Melissa took it, her eyes going stormy, her lips pinched. "You had this last night?"

"I did. But—other things took my attention and I never thought about it again until now. I'm sorry, Melissa. Sit down, James," Lucky said. "You'd better know what happened."

"Do I understand this right? You claimed to be James Harold Pickney IV and married Melissa?" James asked. "I knew I was late and Melissa had a deadline. Finding her married to someone else doesn't surprise me. But you, sir, a well-known gambler, for you to misrepresent yourself as me is a fraud. I am certain Melissa could be forgiven. But why would you do such a thing?"

Lucky took the shirt Melissa was handing to him and slid his arms into the sleeves. He couldn't read her face and he didn't know whether she was angry or happy, but James was another story. His pale face was even paler, and the way Agnes was fussing around him made it obvious that James was a man who'd traveled a long way. "I had no idea what would happen. It was a spur of the moment opportunity for me to hole up until . . . doesn't matter now. It was a mistake."

"I'm thinking that Mr. Pickney needs to rest," Agnes

interrupted. "This is something we can resolve later. Miss Grayson, please show us to Mr. Pickney's room?"

"She's not Miss Grayson," Lucky snapped. "She's Mrs. Lawrence."

Agnes looked from Melissa's wrapper to Lucky's bare feet with confusion. "Mrs. Lawrence?"

Melissa let out a very unladylike swear. "I don't know who I am. I just know that if I had Black Bart here, I'd shoot his black heart out! This is all his fault."

"Black Bart, the outlaw?" James asked, suddenly awestruck.

"Not the real outlaw. Bart Jamison's a bad character, but he just calls himself Black Bart. He got the town so stirred up that everyone in Silver Wind gathered at the depot to make sure I married James Harold Pickney IV. You weren't on the train. Lucky was."

James glowered at Lucky. "After looking at Melissa, I can see why you wouldn't want to correct them," James said.

"I didn't know he was an imposter," Melissa protested. In truth, she'd expected James to look like the real James: thin, pale, and weak. At the time she hadn't considered what that might mean. But the presence of a nurse made her feel guilty at her own lack of concern. It was unfair to compare him to the man she'd married, but she did. "I'm truly sorry, James. I didn't even question him. I knew he wasn't the kind of man I'd expected, but, well, everything just moved so fast. Then later, well, by the time I found out he wasn't you, it was too late."

Agnes said timidly, "But now that you're here, Mr. Pickney, the mistake can be rectified. If the minister married Melissa Grayson to James Harold Pickney IV, then she's your wife. Or maybe she's not married at all."

James cleared his throat. "Mind you, I'm a scholar and not an attorney, but I believe that using a false name in a legal procedure would make the marriage null and void."

"In plain words, you're saying we aren't really married?" Lucky asked.

Melissa groaned. "Ohhhh! I think I should tell you, Jamie," Melissa began, hesitantly, "it's too late. Lucky and I...I mean, we've..."

"You've not been as brother and sister. I can see that," Jamie finished. "Well," he said with an effort at enthusiasm, "let's look at it realistically. I came out here for an adventure. I wanted to experience the West and what it meant, and it looks like I may have stepped into the pages of one of those dime novels. You needed my help to save your school. I'm here. If Lucky Lawrence is James Harold Pickney, then James Harold Pickney will have to become Lucky Lawrence. I don't know how to play poker, but I shall learn. Being Lucky Lawrence sounds much more exciting than being James Pickney."

"Not anymore," Lucky said under his breath.

"You intend to stay, James?" Melissa asked in shock. There was no way that James could convince the town fathers that he was a quick-drawing gambler.

"I do, indeed. You offered me a job as a teacher and I accepted. I shall endeavor to impart whatever knowledge I may have to those without. Where are our rooms?"

"Rooms?" Melissa repeated weakly, emphasizing the plural.

"Why, yes. Miss Fulbright only accompanied me as my nurse. I told her that I expected a town like Silver Wind would have use of a trained medical person. But she will need quarters until we make proper arrangements. Does your doctor have an assistant?"

"I don't think so," Melissa answered, thanking her father for the dormitories. With James's arrival, everything had changed. Except for the expense of feeding her newcomers, the situation might even be a plus. Now she had a dormitory resident for both the girls and the boys—if any boarding students ever arrived. "But I have room for both of you. In fact, you'll have plenty of space."

Suddenly it hit her, she and Lucky couldn't be together like last night again. What would happen to them? She winced. Her head ached and her stomach didn't feel quite right.

"Good," James said as he started rocking back and forth on his feet. "In a couple of days, I'll go into town with you, Agnes, and we'll call on the doctor."

"Thank you, Mr. Pickney," Agnes said.

"From now on, Agnes, I'm Lucky Lawrence," James said with a quirky grin. "Lucky. Hmm. I think I like that."

Lucky looked around. He'd never encountered such a situation before. James was sitting in Melissa's rocking chair, excitement flushing his pale cheeks. Agnes was sitting on the bench at the kitchen table clutching a small medical bag and an umbrella, her red hair frizzing about her round face. Melissa, looking totally bewildered, was leaning against the cook table, rubbing her neck as if she'd slept on a saddlebag instead of in his arms.

"James, *I'm* Lucky Lawrence. You don't want to be me. Right now that isn't healthy. Lucky Lawrence is being hunted by a very bad man who intends to kill him. Do you even know how to shoot a gun?"

"No, but you can teach me. What about that, Agnes? If I get shot, can you fix me up?"

Melissa let out an odd, anguished scream and collapsed dramatically. For all appearances, she looked as if she'd fainted.

"Let me," Agnes called out, and hurried to Melissa's side.

"No!" Lucky scooped her up and rushed into the bedroom, kicking the door closed behind him. "Melissa! Melissa!" he called out as he laid her on the bed and began slapping her face. "Wake up!"

"Stop hitting me!" she hissed.

"You're okay?"

"Of course. It's just that everything is moving too fast. My head is aching so that I can't think—"

"That's from drinking too much lemonade with who knows what mixed in."

"—and my eyes sting like I haven't slept."

A quick grin curled his lips. "You haven't." He smoothed her hair back from her face and let his grin relax into a smile. "We've got a mess here, haven't we?"

"We have. I'm so sorry. I never expected anything like this to happen. I just wanted to save my school."

"I wish I could say that I just wanted to help you. But I'm afraid I'm not that good. I wanted a place to hide, and being James gave me that. But now . . ."

"Lucky, you didn't tell me. Why is that man going to kill you?"

"There was a girl. Her father gambled with Cerqueda. He lost his ranch in Texas and finally, in desperation, agreed to use his daughter to cover his bet. He was certain he was going to win. He didn't. Cerqueda took the ranch and the girl away. Her father hired me to win her back. Cerqueda didn't take it well. I didn't know it at the time, but it seems he swore to hunt me down and kill me. When the opportunity came along for me to become someone else for a while, I took it without realizing that I was putting you in danger. I guess I can't expect you to believe that."

"But I do, Lucky. Except now, in order to protect me, we've put James in danger."

"I thought about that, but once Cerqueda sees James, he'll know James is not the man he's looking for."

"That's true. He'll be looking for you. Oh, Lucky, what are we going to do?"

He looked down at her blue eyes awash in moisture, her beautiful hair all tousled and wild, lips swollen from his kisses, and knew that he had to find an answer.

But that was after he kissed her.

It was the sound of James's dramatic coughing that pulled Lucky back to the present.

He pulled her up, kissed her one last time, swatting her on the bottom as he passed.

"You get dressed. Right now, I'm going to show Miss Fulbright to the girls' dormitory. Then, while you show James the schoolhouse, I'll gather up my things and move them in here."

"But, Lucky, surely you don't mean...I mean, we can't..."

"Oh, yes, I do and we will—or maybe we won't. We'll have to figure it out. Get dressed, wife, before that ex-fiancé of yours dies of consumption from all that fake coughing."

"Lucky, what are we going to do?"

He stopped at the door and looked back at her, her blue eyes veiled in moisture. "Right now, I'm going to drive James's horse and buggy back to town. I'll find out what happened when he came in. Then, decisions have to be made before the real James Harold Pickney IV gets himself killed."

12

Lucky tied Arthur to the back of the wagon and told James that he was returning the rented horse and buggy to the livery stable in town. To Melissa's relief, James, with Agnes in attendance, went to the dormitory for the rest of the afternoon. While everyone was gone, Melissa moved Lucky's things into the sleeping loft. Everything had changed. Until she learned who she was married to or even if she was married at all, she and Lucky shouldn't... couldn't.... Lucky would have to sleep in the loft—so near but so far.

Time passed. Melissa paced. Suppose Lucky had run into trouble? Suppose he'd run into Cerqueda?

Agnes helped with supper in silence, then took food for herself and James into the dormitory. When she returned, she pronounced him weak but regaining his strength.

"I'm sure we've created a problem for you, but I think you ought to know that Mr. Pickney is determined to become Lucky Lawrence. He's like a little boy with his first toy. I've never seen him so excited."

"But, Agnes, we can't let him pretend to be Lucky. It isn't safe."

"That's what I told him, but for the first time in his life he has a chance to be a real man, a man who isn't sick. I haven't the heart to argue with him now. I . . . I thought, maybe we could let it go for a few days. Let him be the man he's always wanted to be. Once he gets involved in the school, he'll forget all this nonsense."

Reluctantly, Melissa agreed. She gave Agnes a lamp and told her good night. With a heavy heart, she paced the confines of the house until she could no longer stand it. Either something had happened or Lucky wasn't coming back. He could have ridden into town and back several times by now.

She couldn't blame him. He'd done everything she'd needed. He'd married her, then once he understood the situation, he'd confessed to his deception right away. Then he'd promised to stay for three months to satisfy the requirements of the town fathers. And she'd agreed. She played as big a part as Lucky in the deception. There'd been no reason for him to restring the wire around the corral or put heat in her bedroom or help with the children. But he had. He'd played the role of her husband convincingly. Everyone in town liked him. But things had become too complicated.

Finally, she wrapped herself in a shawl, opened the door, and stepped into the yard. She walked down to the stream and along its bank toward the mountains, with Mac trailing silently beside her. This place, this beautiful place where she expected to build a life for herself, had changed. Life was repeating itself. For the third time, people she loved had made her promises they didn't keep. Her mother had said she'd get well. Her father had told her he'd come back for her. Lucky had said he'd stay. But he was gone.

The legal ramifications of their marriage would have to be resolved. What would the citizens of Silver Wind think when they found out that the James they knew was really Lucky Lawrence, the gambler, and the man arriving on this morning's train was the real James? They'd have to be told eventually. Maybe sooner than later. What would her father have done? The school was at stake, so it would have to be done in such a way as to save her father's dream. The thing she couldn't acknowledge was tearing her heart out. Did last night mean as much to Lucky as it had to her?

"Oh, Lucky," she whispered. "I had no right to expect anything to change because I let you make love to me. I practically forced myself on you. What I want doesn't matter. I made a promise to myself to follow through on the school. I can't let what I feel change that. I cannot fail."

"You aren't going to," Lucky's voice came out of the darkness behind her.

"Lucky, you're back. I was afraid something had happened to you." Despite her resolve to keep her distance, she threw herself into his arms.

"I didn't think you'd welcome me back," he said.

"Why not?"

"Well, James is here now."

"But it's you—" She stopped herself before she said she cared about him. She had no idea how he felt. Her emotions seemed to rise and dip like the water in the creek rushing downhill.

She leaned back, gazing up at him, memorizing the way his lean dark face looked in the moonlight.

He grazed her cheek with his knuckles, silencing her before finishing her sentence. "It's me who got us into this mess. Now I have to find a way to straighten it out."

She caught his fist and uncurled his fingers, pressing her cheek into his palm. "You didn't do anything."

"Oh, but I did. You and I know what happened between us was a mistake." There was a silence between them.

She wouldn't lie to Lucky. "It wasn't a mistake, not for me." In the moonlight she could see a perplexed look cross his face.

"Don't do this, Melissa. Don't ask me for something I can't give. You're a lady and I'm just a gambler. I'm not the kind of man for you. I only came back here to protect you and James. I can't have him getting killed because of me."

She let go of his hand and turned away. He was lying. She knew it. The set of his mouth gave him away. Lucky Lawrence had a laughing mouth. Now it was tight and grim. He might be a drifter, but he was a caring man with a purpose. For whatever reason, he hadn't left her. He'd come back, something he didn't have to do. But it was obvious Lucky didn't think he was the right man for her.

She'd have to change his mind.

"What happened in town?" she asked.

"Nothing. It seems your James was closemouthed. He just claimed he was an old friend coming to help out at the school."

Melissa let out a sigh of relief. "So we have time, then?"

"Time for what?" Lucky asked. "We can't change anything and yet we can't let it stay like it is. Now that James has arrived, everything is different. I don't know what we would have done had he not come. But he's here now, and we have to deal with it."

"I know," she said, "but I want it to be the way it was before."

"I'm moving my things out to the lean-to," Lucky said finally. "I don't think I can stay so close to you and stay away from you."

"I moved your things up to the sleeping loft, Lucky, unless you'd rather..."

"No, I'm moving out to the barn's lean-to."

She shivered. "It's getting colder. The wind has picked up and we're likely to have our first snow soon. You can't sleep in the lean-to; you'd freeze. We'll work it out. Sleep in the loft. It's above my bedroom. We won't be together."

"I'll know you're down there," he said.

"Yes," she answered, sliding her arm around his waist and laying her head on his shoulder as they headed back to the house. "And I'll know you're up there."

When Cerqueda's search for the gambler who had defeated him failed, he returned to his home base, Arido, Texas.

Arido was little more than a mecca for thieves and gamblers, but it was one of the few places Cerqueda had friends, friends he'd bought and paid for lavishly, including the sheriff, who kept him informed of the activities of the lawmen of the Southwest.

As the days passed, his fury grew. Cerqueda finally

admitted the man-in-black had outwitted him. Nobody had seen him, or if they had, they wouldn't admit it. Logically he knew he ought to give it up and get back to his ranch, but nobody bested Cerqueda. His reputation had been carefully built and he refused to let it go. Now he sat in the corner of the bar emanating a fury that warned the others to stay away. It was bad enough that he hadn't found his man, but he'd been forced to ride in on a horse that he wouldn't have even bothered to steal. He would track down the gringo and find the high-and-mighty Louisa Hidalgo and bring her back if it was the last thing he ever did.

"Lem," he shouted to the bartender, "bring me a new bottle and find the sheriff! I want him here now!"

"Sure thing, Cerqueda. I'll get him for you." Whiskey forgotten, Lem scurried from behind the bar.

Moments later, a short nervous man appeared at Cerqueda's table. "Haven't seen you in a while, Cerqueda. Something wrong?"

"Sit down, sheriff. I have a little job for you."

"Sure thing, boss."

"I want you to check around and see if there's any news about a gambler who dresses all in black and carries a pearl-handled Colt 45 and a lucky gold coin with a diamond in the center."

"You want me to send telegrams?"

Cerqueda looked at him, tapped his fingers on the table and asked in a low, threatening voice, "How else are you going to find out?"

The sheriff stood nodding his head. "Yes, sir. I'll send them out right away. Are you going to be here?"

"I'm staying here until you get back to me," Cerqueda said.

"What am I going to say? Why am I looking for him?"

"You're looking for him because I want to know where he is. I'm looking for him because I'm going to kill him."

Melissa lay wide-awake in the same bed she'd shared with Lucky the night before. He hadn't protested when she'd told him she'd moved his clothes to the sleeping loft, and he hadn't come to her, either. A frequent creak in the ceiling told her he was not having any more luck at sleeping than she. Poor Mac couldn't be still either. He slept for a time just outside her door before moving back to the loft steps. There was only silence in the girls' wing on one side and the boys' dormitory on the other. Obviously James and Agnes were having a better night than she was. She wrestled with the problems of dissolving her marriage to James Harold Pickney IV without hurting her school, and convincing Lucky Lawrence that he needed a wife. But there was no answer. Only two things seemed to be in her favor: one, Lucky appeared to like making love to her; and two, he had returned to the school last night when he could have kept on going. He was here. He'd wanted her once, and she'd just have to make him want her again.

When the sun came up, she still didn't have a plan for accomplishing her goal, but at least she had a goal. How she'd accomplish that with Agnes and James on the premises remained to be seen. She heard Lucky moving around and then come down the ladder. Every morning he'd start the fire in her cook stove and make

the coffee and then head for the schoolhouse to light
the fire that he laid the night before. This morning was
no exception. After he was gone, Melissa rose, dressed,
and readied herself for the day. The children would arrive shortly and she needed to talk with James about his
plan to help with the teaching.

As it turned out, she didn't need to give James any instructions. The children were chattering, energetic as
usual—except for Ellen—when suddenly they grew
quiet. She assumed by the expression on Ellen's face
that Lucky had arrived. But when she turned, it wasn't
Lucky; it was James. He looked fresh and eager and he
was looking at Ellen. After introducing himself to the
children as "Professor" Lawrence, he won them over
quickly with his tall tales of history and times past, tying
them to the literature and poetry that they were studying. For the little ones, he wrote the ABCs on the chalk-
board, then made little figures out of each letter. Their
delight was proven in their attention to their slates. By
lunchtime she could tell that he was beginning to tire.
As it turned out, she didn't see Lucky; she didn't know
where he was. Arthur was still in the corral, so unless
he'd taken off on foot or been abducted by Indians, he
was still somewhere around the place. The children ate
their lunch, James retired to the house to rest, and
Melissa continued the afternoon session. At one point
she heard a commotion in the corral, and looked up to
see Lucky hitching Arthur to the wagon. James and
Agnes were standing beside him. She gave the children
an assignment and wandered out to where the three
were standing. "What's going on here?" she asked.

James beamed broadly and said, "Lucky and I are going into town to talk to the doctor about Agnes working with him." Agnes looked anxious until Melissa gave her a smile of approval.

James climbed into the wagon. "We'll be back before supper, won't we, Lucky—excuse me—won't we, James?" The twinkle in James's eye said how much he was going to enjoy being Lucky. The chagrin on Lucky's face told how little he was going to enjoy being James. Agnes allowed Lucky to help her into the wagon, drawing up as small as she could between the two men. Off they went leaving a perplexed Melissa standing in the schoolhouse doorway, wondering what they were really up to.

In town, Lucky took James and Agnes to meet the doctor, only to find out he was away making a house call. The sign on his door said he'd be back shortly. Lucky and James decided to go to the general store, leaving Agnes to sit in the doctor's office and wait. When a small boy came into the doctor's office with a cut that needed a dressing, Agnes searched the supply cabinet, pulled out what she needed, and dressed the boy's wound. When she was finished, she gave him a pat on the head and a piece of hard candy from the jar on the doctor's desk. Then she proceeded to clean up the doctor's office and clinic.

"James," Lucky said, "what do you say we go over to the saloon and check it out? There's someone there I want you to meet."

James looked at Lucky, glanced at the general store and back again. "You go on, Lucky. I've got a stop to make over here at the store. I'll join you shortly. Remember, you're me, James Harold Pickney IV."

"Remember, you're me. Be careful."

"Don't worry, I'll stay out of trouble." As Lucky watched the Easterner go into the general store, he turned and headed toward the saloon. Later—no matter what happened—he needed funds, and the only way he knew how to make money was by gambling. He just had to figure out a way to do it without offending the town fathers, and that answer hadn't come to him yet.

Under the pretense of speaking to Sable and sending her Melissa's regards, he could at least survey the place. Surely some of the town fathers indulged in a friendly game.

In the meantime, James entered the dimly-lit store and looked around. He knew just what he was looking for. He only hoped the storekeeper carried black trousers, a shirt, and a vest like Lucky's. If he was going to be a gambler, he intended to look the part.

"Good afternoon, sir," Alfred Sizemore said. "You must be the new teacher at the school. Ida enrolled our girls out there, though I'm still not sure it was the right thing to do. If they don't behave themselves, you just let me know."

"Oh, they're splendid little ladies," James said. "I worked with them this morning. You're to be congratulated on such well-behaved girls."

"What can I do for you?" the storekeeper asked, giving James a smile.

"Well, I'm thinking I need some different clothes. These are all right for the city, but I feel a little overdressed here. I'm thinking what I want is a nice pair of black trousers, um, like James is wearing, and a shirt perhaps like his. Do you have such items?"

Alfred Sizemore looked at him, a bit puzzled. "I think so. Are you sure that's what you want?"

"Oh, yes," he said. "I wanted to make a good first impression on Mrs. Pickney's friends, so I didn't wear my regular clothes." Moments later, the new Lucky was wearing a pair of black boots that added at least two inches to his height, and would be perfect once he learned to walk in them; a pair of black trousers with a kind of cording up the side, just like the ones he'd seen the men wearing on the covers of the dime novels, a black shirt, and a vest with silver buttons. "Now all I need is a hat. I fancy one of those ten-gallon ones," he said to the storekeeper.

The only one Sizemore had in stock was a half size too big for James, but that didn't matter. James bought two handkerchiefs and wrapped them around the inside band of the hat and tried it again. As long as he didn't jiggle too much, it stayed right where he put it. He would never have dared wear a ten-gallon hat back in New York, but the moment he donned the oversized head covering, he was set. Perfect. He looked in the mirror. More than perfect. It was exactly what he dreamed of. He paid Sizemore and started out the door, then stopped abruptly and turned back. "One more thing, I seem to have left my guns at home, so I need to replace them. What about a gun belt and two pearl-handled revolvers?"

The expression on Sizemore's face was one of incredulity. "You want two pistols? What for?"

"Well, I always wear my pistols when I travel. A man

like me in the West, well, I can't be without my weapons. You never know when you'll run into a bad guy that needs a little taking down."

"Taking down? Are you sure you know how to shoot?"

"Of course I know how to shoot," James protested indignantly. "I'm one of the best shots in New York State. I'm quick. Back home they call me Dead Eye . . . Dead Eye Lawrence."

"Lawrence? Mmmm. Pearl-handled guns, black clothes, black hat. What exactly do you do back East? I thought you were a teacher."

"Well, uh, uh, I help out now and then when I'm between job assignments," James said. "Where I make my funds, though, partner, is through my gambling. I'm almost as good at gambling as I am with a gun."

"I understand you're helping Miss Melissa. You're actually teaching out at the school? I don't know what I think about this," he said with a crease in his forehead. "We don't much like trouble here in Silver Wind."

"And you're not likely to have any now that I'm here," James said, strapping on the gun belt.

Unfortunately the belt was a little too large, and though he fastened it as tightly as it would go, it slid down his slim body once he turned, catching at his knees. "Oops, looks like I need another hole in the belt," he said. "Could you make me one, so I could cinch it up about here?" He pulled the belt at least two notches tighter and held it out.

With a nod, Sizemore turned to the counter behind him and picked up an ice pick with which he made a hole in the belt. He slid it back through the buckle and fastened it, then looked a long time at James before he said skeptically, "You tie the string around your thigh, so it'll stay in place."

"Oh, yeah, sure. I was going to do that." James tied the rawhide strings around his legs, took a wide-open stance and laid his hands on the top of the gun handles. Patting them a couple of times, he nodded his head. "Just right."

"Oh, Mr. Lawrence, did you intend to buy any bullets?"

James focused on his guns with affected surprise. "You mean they aren't loaded?"

"Nope."

"Then let me have a few . . . some ammunition."

Sizemore reached under the counter and pulled out a box and loaded the guns. He gave James a total and collected his bill. Regaining his swagger, James marched out the door onto the sidewalk, stepped down in his new boots and tripped. Only the hitching post saved him from falling into the water trough. He collected himself and looked around to make sure no one was watching.

Everyone was watching!

He lifted himself to his full height of five feet, plus the eight-inch crown of his ten-gallon hat. Today he could do no wrong. He was no longer James Harold Pickney IV. Today he was Lucky Lawrence. He marched across the rutted road and through the batwinged doors into the saloon. Taking a wide stance once more, he put his hands on his guns and cleared his throat.

Unfortunately his voice cracked a bit, and instead of the threatening manner he intended, he started

with a growl and ended with a squeak. "Name's Lucky
Lawrence." He swaggered to the bar. "I'm meeting my
friend...James here." He put his foot on the rail without accounting for the slickness of the bottom of the
new boots. His foot slid forward between the rail and
the bar, and he ended up with his chin on the smooth
wooden surface and his hat over his eyes.

"Over here," the real Lucky called out as he came to
the assistance of Melissa's friend, who was trying to gain
purchase with his new boots. At the same time, he was
fumbling with the biggest hat Lucky had ever seen.
"Come over to the table and have a seat; I've been waiting for you."

"Sure, sure. I've been hankering for a drink of
straight whiskey," the new Lucky said. When he lifted
his hat, his handkerchiefs drifted to the floor like flags
of surrender.

Lucky groaned, picked up the handkerchiefs, and
turned James around. With his hand on his shoulder, he
maneuvered poor James to a chair at the table in the
corner.

"What the hell are you doing?" Lucky said under his
breath. "You're supposed to be a teacher out here. Why
this getup?"

"No," James said. "I'm supposed to be Lucky
Lawrence, the gambler, and that's who I am. Bring the
cards and my whiskey!" he said loudly, while muttering
under his breath, "Don't worry, partner, we can do this."

"You're supposed to be helping out at the school,"
Lucky corrected. "A teacher wouldn't be in this saloon
gambling. You're going to ruin everything."

Looking straight at Lucky, James said, "So what are
you doing in here?"

"Looking after you," Lucky growled under his breath.

Somebody slapped a deck of cards on the table and stood towering over Lucky. "I'll play," he said.

Lucky raised his eyes. "Bart, what are you doing here?"

"Mr. Pickney and Mr. Lawrence, is it?" Bart said. "I believe I've heard of Lucky Lawrence. If he wants to gamble, I'll play him a hand. I'm going to be needing some money now. Seems I got fired yesterday. I hold you responsible for that, Pickney. If you hadn't come into town and stirred things up, the colonel wouldn't have taken no interest in that schoolmarm. She'd of seen the light and picked me. But no, you suddenly turned up, then I lost her and now I've lost my job."

Lucky could see trouble brewing higher than the San Juan Mountains behind him. Now Bart was blaming him and Melissa for losing a job he was bent on losing anyhow; James was strutting around like some sort of peacock, pretending to be a rough-and-tough gambler with not one gun but two; and Cerqueda was God only knew where. Not to mention Melissa sleeping below him every night. He could see the storm gathering on the horizon. He just didn't know how he could stop it.

Bart dragged up a chair and flopped down. "Think I'll let you deal the cards, Mr. Lawrence. But I believe I'll shuffle them."

"No, that's okay; I'm a little superstitious about that," the new Lucky said. "You go ahead and deal. You choose the game. Of course, we might play it different back East. But I'm a fast learner. I'm sure I can handle it."

Lucky groaned, wondering how in the hell he was go-

ing to play a game with the coins he had in his pocket,
keep James from making a fool of himself, and keep Bart
from knowing the truth. He needed a miracle.

"Afternoon, boys. Didn't expect to see you in my establishment." It was Sable, come to stand behind Bart.

"Melissa just wanted me to stop in," Lucky started
with his rehearsed invitation. "We'd like you to join us
for supper one evening, to meet her new *teacher,*
Lawrence here, and Miss Fulbright, the nurse who
came in on the train with him."

"My, my, another new woman in town? Will she be a
teacher too?

"Agnes isn't a teacher," James corrected impatiently.
"She expects to help the doctor and probably Melissa as
well."

"Okay, enough talk," Bart interrupted. "Let's play
five-card stud. Deuces wild."

Lucky was worried. He didn't know whether James
knew how to play poker or not. He suspected the only
games James had ever played had been with a group of
ladies who gossiped more than they played cards. Getting them out of this situation now that Bart had in-
truded would be difficult.

Lucky put a worried expression on his face for Bart's
benefit. Referring to himself as James and to James as
the gambler named Lucky Lawrence was going to be
even harder. "I don't think it would be fair for an experienced gambler like you to take on Bart. After all, he's a
miner. So I'll tell you what. I'll play Bart a couple hands
while you observe."

Bart shook his head. "I don't think so. When I win, I
want to have beaten Lucky Lawrence, not some Eastern pipsqueak nobody ever heard of."

James looked relieved. He knew he was out of his element, but this made him look bad. He raised his eyebrows so high they almost disappeared under his hatband. It hadn't occurred to him that he was the only man at the poker table still wearing one. "You know that's not a bad idea, Pickney. It would be unfair of me to take advantage of Bart when he's just lost his job. You, on the other hand, will be an easy mark for him. He's a man who needs the money, so I'll just observe for a hand or two."

"I'll even let you deal," the real Lucky said, in his role as James. "But I warn you, I don't know much about cards. I may have to ask questions. Will that be allowed?"

Bart gave a shrewd grin and nodded his head. "Sure thing, dude. Ask whatever you like."

To follow through, the pseudo-James asked a couple of questions as they played the first hand. He let Bart win. It was hard to play that badly, particularly when he knew he'd just used all his money.

To his credit, the real James sensed Lucky's dilemma and pushed forward a folded roll of bills, with the statement, "If I can't play, at least let me show my appreciation for your hospitality by investing in the game. I'll just take half your earnings when you're done, Pickney."

"Well, I don't know," said Bart.

Lucky pretended to fumble his cards. "I'm not very good at this, but I'm not ready to give up. I think I can beat you, Bart."

"Money's money," Bart said gleefully.

Lucky let out a sigh of relief. Greed always won. This might just work. If he let Bart win just enough to stay in the game, he could save the real Lucky and the real James and win some money for himself.

Lucky took the next hand, then let Bart win again. They were beginning to attract a crowd. The time had come for him to take one big pot and depart before something happened. He already knew that Bart was dealing marked cards. It hadn't taken him long to figure out his system.

The next time Lucky had the deal, he made sure Bart's hand was good enough to build a good-sized pot. This time he was forced to add his lucky coin to the pot. His plan would have worked except Bart made the mistake of swapping a card he'd had up his sleeve for one in his hand. James was more observant than Lucky had expected. He'd seen Bart's move and scrambled to his feet, drawing his gun and waving it around wildly as he stood.

"You're a cheat! I saw you swap that card."

Lucky didn't think James actually meant to fire the gun, but he did, and the bullet sailed across the room toward the mirror behind the bar. For one instant, the hole looked like a fat spider as the glass cracked in sharp lines like a web before it shattered and plunged to the floor. The men watching, climbed under the table. And James stood looking at the broken mirror with a dazed expression on his face. Lucky turned to Bart, noting the expression on Bart's face was about as surprised as James's.

What was he going to do now? "Hold on there, Lucky. You're in friendly territory here. Put down your gun. Sorry about that, Bart. We'll just call this hand yours."

But James had an image to uphold and he was having no part of letting Bart cheat. "Hold on there, eh, uh, uhhh, James; Lucky Lawrence plays a clean game."

"And so does Bart, normally," Sable offered, giving her box-supper dinner partner an odd look. "I'm sure this wouldn't have happened if he hadn't just lost his job. So why don't you just split the pot and call it even."

It was clear that Bart didn't want to go along, but with Sable standing there, hands on hips, he agreed. The look on his face said that didn't mean he wouldn't get even later, it just meant he wouldn't do it with an audience. Silently he raked half the money from the table, being careful that his half contained the most bills.

"Next time, Lawrence, it'll be between me and you," he said as he left.

A shaken James faced Sable. "Send me the bill, ma'am. I'm sorry for the damage I did. I just needed to get Bart's attention."

"Well you certainly did that," Sable said.

At that point, Agnes appeared in the doorway, ready to take care of a gunshot victim. "Mr. Pickney?" she said, "are you hurt?"

"No," Lucky hastened to assure her before James gave an automatic response to his name. "But I imagine Mrs. Pickney is wondering where we are. Don't forget we're expecting you for supper, Miss Sable. Now I think it's time for us to get home, *Lucky*."

13

"James did what?" Melissa stared at Lucky and Agnes incredulously.

Agnes swallowed hard and tried to explain. "He shot his pistol, but I'm certain it was just to get everyone's attention."

"I'd say he succeeded," Melissa said.

"Unfortunately," Agnes went on, "the bullet hit the mirror behind the bar and shattered it. But don't worry, the proprietor accepted James's apology and his offer to pay for a replacement."

"But why was James trying to get their attention?"

James spoke up. "Bart was cheating. As Lucky Lawrence, I couldn't let him get away with cheating. Could I?"

"And you thought if you bought those clothes, you could do anything," Melissa snapped, and frowned at Lucky and Agnes. "And what about the two of you, you let him get away with it? What were you thinking, and where was the sheriff?"

Lucky started to explain, then saw the disappointment on James's face and said, "Your sheriff never seems to be around when he's needed. And from what I hear, he might have shot the mirror too. Look, Melissa, I don't think too much harm was done. He was right. James—excuse me—Lucky was warning the townsfolk that he wouldn't tolerate dishonesty, which is exactly what I might have done."

"But you wouldn't have broken the mirror," James said. "And I left without even cleaning it up."

Melissa would have taken all three of them to task but she remembered her own shot that had wounded Ted and caused the church bell to fall, starting this whole chain of events. She couldn't hold James accountable for the same kind of error in judgment she'd made. "All right, but take off that ridiculous hat and give me a hand in the classroom. This afternoon we've been reading Walt Whitman. Ellen seems to have taken an interest in poetry, so I hope you'll give her some special attention, James."

A wilted James suddenly drew himself erect and gained a fresh strength. "I'll be right there, Melissa. Just give me a minute."

Gathering her shawl, Melissa strode across the courtyard, her body as taut as a bowstring. It took a Herculean effort not to turn back and continue the conversation. She still wanted to ask Agnes what she'd been thinking by allowing James to dress that way, and she wanted to scold James for putting himself in a position where he might either be hurt or harm someone else—the school included. But the thing she wanted most was to lean against Lucky's chest and feel his arms around her. Just as she thought things couldn't get any worse, they had. The townsfolk were still giving her a jaundiced eye. For all she knew, Cerqueda was still searching for Lucky, and now, if she knew Bart, he'd be after James.

For the rest of the afternoon Melissa waited for the sheriff, the mayor, or even Bart to appear. But it was Colonel Curtis who entered the classroom.

"Thought I'd just ride up and see how things were going," he said casually. "I understand you have a nurse and another teacher, a part-time *gambler*? The nurse is a good idea. Can't say the same about the new one. Seems a little odd to me. What do you know about him?"

Ellen rolled her chair to James's side. "Father, this is Mr. Lawrence. He was educated at the university. He knows just about everything about poetry. He knows about Rome and Venice and Switzerland, and he knows about the pyramids."

His daughter seemed to have transferred her admiration for Pickney to Mr. Lawrence. He sighed. At least he was single, even if he did look like the last person in the world to be a gambler—part-time or otherwise. Something about this whole thing was fishy. "Have you been to all those places, Lawrence?"

"Well, I haven't actually been there but I've read about them."

The colonel scoffed. "Rich men go. Poor men read."

"And ignorant men do neither," James said.

Melissa spoke up, "I'm afraid you have the wrong idea, Colonel Curtis." She started to say James and then remembered the switch and said instead, "Mr.

Lawrence here"—she gestured toward James—"has been too ill to travel. But he is a scholar and a brilliant teacher. We're very fortunate to have him."

The colonel said, "I thought you were a gambler, Mr. Lawrence. In fact, I'm told you are very good at what you do. That seems pretty strange, being a scholar and a gambler. You look too puny to be either one. What's wrong with you?"

"Lung problems, sir. But since I've been out here, I haven't had an attack."

The colonel jutted out his chin. "So, our fine mountain air is what brought you to Colorado. That's what brought us also. The doctors in South Carolina said it would be good for my Ellen. We thought it might make her well. Could have if she'd done her exercises, but she has a mind of her own and it's easier to ride in her chair than try to walk. I hope you have better luck."

"Father," Ellen interrupted, "could we ask Mr. and Mrs. Pickney, Miss Fulbright, and Mr. Lawrence out to the ranch for dinner on Saturday evening? You could get to know them that way." When she saw he was about to refuse, she threw in a bribe. "We never have anybody come to the ranch. I get so lonely. If you let them come," she said with a smile of sudden inspiration, "I'll start back on my exercises."

"You promise? I don't take lightly to broken promises, girl."

The children giggled. The older boys nudged each other and grinned broadly.

"Behave yourselves, children," Melissa said.

"Oh, yes, Papa. I promise. Can you come, Mrs. Pickney, Mr. Lawrence?"

"We'd be delighted."

She wasn't sure of that statement, but of late, everybody seemed to be happy except her.

Dinner with the colonel was a possible answer to their problems—if the fake Lucky hadn't ruined everything. Melissa didn't know what to say. For tonight, she and her new family had to get through supper. Agnes saved the awkwardness by announcing that the doctor was pleased at her handling of the child's injury. He offered her a position and she'd start right away. Now that she was employed, she could pay rent, if Melissa would allow her to stay at the school. In return for her help with the students, the deal was set at a rate more reasonable than Agnes had expected. She'd just have to learn to drive a buggy or—heaven forbid—ride a horse.

Lucky remained silent, electing to bring in more wood, while Agnes and James retired and Melissa cleared away the supper leavings. But sooner or later, he knew he'd have to face the woman he'd married and the responsibility for what had happened in town.

It was nearly November now and the first snow wasn't too far away. He could smell it in the sharp night air as he pulled the collar of his jacket closed and buttoned it. With James and Agnes out here, at least Melissa wouldn't be alone. That was a useless thought. James had already proved that he was a teacher, not a gunfighter. And Agnes? Well, at least she could take care of any medical problem. The lie he'd perpetuated about his identity and his marriage to Melissa weighed heavier and heavier on his conscience. He was at the end of the charade. And it was up to him to take the responsibility. Tomorrow he'd go into town and talk with the mayor. He'd make certain that Cerqueda knew he'd moved on. Melissa and James could marry as they'd planned, and life would get back to normal.

He'd have to leave the woman he'd fallen in love with.

The cabin was dark when Lucky opened the door. Not even a lamp was burning. He quietly made his way to the ladder, and looked into the open doorway of Melissa's room. He didn't have to see it. He knew that everything about it said "Melissa": the spread, the curtains, the smell of her soap, a blue hair ribbon curled across her bureau. The furnishings might not be fine, but they were permanent. He'd never had a room—not really. He had the butler's pantry off the dining area in his mother's boardinghouse. But his room had to be portable in case a guest arrived and there was no space. Sometimes he moved to the kitchen floor, the porch, or even the shed.

In the long run, Melissa would be better off without him. She would marry James and that was the way it should be. It was too early yet to tell whether or not he'd given her a child, but the way he had it figured, she'd be married by the time she knew for sure, and James was the kind of man who'd look after Melissa's baby.

He climbed the stairs to the loft, undressed down to his bare skin, and slid beneath the covers. With his hands behind his head, he took a deep breath and stretched out. His knee touched bare flesh. That's when he found out that he was not alone. He froze. *Melissa*. He recognized that same scent from her bedroom—lavender. He breathed in again, allowing the scent of her to intoxicate him just for a second. "What are you doing?" His voice was so hoarse it was difficult even for him to hear what he'd said.

"You've been avoiding me," she whispered. "I don't care if it's right or wrong, I consider myself married to you, and I want to be with you. I think you want that too. If a person doesn't go after what she wants, she'll never get it. I want you to make love to me, but I'll get up and go downstairs if you tell me to."

Silence.

She turned to her side and laid a tentative hand on his chest. "Please don't tell me to go, Lucky."

He caught her hand in his. "I can't, but I ought to go. This is wrong. Only, I want you to stay." He groaned and pulled her over him, capturing her mouth with his, and kissed her. "Suppose I've already given you a child?"

"Suppose you have? And if you haven't, Lucky, I want you to give me a son, tonight. Having your child would be more than I ever expected. I would love him and raise him to be just like his father."

"Like his father? A gambler who never stays in one place? A man who has less than twenty dollars in his pocket and no way to earn more?"

"No. A man who looks after and protects others. A man who doesn't run away. A good and honest man."

How could this woman see him this way, even after he'd told her about his sister? He had no future to offer a wife or a child. He couldn't do any more damage with his wants. He'd done enough already. "Melissa, you're seeing me through the eyes of desire. You can't love me. You're too smart for that."

"You're right. And I'm the only one who can decide what I want, because I'm going to have your child."

His blood went cold. "Are you with child, Melissa?"

"Not yet," she whispered, and kissed him. Any restraint he might have had was instantly lost. Melting against him, she responded with an eagerness that reached inside him and burned away any thoughts of refusal. It was already too late. Whatever the names under which they had married, they belonged together.

She whispered his name, threaded her arms behind his head, and rolled to her back, carrying him with her. He tried to pull away—just once—but when she lifted herself to meet him, he groaned and thrust inside her.

Later, as they lay in each other's arms, sated with fulfilled desire, Lucky knew he was lost. He could no more leave her than he could give up on finding his sister someday. It was almost as if Melissa had been sent to fill the void in his heart. Lying with a woman gave a man satisfaction, but after the first woman, the satisfaction was temporary and the act was quickly forgotten. Or at least that's the way it had been—until now. Until Melissa.

He could hear her breathing softly in the darkness, trusting him, offering herself to him as if she truly were his wife. *Wife*. No matter how hard he tried to deny it, the very word made his heart swell. There had to be a way. He couldn't help Melissa in the classroom. And a husband had to protect and provide for his family. But how? He couldn't gamble. The people in town wouldn't tolerate that, and he didn't blame them. He wasn't a miner, a farmer, or a storekeeper. Maybe the colonel could use some help on his ranch.

Melissa stirred, nuzzling her cheek against his chest. "Are you asleep?"

"No, I was just lying here thinking. I may have to leave. I can't live here and keep making love to you, no matter what you want."

"Don't think. My father used to say that thinking just complicates things." She planted a kiss on his chest and rubbed her palm back and forth across his nipples. "Making love is much better. After all, we're married."

He groaned and drew in a deep breath. Smoke! He smelled smoke.

The sound of Arthur's hooves pounding the hard earth of the corral announced his agitation. About that time, Mac started barking wildly, and he heard James yell "Lucky! Lucky! Come quick. The school's on fire."

"Oh, no!" Melissa screamed, scrambling to her feet.

By the time Melissa and Lucky got their clothes on, there was no doubt. Flames licked at the window and between the cracks in the wall. Agnes was standing in the doorway wailing helplessly. The roof blazed. The wind whipped down through the mountains, picked up the sparks, and flung them into the creek, making a sound like that of huge drops of water falling on a hot griddle. Lucky quickly realized that they had a disaster in the making. If they didn't get the schoolhouse fire under control, it could spread to the lean-to, the house, and the dormitories. "Forget the school," Lucky shouted. "We have to save the other buildings. Let's try to wet them down."

The thick smoke caught in her throat and burned her eyes. She knew it was hopeless but they had to try.

"Where's James?" Melissa called out, following Lucky to the water trough by the barn. She could only guess what this would do to his damaged lungs.

"I don't know," Agnes answered. "Wait, I just saw a shadow through the schoolroom window. He must be inside." But her voice was lost in the crackle of the flames.

By the time Lucky realized what she said, she was already inside the burning building. He threw the bucket of water he was carrying on the blaze and went after her. "Agnes, where are you?"

"Here, I'm over here. Help me drag him out; he must have passed out from the smoke."

Melissa had given up on the fire. Her heart fell to her stomach when she saw Lucky rush into the flames. Before she could reach him, two shadowy figures backed through the doorway onto the grass and to the creek.

"Support his head," Agnes said. "Let's drag him into the water. His clothing has burned him and the cold water will help relieve his pain."

Melissa ran to help. "James, I'm so sorry."

"Don't worry, Melissa," the real James said from behind her, chocking back a spasm of coughing. "We'll just rebuild the school."

Melissa looked behind her in surprise. "Are you all right?"

"No, but I'll make it." He was wheezing heavily.

"James, where were you?"

"I let Arthur go." He coughed. "I think there's another horse back in the woods. I heard him neigh."

Lucky slipped, and for a moment the man they were carrying went under. "If this is not James we're putting in the water, then who is it?"

"The smoke is so thick, I can't see," Melissa said.

"I guess we'll find out soon enough. Let's get him inside now," Agnes said. "We'll remove his clothes and I'll examine him. James, you go light the lamp and build up the fire."

"Where do you want him, Agnes?" Lucky asked, the fire forgotten in the shock of finding the injured man.

It was Agnes who took over. "Put him in the girls' dormitory. He's going to require around-the-clock nursing and there is no point in disturbing the rest of you."

"Are you sure you want to do this?" Melissa asked. "He's probably the one who started the fire. We don't even know who he is."

But as soon as they got inside and the lamplight fell across the injured man's face, they knew. In a collective voice they all whispered, "Bart."

The schoolhouse turned out to be a total loss. Lucky's fears were soon realized, as the wind blew sparks onto the roofs of the other buildings and quickly fanned them into flames. For the next hour, Lucky, Melissa, and James ran from one spot to the next beating out the fires. The same abutment that protected Grayson Academy from public view also kept the townspeople from seeing the fire until it was almost too late.

Finally, James collapsed in a burst of wheezing on the porch. Alarmed, Melissa went to check on him.

"I'll be fine, Melissa—honest. Lucky Lawrence is tough."

James looked like a coal miner. His new clothes were ruined, but he managed a grin. "You're a mess, teacher."

Melissa didn't have to see herself in the mirror to know that her face was covered with soot. The blisters on her hands had long since burst from carrying the bucket filled with water. She looked back at the school and realized they'd done all they could do. She was about to lose everything in a way she'd never considered. Swallowing back the lump in her throat, she leaned against the porch post and felt cold moisture on her cheeks. Lucky was still carrying water. She walked toward him, touching his shoulder. He jerked around as if he'd forgotten anyone else was there.

"Stop, Lucky. It's no use."

At that moment Mac headed down the road barking wildly. Someone was coming. A lot of people were coming. Wagons filled with townspeople. Men on horseback. They all attacked the fire. But even with their help, the lean-to was lost. Melissa watched, proud that the very people who'd once condemned her had come to her rescue. But the water trough was soon empty and they had to transfer their buckets to the creek, which was farther away. But with their help, they were going to save the house and dormitories.

That was when Melissa realized that at some point the colonel had arrived, bringing Ellen, who was sitting on the steps with James. Their heads were close, as Ellen wiped soot from his face. Suddenly she didn't seem so young and James didn't seem so weak.

Melissa felt moisture on her face. It was snowing. As the flakes hit the fire, they sizzled and went out. In twenty minutes, mother nature had done what Melissa and Lucky had tried to accomplish in what seemed like hours.

"How'd it happen, Pickney?" Colonel Curtis asked.

"We're not sure," Lucky said guardedly.

James spoke up, "I can tell you how it started. Somebody set it. We pulled him out of the fire. He's in the girls' dormitory."

"Probably one of the miners, just trying to stay warm?" came from a voice in the crowd.

"If he was trying to stay warm, I think he succeeded," Melissa said.

"Well, who is it? Do we know him?" Mayor Dawson asked, and wiped the sweat from his face with his arm.

"We do," Lucky said. "It's Bart Jamison. At least, we pulled him out of the schoolhouse. And I don't think he was trying to save the books."

An angry murmur rose from the crowd behind them. They could tolerate a lot of things—fighting over claim sites, gambling, petty theft—but to burn down a man's property at the beginning of winter was a hanging offense.

The mayor held up his hands, indicating that the crowd should hush. "How bad is he hurt? Can he be moved to town?"

"The doctor is over at the mine," the colonel answered. "One of my men fell and hurt himself."

The door to the girls' section opened and Agnes stepped out. "Mr. Jamison is pretty bad but he has a chance. If you move him, you'll kill him. When the doctor returns, please tell him I could use some sulfur powder and bandages."

Melissa planted her palm in the small of her back and leaned her head on Lucky's shoulder. "Thank you for trying to help. It may take me a day or two to figure out what I'm going to do about the school."

"What *we're* going to do," Lucky said, drawing her closer.

Reluctantly, Ellen allowed herself to be moved into the carriage, and she and the colonel left. The rest of the townspeople followed, their sooty clothing being peppered with white. Winter had come to Silver Wind, Colorado. By morning, if the snow continued to fall as heavily as it was falling now, the ruins of a fire would be covered with white. Inside, each turned in a different direction. Agnes, though she assured them she did not need any assistance, accepted James's help with her patient. Lucky and Melissa went into the house. Melissa went to her bedroom and Lucky to the loft. It was as cold inside as it was outside. The sanctuary they shared only hours ago was gone.

14

October 24, 1888
Arido, Texas

Cerqueda was growing restless. Along the West Texas border, the wind swept across the flat land relentlessly. Now the snow had started. He didn't like either. He preferred warm luxury, cheerful music, and beautiful women; and he was tired of waiting for news that did not seem to be forthcoming. He was about ready to make up some story that would account for his returning to Texas. But he couldn't quite bring himself to do it.

He'd been in Arido for less than a week. But this time, even those he'd welcomed to Arido seemed wary of him. He finally figured out they'd heard about the man he shot. Their reaction surprised him. Cerqueda had shot men before, for less reason. But this time it was one of theirs, and the trust was gone. When this last business was done, he'd run them all off. He'd built this town and he'd close it down.

He had paid Sheriff Wake Boland to send off enough telegrams to find Geronimo, but nobody had responded. A bounty with a time limit was his last option. If he had no response in a week, he'd give up—for now.

He summoned Boland. "I'm gonna make this real easy. Send a telegram to every operator in a hundred miles. Tell them you're looking for a stranger, a gambler who dresses in black. Say he probably turned up about a month ago. He carries a lucky gold piece with a diamond in the middle."

"Who do I tell them wants to know?"

"You, idiot. You're the sheriff, aren't you? Tell 'em there's a $500 reward for the man who finds him."

By morning, the snow blowing down the San Juan Mountains had stopped. The rocky cliffs and the bare limbs of the aspen trees were frosted with white, but the smoldering wood from the fire had melted the snow on the schoolhouse and the surrounding grounds. Melissa had never been in a war, had never seen the aftermath of a battle. But she was sure that what she was looking at was just as bad. The only difference was that the war was over. There was only one body, and unless he'd died since she last checked, Bart Jamison was still her enemy.

Melissa stood on the porch and felt a lump form in her throat. Everything was lost; all she'd done was for nothing. Even if she wanted to rebuild the school, there was no money to pay for it. She could move into one of the dormitories, but somehow the incentive was gone.

Grayson Academy had failed. She'd have to go back East and find a job in one of the boarding schools for young women. Well, so be it. She'd done the best she could. Now she had the responsibility of the three lives she interrupted. Agnes seemed to be the kind of woman who'd always find a place for herself. James? She didn't know. In spite of his exertion in helping fight the fire last night and the smoky air he was forced to breathe, he hadn't given up. Once she'd confessed their deception, James might elect to stay in Colorado and take advantage of the offer the citizens in town had made to her father. He could operate his own school in the church. Lucky—well, that was harder. He told her in the beginning that he was a drifter searching for his sister. Now he could go back to that and his gambling.

It was then she noticed Lucky step out from behind the burned-out lean-to with the reins of Arthur in one hand and a strange horse in the other. He herded them into the corral and fastened it. Then he did an odd thing. He began gathering what was left of the schoolhouse timbers and stacked them like firewood. Why would he do that? The horses didn't need a fire, and once Bart could be moved, everyone would be gone.

Too weary to concern herself further, Melissa went to the kitchen to start breakfast. For the first time, Lucky hadn't made the coffee. There was no fire in the stove, so she added kindling wood and struck a match. While the oven heated, she made biscuits and fried thick slices of bacon. Once the biscuits were done, the coffee had perked, and the food was ready; she'd better check on James and Agnes.

But James was not in the boys' dormitory. She

searched until she found him in the girls' wing with Agnes. At some point during the night, he'd moved the rocking chair from the main house next to Bart's bed. Now he was sprawled back against the chair, his legs covered with a blanket, his feet resting on the foot of Bart's bunk. Agnes was in the bunk next to Bart, sound asleep. Bart seemed to be sleeping too. His clothes had been removed and dropped in a pile by the door. There was a bandage covering his forehead and his left arm. A white powdery substance covered one cheek and the side of his neck.

She'd never wished a man dead before, but it was hard not to this time. For her father's dream to be so nearly recognized, then go up in smoke because of one man's anger, was hard to accept.

"I'm sorry, Father," she whispered. "It wasn't you who failed. It was me. We are ruined."

The chair squeaked as James lifted his feet from the bed and planted them on the floor. "You aren't ruined," he said. *"A ruin—yet what ruin! From its mass, walk, palaces, half cities have been reared..."*

"Childe Harold," Melissa whispered. "That may be good enough for France, but Silver Wind, Colorado, is just a mining town. Nobody will even miss it when we're gone."

"I think you're wrong, Melissa," he said. "Don't be too quick to give up on the school. We'll think of something."

He stood, caught Melissa's arm, and indicated they should go outside. "I don't think Black Bart is fatally injured. Apparently, he stumbled and hit his head from having too much to drink. But Agnes did have to sedate him so she could dress his burns and keep him in the bunk. I suspect he'll have to be moved into town in a day or two, or we'll be forced to restrain him."

"I don't suppose it matters now that the school has burned. Will Agnes be all right in there with him while we have breakfast?"

"Breakfast? Oh, yes. Agnes could take on the Apaches and win. All she'd have to do is show Bart her syringe and he'd faint."

"Are you feeling okay?" she asked as they stepped on the porch.

"I could probably eat a cow. Fighting a fire builds up an appetite."

James looked able to eat a cow. His color was good and he was standing straight.

"Say, did you see Ellen's father last night? He was right in there working with the others."

Melissa smiled. "Yes, and I noticed Nurse Ellen looking after you."

James blushed. "She's very concerned. If she'd been able to walk, she'd have done more."

Melissa opened the door. "Well, her father said the doctors told her she could walk if she were willing to exercise. Maybe you could convince her."

"Maybe I can." He blushed even more, then added hurriedly, "Where's Lucky?"

"In here eating biscuits," Lucky answered. "How's Bart?"

"He won't be burning anything else down for a while," James said. "If the heat in hell is anything like the fire he just went through, he might even rethink his ways."

James filled his coffee cup, grabbed two biscuits, and sat down.

"Lack of sleep hasn't affected your appetite," Lucky observed.

"Not a bit. Don't think I'd choose to be a fireman, but I've never done anything physical before. Quite exhilarating really, and no more taxing than a stroll down Fifth Avenue in New York. When do we start rebuilding?"

"We don't," Melissa said in a taut voice. "All the equipment has been destroyed: my father's books, the slates, the benches. Everything's gone." She closed her eyes, rocking back and forth on the balls of her feet as if she were swaying in the wind. The schoolhouse was gone, her punishment for going after something she was not intended to have.

She should never have let Lucky make love to her. She'd given in to her own desire. They made love, not one night but two; each time he'd told her that it was wrong. Now he was gazing at her with something almost like anger. What did he expect of her?

"Tell me again why you came out here, Melissa. Was this your dream or your father's?" She frowned. A sudden wave of fury swept up her back and she wanted to hit him. "I came for my father," she said. "You know that. This was his dream, the one thing he wanted to accomplish. He needed to prove to the world that he was not a failure."

"He wasn't a failure. He accomplished what he said he wanted to do. The only thing he failed at was coming back for you. You came to him. I think the thing you're really afraid of is your own failure."

Melissa ran out the door and up the canyon along the creek. Mac was running ahead of her, chasing the imaginary rabbits, loudly proclaiming his joy. How much easier it was for him.

How dare Lucky criticize her? How many women would have left the only life they knew to go out West? She'd done what she had promised her father. No ... she'd come here because it was important to her.

"Hey, take it easy," Lucky called from behind. "Melissa, stop! We need to talk about this." Then he stopped. He didn't have the right to confuse her life any further. She'd been right when she tried not to let him get close to her, creating a vast wall between them. What he wanted to do was take her in his arms and tell her everything would be all right. But he couldn't do that. He'd spent most of his adult life helping strangers. But he'd never been able to do anything for the people he loved. His mother had died and his sister had disappeared off the face of the earth while he'd been off looking for gold. Gold! One way or another he'd always been searching for something. Now he'd fallen in love and there was no way he could see to save her. But he wouldn't give up.

She turned back, looking past him at the burned building. "You just don't understand, Lucky. I should have been able to stop this. It never should have happened. My father managed to pan enough gold to build this, but I don't know anything about panning and I have no gold. I can't charge the citizens for teaching those children without the necessary supplies. This is 1888. We don't draw with sticks in the sand anymore. We have nothing left."

"We have four pairs of willing hands, and we have the children. That's it," Lucky said. "We have an invitation to dinner with the colonel, remember? I say we take him up on it. We'll ask his advice."

Melissa blinked. "You want us to go to the colonel's ranch for dinner?"

Lucky smiled and nodded. "Why not? We have to eat somewhere."

"What makes you think the colonel would help even if he could?"

For the first time in days, Melissa saw that wicked grin return to Lucky's face. "Because, my dear wife, we have Ellen on our side."

Melissa gasped. "You're going to court Ellen?"

Lucky laughed. "Of course not. James is. And I don't think either of them will object."

"She's too young."

"Well, he has plenty of time."

Bart groaned and tried to open his eyes. He felt as if they'd been glued shut. Every effort he made set off a chain of thunder and pain in his head. He couldn't move his upper body. Concentrating, in spite of the pain, he wiggled his toes. Good. Now the foot, then the leg. They all moved. He tried to remember what happened. There had been smoke and fire, fire that leaped ahead of him and he couldn't see. He'd tripped and fallen and then there was an explosion of pain.

"Be still, Mr. Jamison. Don't try to touch your head."

It was a woman's voice that came to him out of the darkness. A voice he didn't recognize. "Melissa?" His voice was tight and gravelly, his mouth so dry he could barely speak. He felt as if he'd swallowed coffee that was too hot. "Thirsty," he managed to say.

Something cold and smooth suddenly pressed against his lower lip. When he tried to push himself up to accept the liquid dribbling into his mouth, a wave of pain started to form at the base of his skull, then sliced across the top of his head and down his right arm like a bolt of lightning. "Awww. What happened?"

"You were in a fire, Mr. Jamison. Don't you remember?"

"Fire? Where?" He frowned, wrinkling his forehead against . . . ? His eyebrows touched fabric. Once again, he reached to examine it, but the pain stopped him. He closed his eyes. The cup appeared at his mouth again and he drank clumsily, unable to stop the liquid from dribbling out of the corners of his mouth and down his neck. But a soft cloth blotted the liquid.

"No," he whispered. "I don't remember."

The woman sighed. "It's probably best you don't try to remember now. You have a head injury and burns. For now, you simply need to sleep. I'll be here to take care of you."

Take care of me? Suddenly he was a boy again, a boy who still had a mother to comfort him. But that was a long time ago. Perhaps his want had made him dream this. Maybe he was dying. "You must be an angel."

This wasn't the first time Agnes had been called an angel. Nurses often were. But this was the first time she'd been called that by a big, dark, wicked-looking man who'd hurt people she cared about. She neither understood nor could explain the odd feeling of need this man evoked in her.

It started back in Silver Wind when she rushed into the saloon and found James brandishing a pistol. Bart had been standing by the poker table, totally amazed by what he was seeing. It was obvious that he was not afraid of James. But it was Lucky who caught the brunt of Bart's reaction. He hadn't even noticed her, but she hadn't been able to forget him.

Now she had Silver Wind's bad man in her control. He was helpless. She didn't think he would die, but as a burn patient, he might. That gave her a sense of power. She liked that. Sooner or later he'd have to see her as a person. Until then ... well, until then, she was living her own dime novel—where the heroine tamed the bad guy.

Or perhaps she wouldn't tame him. She had time to decide. One thing she did know was that the West was turning out to be more exciting than she'd ever expected.

The night came for the Grayson Academy staff to dress for dinner at the Curtis Ranch. The colonel was sending his buggy and a driver who would fetch and return them. Lucky took James to the barbershop in town, where they'd get their baths, haircuts, and a shave—at James's expense. At the same time, Lucky wanted to have a word with Sheriff Vance about his plans for Bart. Agnes had declined an invitation to join them, insisting that Bart could neither be left alone nor moved. Taking her duties seriously, she rarely left the dormitory turned hospital.

Melissa, grateful for the solitude, heated water for her tin tub, found her last cake of sweet smelling soap, and stripped off her clothes. As she climbed in, the smell of smoke in her hair made her realize she needed to look her best. If she took a real bath, maybe she'd stop dreading the evening. It wasn't her way to ask for help, and she was uncomfortable with what they were doing. Still, the Academy was more important to the children than her discomfort, and that was the reason for accepting the invitation. Even more awkward was being forced to take the stage as Lucky's wife before an audience. Their relationship was such a change from one day to the next. Over and over again she'd gone over their situation. It was as if they'd been caught in a summer wind, had come together in a blast of heat, then had been blown apart. Just when it seemed that they could get past the reality and allow themselves to be two people who fit together, something happened to tear them apart.

But aside from her private fears, the one that had her so uneasy was Lucky's statement that James would be the one to win Ellen to their side. James was a bit older in years than Ellen, but the truth was, he was just as innocent. Since both had similar backgrounds in fighting medical problems, they might be a good match—if James was content to wait. But she couldn't quite see him as the colonel's heir.

At this point it was out of her hands. She'd feel better if everything weren't based on deception. Lucky, pretending to be James, was really a gambler being tracked by a killer from whom he'd rescued a kidnapped young woman. James, a formerly sickly scholar, was having the time of his life playing the role of Lucky. Agnes had traded her position as James's nurse for that of caring for the man who'd tormented Melissa and apparently burned down the school in revenge—Black Bart.

As for herself, Melissa couldn't string a line of words together to describe her situation. She'd come out here determined to make a success of her father's school. When faced with failure, she'd taken what she thought would be a reasonable step in proposing to James. Then everything had gone wrong. If only Lucky Lawrence had never stepped off that train. She'd never seen James, but she'd sensed from the beginning that there was something wrong about the man. Lucky could have stopped it right away. She should have stopped it but she hadn't. That made the deception more damning to herself.

She couldn't escape the truth. Her conscience forced her to admit that she'd turned into some kind of jezebel. She scooted down in the tub and let her legs hang out, immersing her hair in the warm water. *Jezebel.* She closed her eyes and tried to imagine what would have happened if she'd met Lucky back in Philadelphia. Would they have ever met? Would he have noticed her? Would he ever have kissed her? Would she have let him?

The answer to all those questions was probably not.

By the time she'd dried her hair and emptied her bathwater, she was just as befuddled as before. Standing before her wardrobe, she studied her garments. The truth was, she was in the midst of a dilemma. Whichever direction she chose was likely to be a disaster. Reaching into the back of the cabinet, she pulled out her only real dinner gown—a low-cut blue silky garment trimmed with an apron of shimmery silver. There were matching blue gloves and white flowers for her hair, and a fur-trimmed white velvet cape.

She was almost dressed when she heard the front door open and the voices of James and Lucky. They were joshing each other about how well they looked in spite of the rustic facilities available to them.

"Look," James said, "the floor's wet. There's the tub. Looks like Melissa's been doing a little washing too."

If they hadn't stopped by the sheriff's office to report on Bart, they would have arrived sooner. He was gone and they'd wasted too much time. If they'd returned to the Academy sooner, he could have scrubbed his wife's back. Or dried her beautiful hair. Or... On the other hand, she might have emptied the water over his newly trimmed haircut and destroyed his brushed and pressed clothing. He let out a deep chuckle. "Looks like it. Too bad," Lucky said loudly, "if she'd waited, I could have helped her."

"Help her wash clothes?" James asked innocently. "You don't look like a washwoman."

"Neither does my wife. But getting wet does strange things to a person."

"I still think wearing this tan jacket and trousers is a mistake," James said.

"Trust me," Lucky assured him. "You're about to call on the daughter of a wealthy man who's attended the best parties in our state's capital. Looking like a gambler might appeal to you, and even to Ellen, but tonight you need to be a gentleman."

"Why?"

"Because if you want to impress Ellen, you need to win over her father."

"But I like being you," James argued. "And Ellen likes my clothes."

"Tonight you have to be yourself. Tonight you're James Harold Pickney IV."

Melissa opened her bedroom door. "I was always told a person is what he or she wears. What do you think, Lucky? How do I look?"

15

— ❧ —

Lucky tried to answer, but the picture of his pretend wife standing in the doorway, took his breath away. Shimmering in a gown the color of moonlight and blue sky, in the light of the lamp, Melissa was absolutely enchanting. She was an angel with a naughty look in her eyes and a gaze firmly planted on him.

James grinned at Lucky. "May I?" He took Melissa's velvet cape and draped it around her shoulders in his most gallant manner. "You are absolutely beautiful, Mrs. Pickney. And you have a nice name too." He extended his arm as if she were royalty. "Coming, Lucky?" he teased, leaving the gambler turned husband, stunned.

"Now just a minute, Pickney," Lucky blustered, "that's my wife you're running off with."

"Yes, but she was supposed to be mine. You stole her from me."

Lucky closed the house and hurried to catch up.

Agnes waved from the dormitory doorway. "Have a good time. Try not to worry. I'm certain the colonel will listen favorably."

"I wish I was that sure," Lucky said, brushing James aside to take Melissa's arm. "Just remember, James, we need Ellen on our side. I hate to wish her on you, but it's your job to make her feel like a princess. She's the only one who can persuade the colonel to help."

"She's really not spoiled," James argued. "She's just lonely and afraid. I know what it means to be different. It will be nice helping someone else instead of being the one who needs help."

The colonel's carriage and driver were waiting in the yard. "Evening, folks. My name's Willis. The colonel sent me to fetch you. There's a blanket in the buggy."

James climbed in first, taking Melissa's hand. Unfortunately, Melissa's dress, her short stature, and the step up into the buggy presented a problem; a problem Lucky was only too happy to solve. He put his hands on Melissa's waist, held her for a moment, and then lifted her. "Drive on, Willis," Lucky said, taking advantage of the short seat to snuggle close to his wife. As he slipped his arm around her shoulder, he encountered James's hand. Apparently, James had the same objective in mind. Lucky shoved it away and leaned forward to speak to James. "I assume, *Mr. Lawrence*," he said under his breath, "that you're making plans to handle your assignment for the evening?"

James grinned. "I always have plans."

Lucky groaned. *James has plans*. Unless he'd taken on a job, the real Lucky had bounced around the country for years with no plan of any kind except to find his sister, Rainey. Now, in the last month, he'd been forced to think about protecting a school and building its future and—being a husband.

The buggy was open in the front, and once they'd rounded the abutment and turned back toward the mountains, the light of the moon capped the snow-covered mountain peaks with silver. A brisk wind caught the loose snow and flung it down the valley like a white veil. "Did you see the wind shower? That's how Silver Wind got its name," Melissa explained. "When the conditions are just right, the wind turns silver with snow."

"Your Colorado is very beautiful," James said. "Its air is fresh and pure. It gives a man a promise of forever."

James's words touched both Melissa and Lucky. Melissa had felt that instinctively from the beginning, but she'd never put her feelings into words before. James was the dreamer, the peacemaker, the mountain. And Lucky? Lucky was a challenger, powerful and as unpredictable as the wind. And she, what was she?

"Sometimes, when I breathe in the air and look at the mountains, I feel very small," Melissa said. "According to Longfellow, *'Great men make their Footprints on the sands of time.'* I thought I could do what no other member in my family had done—finish something we started."

"You're not walking on sand, Melissa," James admonished. "Mr. Longfellow also said, *'It is the heart, not the brain, that to the highest doth attain.'* You have a very big heart, and you light up your students with your enthusiasm and determination."

Lucky couldn't argue with the tribute to her determination. Under the blanket, Melissa's fingertips were dancing up and down his thigh. Under the guise of allowing the blanket to slip off his lap, he reached down and retrieved it, removing her hand in the process. Just as he leaned back, the Curtis ranch came into view, lit up like a birthday cake covered in candles.

"Will you look at that?" James said. "Charleston in the middle of the Colorado mountains."

The white two-story colonial mansion lacked only a long tree-lined drive, cotton fields, and ladies dressed in hoop skirts waiting to greet them. Lucky observed, "I'm surprised he calls it a ranch. It ought to be Curtis Plantation."

The buggy stopped at the front door and the driver climbed down, ready to assist the guests. He needn't have bothered, James thought, as Lucky scrambled out and then swung Melissa to the ground. At that moment, Colonel Curtis walked through the door and greeted them. "Good evening, Mrs. Pickney. You are a vision of loveliness tonight." He held out his hand. When she placed hers inside it, he leaned forward and gallantly brushed her fingertips with his lips. A firm handshake for the man he believed to be Melissa's husband followed, and a lesser acknowledgment of the new teacher.

"Let's go inside and get out of the cold. Ellen is waiting for us in the drawing room." A servant standing just inside the door took Melissa's cape and opened the large double doors off the foyer. Everything inside the drawing room was oversized: a large fireplace with a blazing fire, a huge Oriental rug on which two brocade sofas seemed boxed in by ornate mahogany library tables. Shelves filled with books and statues lined one wall. The other two walls contained French doors leading out onto a snow-dusted veranda. At the point where they intersected was a small, highly polished piano upon which sat a candelabra holding more candles than Melissa could count. Ellen was sitting in her wheelchair near the fire.

"Do come in," Ellen called out. "I'm so glad you came. We don't often have intellectual company out here."

"I'm certain they just don't know what they're missing," James said, moving to her side. "What a lovely home you have, Miss Curtis."

Ellen smiled, suddenly becoming the chatelaine of the castle. "Please, Mr. Lawrence, I've asked you to call me Ellen. After all, we are friends, aren't we?" She held out her hand, drawing him down to the sofa next to her.

"I very much hope so," James answered. "Do you play the piano—Ellen?"

"A little."

"Personally I like Mozart," James said. "I suppose I'm a little prejudiced."

"Oh? Why is that?"

James blushed a bit, then straightened his back and said, "Mozart was small in stature—something like me—and yet the world loved him."

"And he had such a glorious name. Wolfgang Amadeus Mozart. One of a kind. Something like Lucky Lawrence."

Lucky, still standing in the middle of the foyer, choked back a laugh. He did not consider himself to be a well-educated man, but even he knew Lucky Lawrence and Wolfgang Amadeus Mozart could only be equal in the eyes of an impressionable girl. The best he could hope was that nobody learned his real name.

"Dinner is served, Colonel Curtis," the same servant who'd taken Melissa's cape announced.

"Allow me," the colonel said, holding out his arm to Melissa. "I hope you'll enjoy the meal our cook has prepared. We're too far from the ocean here to make good use of the seafoods we might have enjoyed back home in South Carolina, but I think you'll enjoy our roast beef and the vegetables grown here on the range."

Like a fish out of water, Lucky trailed the colonel and Melissa. It was all he could do not to reach out and pat her sassy little bottom as she sashayed down the hallway.

The colonel pulled the chair out for Melissa to sit. In the mirror over the sideboard, Lucky watched James push Ellen down the hall. The flush on their cheeks indicated their interest in each other. Lucky took the seat by Melissa, leaving the seats across the table for James and Ellen.

Water glasses and wine goblets were being filled when the colonel said, "Sorry about your bad luck down at the school."

Melissa waved off the wine, refusing to look at Lucky as she did so. She didn't have to. He could see she was remembering her last alcohol indulgence. Too bad. Overindulging had taken them to a place neither would have gone without help.

"Yes," she said with a catch in her voice. "Thanks to all the help, the house and dormitories survived."

"So? You going to build it back?"

"I'm not sure," she said.

"Of course you are," Ellen piped up as James pushed her chair to the table.

The colonel came around to stand beside Ellen. "Do you want to sit in your rolling chair or in the regular one?" he asked.

She looked up at James and held up her arms. "The regular one, next to Mr. Lawrence," she said. "Don't strain your back, Father; he can lift me."

Lucky turned a laugh into a cough when he saw the expression on James's face. But he had to hand it to James, the man was game. Using what was probably his last ounce of strength, he lifted Ellen, who gazed up at him sweetly, and placed her in the chair. Then he sank down into the one next to her.

"Let me offer a toast," the colonel said. "To the intellectual additions to our community. We expect you to turn our children into educated citizens who will in turn make Colorado as gracious and gentle as..." he broke off, finishing with, "as my Ellen."

Over a menu as lavish as any he'd experienced anywhere, the real Lucky watched Melissa charm the colonel and James win over his daughter. He faced a painful truth. They both belonged in this kind of elegant setting. Lucky Lawrence, gambler, didn't. At the close of the meal, Lucky rose quickly, offering to assist Ellen to her chair before an exhausted James collapsed into his half-finished dish of custard.

"Will you play for us?" James asked as he pushed her chair back to the drawing room.

"I'm afraid I'm not really very good," Ellen said.

Melissa sent James a quizzical glance. "You play, don't you, James—I mean, Lucky? I'm sorry," she apologized to her guests. "I'm continually calling them by the wrong name."

James answered quickly. "Yes, though I don't often do it. People don't expect a man in my profession to have musical talent."

The colonel offered both James and Lucky cigars. Lucky bit off the end and accepted the colonel's light. James was in the process of declining when the colonel said, "Just what is your profession, Mr. Lawrence? I'm not too clear on that. You really don't look like the gamblers I know. There was Doc Holliday, of course, but he died of consumption. How are the lungs?"

"They continue to improve," James assured, biting off the end of his cigar as Lucky had done and allowing the colonel to light it. Lucky wondered how many men there could be in the year 1888 who had never smoked a cigar.

Obviously James had never hidden behind the woodshed smoking rolled-up rabbit tobacco. He drew in the smoke and—swallowed it. The fit of coughing that followed left James pale and spent.

"Let's step outside...Lucky." The imposter James took his friend by the arm and pushed him out onto the veranda. "What do you think you are doing, James? I'm sure you're not supposed to smoke."

"I'm not supposed to do a lot of the things I've been doing, but I am."

"Yes, you are." Lucky looked through the glass doors at the woman he was illegally married to. She was frowning at the colonel, then shaking her head sharply. Lucky didn't know what Melissa said to the colonel, but soon after, they were out the door and on the way back to the Academy. Apparently, Melissa was the only one intent on rebuilding.

"I guess I ruined it," James said weakly on the drive back.

"You couldn't ruin anything that wasn't already ruined," Melissa said. "Don't feel bad, James. We tried. There're just some things that aren't meant to be."

"And there are some things that are," Lucky said in a tight voice. "We just have to find a way to make it happen."

We? Melissa couldn't tell Lucky that Colonel Curtis had warned her about him. "Seems like there's some kind of bounty out on the man," he'd said. "Five hundred dollars. He must have done something pretty bad. While I'm not against rebuilding the school, I'm more concerned about the safety of my daughter."

"If you're worried about Ellen," she'd said, "don't be. I'd never allow any man around who might be a risk to my students."

Only a risk to me.

16

—❧—

Agnes had kept him sedated for days. Now it was time to let the man who called himself Black Bart wake up. She leaned over and blotted the sheen of perspiration from his upper lip. Even beneath her cloth, the stubble of face hair grated against her fingertips like a file. Sooner or later she'd have to shave him. Sooner was better. His gaunt face was stubbled with a cold black beard that made him look the part of the criminal he had become. She didn't understand the strong response she felt, not fear exactly, nor was it anxiety. The sensation was illusive and she directed herself to put it out of her mind.

The odd feeling had started when she'd removed his clothing. She'd had to bathe him before she could treat his burns. Now he lay naked beneath his blankets. As a nurse, she'd treated many men, directing her thoughts away from their masculinity. But this man was extraordinarily...male. She felt herself blush and her pulse raced.

Suddenly he raised up and grabbed her shoulders. "Are you trying to kill me?"

"I am not!" Agnes tried to pull away, but the man had a superhuman grip. She'd seen it before. Fear or pain sometimes gave a patient a sudden burst of strength. "I'm trying to save your life."

Bart groaned. "What have you done to me? My skin is on fire and my skull feels like it's been run over by a wagon."

"I'm not surprised. You were hit in the head by a beam and your skin was burned by the fire you set."

He pulled her closer. "Fire? I don't remember setting any fire."

"I'm surprised you remember anything. You have a head injury. Be still, Mr. Jamison. I'm not certain that you'll die if I go, but if you thrash about, I can promise you'll suffer a lot of pain."

His lips were tightly set in a grim line, parting only as he gasped for air. "I've suffered pain most of my life, lady. Who are you anyway?"

"I'm Agnes Fulbright. I'm a nurse, and if you don't unhand me, I'm going to let you keep on hurting. Now let me go. I need to treat your burns."

He groaned and fell back to the cot. "I think I'd rather go for a swim in that creek."

"You've already been there. The only water you're bathing in now is vinegar water. We have to worry about fighting infection." She pulled the blanket down.

"Hellfire, woman! Where're my clothes?"

"In the fireplace, Mr. Jamison; what was left of them."

"You mean you...you've been..."

"I have, and I'm going to remove these bandages on

your head and your arm and do it some more. You're fortunate that the rafter protected most of your body, that and the teacher's desk."

He tried to shimmy up the bed away from her, then realized he was leaving his blanket behind and slid back. She was right about the pain.

"That's better."

As gently as possible she removed the dressing from his head, washing the dried blood away from the wound on the top. "Good. No infection there." She sprinkled it with sulphur powder and lifted his head and rewound it, not realizing until she felt his breath on her neck how close her bosom was to his face. Too quickly she let his head drop, and jerked away. The wicked glint in his eyes said he recognized her reaction. He was enjoying her discomfort.

It was time she let him know that she could make him uncomfortable too. She had her own kind of power. Catching the end of the bandage covering the burned arm, she began to peel it down. The oath he let out forced her to regret her action, and she stopped. He didn't deserve such unprofessional treatment when it was she who'd overreacted. "If you'll be still, Mr. Jamison, I'll try to make this as easy as possible."

Between clenched teeth he muttered. "Easy? You call this easy?"

"I'm going to remove your bandage so that I can change the dressing. Once I'm done, I'll rub it with laudanum ointment and healing powder."

The perspiration beaded up on his forehead. "Laudanum? That's for women. Got any whiskey?"

"No. I do not."

He grinned. "I thought all you sawbones carried whiskey—strictly for medicinal purposes, of course."

"I'm not a doctor. I'm a nurse. Now be still."

Once she'd removed the bandages to reveal the angry, skinless flesh, he closed his eyes. She had to give him credit. He didn't cry out or complain. For a moment she thought he was asleep. "Was anyone else hurt?" he asked.

"No. You were the only one. We managed to get Arthur away from the flames, but the building was destroyed." She stuck her fingers into the ointment and touched his burn. He started, then relaxed as the deadening effect of the paste took effect.

"Who's Arthur?"

"Mrs. Pickney's horse. You ought to be ashamed of yourself for what you did."

"You're assuming I did it."

"Why else would you be skulking around out there?"

"Well...she ought not to have turned me down. I might not be a fancy dude like that Pickney, but I belong out here, and I'd have treated her good. Guess you don't believe that, but there was a time...never mind."

"Yes, I do." And she did. The more of the ointment she applied, the more relaxed he became. The more she touched his lean, muscular body, the more the heat seemed to transfer from his body to hers. "You just can't force yourself on a woman, Mr. Jamison. You have to show her you are a kind, caring person. No woman likes a bully. Who taught you to be like that?"

"My pa, I guess. He said you had to keep a woman in her place. Tell her what's what. People thought he was a good man. My ma didn't complain, so I guess I didn't know no different."

"Well your father was wrong."

"How would you know? You're not married, are you?"

"No. I've never met a man who . . . I mean, men don't seem to like me."

He opened his eyes. "Why not? You're a fair-looking woman. Good teeth. Good eyes. Your hair might be a little peculiar, but you got plenty of it. And you got spunk. I like a woman with spunk."

"I think, Mr. Jamison, that you'd like any woman who'd have you."

"I think," he said, his voice growing thicker, "any woman who's had her hands all over my naked body could call me Bart. By the way, you have nice hands."

Agnes let go, her hands throbbing in time with her pulse. She stood, turned and left the room, slamming the door emphatically behind her.

Bart grinned. The salve she'd rubbed on his arm and shoulder had taken away the pain for the moment. It was probably a good thing Miss Agnes had left the room. To his surprise, his body was responding to the nurse in an embarrassing way. She was a little older than he usually liked his women, but she was kind and gentle. There was something about a gentle woman that a man appreciated. There was something about a kind woman that a man wanted to live up to.

Damn! That knock on the head must have addled his brains.

• • •

Melissa was quiet on the way home. The dinner party at the colonel's had started out good, even if it had ended badly. She shouldn't have reacted the way she had. He was a father concerned about his child. What he'd told her made her just as concerned—about her husband. With a price on Lucky's head, both he and James could be in danger. Suddenly the school had become less important. Maybe it was time they confessed their deceptions. Lucky could disappear the way he'd planned, and James could go back East and become James once more.

"I thought it went well, didn't you?" James asked. "Ellen asked me to come over tomorrow and help her with her exercises. I'm not a nurse like Agnes, but I know that muscles degenerate from lack of use. I want to help her walk."

"I'm not sure that's a good idea, James," Melissa said.

James bristled. "Why not? That's what you wanted. If I make Ellen my assignment, the colonel would be grateful enough to help the school. But you know what? This is more than the school. This is someone who needs my help."

Lucky had been quiet. Now he turned and looked at her.

"I saw you and the colonel talking through the glass doors while James and I were outside. He seemed a little tense. What's wrong, Melissa?"

She gave the driver a quick glance and said in a low voice. "I think it's time for you to go, Lucky. James and I will go back East and you can go wherever it is you'll be safe."

"Go back?" James repeated. "I don't think so."

It wasn't the "go back" that hit Lucky in the gut, it was the word *safe*. "We'll talk about this when we get home," he said, silencing both of his companions with his sharp tone.

A black cloud suddenly covered the moon, and the wind picked up. "Looks like we're going to have a storm," their driver said, urging the horses into a brisk trot. "Don't get so much rain here. Rains on the other side of the mountains, but we get mostly snow or nothing."

By the time they reached the house, the wind was swirling the ashes from the schoolhouse like thick fog. Quickly, they dismounted and hurried toward the house. "Thanks for the ride," James called out, and dashed into his sleeping quarters in the boys' dormitory.

"I'm going to check on Agnes and Bart," Lucky said, raising his voice to be heard over the wind. "Don't go to bed before I get back."

Melissa didn't acknowledge his words, but he knew she'd heard him. Inside the girls' dormitory, Agnes was sitting in the rocking chair sound asleep. She woke up.

"How was dinner?" she asked.

"Too elegant for me," Lucky answered. "What about him? Giving you any trouble?"

"Nothing I can't handle. You know, I think Mr. Jamison is just . . . scared and a little lonely."

"Sure, like a rattlesnake. That's why they hide under rocks. But you get too close and they bite you."

"Don't know anything about snakes," Agnes said, "but I do know a little about men in pain. They're all little boys who need a mother. I'm good at mothering."

"Whatever you say, Agnes. But be careful."

Bart heard the door close. He was about to speak

when he heard Agnes whisper, "Maybe this one time I don't want to be a mother—or careful."

Lucky entered the house and the wind slammed the door shut behind him. "I don't like the feel of that wind. If it keeps up, the schoolhouse site will be swept clean," he said, "or blown away." He was telling her the truth, but it wasn't the wind that made him cold; it was the stiffness of her back, the distance she was deliberately putting between them. Why now?

"I never knew my father," he said. "But you knew yours. This was his dream, the dream he passed on to you. You accepted it, ready to do whatever you had to do to make it come true. That makes you the strongest woman I know. Why would you give up now?"

"A really strong woman should know when to stop. It's time. I couldn't have done what I have were it not for you, Lucky. But when my actions hurt others, it's time to give up."

"Hurt others? What do you mean, Melissa? Do you mean James? He's as happy as a gambler with a full house."

She wouldn't look at him.

"It was the colonel, wasn't it? He said something to you when we were leaving. Tell me, Melissa. You owe me that much."

She turned. "You're right. I owe you the truth. He's investigating Lucky Lawrence. Of course, that means James. But if the word goes out to the world, they'll think he's asking about you, Lucky. I won't be responsible for something happening to you . . . or to James. This has to end before he gets hurt. The only way we can be certain of that is to tell the truth."

"I can look after myself. But you're right. It isn't fair to James. I don't think he's going to give up being Lucky. After all, it's his word against mine. And he does have a way with words, even if he can't shoot a gun and doesn't know beans about playing poker."

"I know. That's why I think it's time for you to go. I'll just say you went prospecting, like we planned. The town won't be surprised. Then later, we'll tell the truth, and James and I . . ."

"James and you?"

"We'll go back East."

She pressed her lips firmly together but she couldn't keep them from trembling. Strong wasn't the word for Melissa Grayson Pickney. Pickney. Even saying the name was wrong. It ought to be Melissa Grayson Lawrence. There was no way he could ride away and leave James to continue his charade as Lucky. He'd be challenged in a fortnight and wouldn't live to wear that ten-gallon hat he was so proud of. She swallowed hard, determined to contain her emotions.

Her cheeks were flushed, the cheeks he'd kissed such a short time ago. Her arms were folded across her chest as if she had to hold herself back. He took a step forward. If he turned away from her now, he'd lose the one thing he'd found that was worth fighting for—a wife.

"Don't do this, Melissa."

"I have to."

"I just want to hold you. I don't know what else to do. I don't know all those fancy words like James, but I know that one way we seem to be able to reach each other is when we're making love."

She stiffened. He had to get through whatever new wall she was constructing before the wall grew too strong.

She held up her hand as if to stop him, but she didn't turn away. "Please..." she whispered. "Don't touch me. Just leave me alone. Tomorrow—tomorrow, we'll talk."

But they didn't talk the next day. Early that morning, James insisted on keeping his promise to Ellen and set out for the ranch before the weather worsened. In order not to be stopped, he left a note, effectively delaying their conference.

"Well, he's growing a backbone," Lucky said.

"I just hope he doesn't become ill. I don't think Agnes could handle another patient."

Melissa looked tired, as if she hadn't slept. The sparkle had gone from her eye and he couldn't see a way to restore it, short of doing what she'd asked—leave. The snow had saved them by putting out the fire. Now the weather seemed determined to take their fate in a different direction. Mac seemed unusually restless, moving from spot to spot inside the house. The rain continued. There was no snow this time. Instead, the heavens unleashed such a deluge that James wouldn't be able to get through the pass. When he didn't return, any plans to work on the school had to be shelved. Throughout the afternoon, the water continued to fall.

Tension inside the house grew. Lucky didn't know what to say, and Melissa went to her room to avoid any attempt at conversation. Finally, he decided to visit the sickroom. Even Bart would be a relief.

He dashed from the porch to the dormitory door.

Mac followed him and slipped inside before Lucky could hold him back. He bounded onto Bart's cot and nuzzled Bart's good arm with his wet nose as if they were old friends.

"Think this building will float?" Bart managed with a grin.

"Pay him no attention," Agnes snapped. "He's having delusions. He keeps saying that he's Noah and this is an ark."

"Now, Aggie, tell the truth. What I've been telling her is that Noah loaded his ark so that those who survived could go forth and multiply. I figure me and Aggie could get a jump on the flood, being as she's not claimed and I'm available."

Agnes's face flushed and she left her rocking chair, giving his bandage a tug that might not entirely have been a nurse's tender ministration.

"You have a talk with him, Mr. Lawrence," Agnes said. "I'm going to get some more firewood."

"Mr. Lawrence, huh? That explains a lot," Bart said. "If you're Lawrence, who's the poetry-quoting dandy?"

Well, he'd known that the truth would eventually get out, but he hadn't expected it to happen this way. Bart had seemed remorseful for what he'd done, and Agnes swore he'd changed, but Lucky didn't trust easily. Agnes hadn't meant to reveal their secret, but she had. And if the colonel was right, everyone would know the truth soon enough. If Cerqueda discovered where Lucky was, they might have to depend on Bart to help protect the women. "The dandy is James Harold Pickney IV."

Bart chortled. "So you're Lawrence and he's Pickney. How in hell did all this get so turned around?"

"Good question. Might as well tell you. Everyone is about to find out anyway. Pickney was coming in on the train that day to marry Melissa. But he got sick in St. Louis and spent two weeks getting well enough to continue his journey. I . . . I just happened to arrive on the same train he was supposed to be on and everyone assumed I was James."

Bart kicked at his covers. "Ah, hah! So you took a look at Miss Grayson and said, 'I do.' How come she went along? Did she decide that anybody was better 'n me?"

Lucky shook his head. "She'd never seen me, Bart. She was expecting the man she'd been corresponding with for over a year. The crowd demanded a wedding and it suited me to spend a little time in Silver Wind. So you burned the school down for nothing."

"Yeah, I'm sorry about that. Once my headache went away it came back to me—what I'd done. Wouldn't have done it if I hadn't just got fired. I'd had too much to drink and I guess I wanted to get even. When I get well, I'll help build it back."

"That's kind of a quick repentance, isn't it?"

"If you had that red-haired witch preaching and poking and washing you twenty-four hours a day, you'd realize the error of your ways just to get away from her."

"And that's why you're suggesting that the two of you repeople the earth after the flood waters recede?"

Bart winked. "I was just teasing her. She's a good woman. She's the first good woman I know who doesn't think I'm a lost cause. You don't really think we're going to have a flood, do you?"

"We'd better hope not. But that creek out there could be a problem. I think I'd better check it out."

He didn't have to. The door burst open and Agnes came scurrying in. "Mr. Lawrence..." she looked stricken and changed her words to, "Mr Pickney, the stream is flooding. The water is up to the schoolhouse."

"Damn! Can you get Bart into the house? We may need to climb up to the loft if the water gets too high."

"Certainly. Mr. Jamison, I'm sorry if I was too rough on you."

"That's okay, darling. Just help me into my pants. You seeing me bare-ass naked is one thing, but I doubt Miss Melissa would think it proper."

With Lucky on one side and Agnes on the other, they dressed Bart, gathered up Agnes's medical supplies, and moved toward the house, getting drenched in the process. Lucky left Agnes to explain to Melissa and get Bart into the loft while he went to check on the water. At least Arthur was at the Curtis ranch and Mac seemed glued to Bart.

The intensity of the rain made it impossible to know how far the stream had overrun its banks, but it sounded like a freight train, crashing forward with such intensity that the ground shook.

Leaving the Academy was out of the question. James had taken the horse and Bart could walk, but not well enough or fast enough to escape. Bart hadn't been far wrong. What they needed was an ark. But first, they'd need firewood. At least for now, he and Melissa didn't have to pretend anymore. Agnes and Bart had the loft, and he and Melissa would share her bedroom.

He brought in two loads of wet wood and dropped them near the stove so that the heat would dry them. Both Bart's and Agnes's clothes suddenly fell from the loft and hit the floor in a sodden thud.

"If you get wet down there," Bart called out, "come on up; but you'd better bring your own blanket. We got just enough up here for us."

"Ah . . . Mr. Lawrence," Agnes's voice called out, "if you go out again, would you bring me my personal bag. I need some dry—clothing."

Bart laughed. "In the morning is soon enough. Come on darling, it's cold up here. Get under this blanket."

"Mr. Jamison!"

"Like I told you, I think it's time you call me Bart."

Melissa turned. "Mr. *Lawrence?*"

"Yep. The cat's out of the bag. Agnes let it slip."

Melissa was picking up the wet clothes, Agnes's dress and Bart's shirt and trousers. "Apparently Agnes has loosened up in other ways too."

"Agnes is a woman with a good head on her shoulders. She knows what she wants," Lucky observed with a grin. "So do I. Come to bed, Mrs. Lawrence."

"What about the floodwater?"

"I'll carry you to the roof. Of course, we could climb up now but I'm not certain Agnes would appreciate it."

Legally, her husband was James Pickney—who was now courting Ellen Curtis. In every other way, she belonged to Lucky Lawrence for as long as the storm raged. Fate continued to intervene. He'd saved her twice; he'd do it again. Melissa held out her hand.

"We've traced the gambler to Colorado," the sheriff told Cerqueda. "From there, he disappeared."

Cerqueda smiled. "Good. What about the girl?"

"If there was a girl with him, nobody saw her."

"Who found him?"

"A miner up in Durango. He had a run-in with the Women's Temperance Union. One of them mentioned a man in a poker game who slipped off the train rather than face the preaching. He didn't think anything about it until he heard there was a reward for a man with a fancy pearl-handled pistol and a gold coin."

"Pick out three or four good men and we'll leave in the morning."

"One of the old Indians that hangs around says there's a bad storm coming. Maybe you might want to wait till it passes."

"Wait! If it weren't dark, we'd head out now. We'll leave at sun-up. Even then it will take us three days to get to Durango. Send that drunk word to meet us there—if he wants to get paid. Better wire him a few dollars to buy a train ticket. I want to question him myself.

"All right gringo, you're about to meet your maker. Lem, give everybody a drink."

17

—⚬—

Maybe it was the storm. Maybe it was because Lucky
knew this might be the last time he'd ever make love to
Melissa, but when he looked into her eyes and saw the
longing there, he knew he had to be with her one more
time.

Inside the bedroom, he put one arm around the
small of her back so that her hips were thrust against his
arousal, and the other hand behind her neck, threading
his fingers through her hair. For a long time he just held
her, rocking her slim body against him until she was
moaning. Then he kissed her. Not gently, not a teasing
taste of her luscious mouth, but a branding of heat that
marked her as his. Rainwater from his hair dripped
down his face and wet her full, lush lips. He opened his
mouth over hers and walked her back to the bed, letting
go of her waist and using that hand to slide beneath her
skirt. Soon his fingers were touching her intimately, as
his lips moved down her neck, nudging her bodice open

and settling on her nipples. He felt her wild response, but when she reached to unbutton his pants, he groaned and pulled away.

"Why?" she gasped. "Why can't I touch you?"

"Because . . . because if you do I'll explode."

"But isn't that what you want? Doesn't it feel— good?"

"Hell, yes! But not without you." She let go of him and pushed his wet trousers down to his ankles, then unbuttoned his shirt and pushed it off his shoulders. He stumbled and knocked her to the feather mattress, falling across her. "You've got me trussed up like a turkey here." He rolled over and sat on the side of the bed, took off his boots, and kicked them into the darkness. The shirt and his underwear followed.

"Stand up, Lucky," she said.

"Why?"

"So I can turn back the covers."

He stood. The bed creaked and he heard the rustle of the covers. "Are you done?" he asked.

"Not nearly," she said, and ran her fingers up his bare leg.

He'd thought he was to be the aggressor. As he slid into the bed she rolled over and covered his body with her own. She was totally naked. As his eyes grew accustomed to the darkness, he could see her face looking down at him, her full breasts grazing his chest, and when he felt the moisture between her legs, his arousal pulsated with desire. His need for her was astounding. Other women, more experienced, had ridden him lustily, but Melissa was different. She was a strong woman who could have her choice of any man, once she was a widow. And that's what he'd decided to do. He'd confess who he was and stage his own death. That would protect James and set Melissa free. Once he'd spent one more night with her, he'd end it. Men like him weren't given the opportunity to love a woman like Melissa. But he had.

He cupped her hips in his hands and lifted her slightly, allowing his penis to slide into the crevice above it. Then he moved her back and forth, teasing her, feeling her arch her back and trying to take him inside her.

"Do you want me, Melissa?"

She moaned.

"Tell me. Just once, tell me you want me."

Her voice was tight and low. "I want you, Lucky Lawrence. You know it. I want you. I feel as if I'm burning on the inside. I want . . . you desperately!"

Even in the darkness, he could see she was biting her lips to keep from crying out. Suddenly she lifted herself and before he could take control, she plunged downward, taking the full length of him inside her.

"Oh, hell!" he said, trying to focus all his efforts on control. She didn't know what she was doing. He'd be through before he'd started. He tightened every muscle in his body. He couldn't. He wouldn't. She clung to him desperately, her fingers digging into his flesh while she kept moving up and down, tightening and loosening her muscles as she kept him inside, then let him go.

"Melissa," he growled. "I want this to be good for you. Stop for just a minute."

She seemed to lock down and stopped moving, and he felt her begin to ripple. "If you're waiting for me, Lucky, you're late."

Like the river raging outside, they were caught up in

the raging current of their release. Then as the last of the spasms died out, she collapsed on top of him, still holding him inside her.

At some point, he'd grasped the bed clothes and held on tight. Now he released his grip and let out a deep sigh. After a long minute she trembled. There was no fire in the room now that their desire had abated. He reached down and pulled up the covers. He moved her into his arms and she cuddled close, her breasts pressed against him. She curled her arm across his chest and ran her fingertips through his hair.

"You're still wet," she said, throwing her leg across his as she edged higher.

He nudged between her legs with his thigh. *Wet.* "So are you, woman."

Melissa sighed and kissed his chest. "This feels so right," she whispered. He didn't know how to answer. It *was* right but he could never say it. Rather than tell her that he was leaving tomorrow, he simply pulled her closer.

She said something, but the words danced out of his mind and he lost them in the aftermath of their love-making. "What?" He finally managed to ask. "What did you say?"

She forced herself forward so that she could whisper in his ear. "No matter what happens, I love you, Lucky Lawrence."

She'd fallen asleep leaving his chest damp with her tears. It would have been so easy to tell her that he loved her too—and so unfair. He knew he'd failed her. She needed something from him that he couldn't give no matter how much he wanted to. Finally, guilt drove him from their bed.

He stood for a long time watching her. Melissa was not a woman who cried. Crying was a sign of weakness. But this woman who loved him was anything but weak. In spite of the cold, damp air, just looking at her in the dark made him hard. The cold and the rain suited his mood. Always before, he'd reacted to things that happened in the past. Now, his actions determined the future. He'd thought that making love to her would extinguish the fire raging inside him. It hadn't. Touching her only made him want her more.

The rain was still pelting the roof. Mac was prowling restlessly in the other room, and an occasional creak of the ceiling suggested Lucky wasn't the only one still awake. He pulled on his damp trousers and shirt. He needed to check the yard and make certain that the main house wasn't in danger of being swept away, knowing that even if it were, there was little he could do to stop it. Once again he wondered why Melissa's father built his lean-to and the school so near the creek. At least the house was on higher ground, even if the dormitory wings weren't.

Leaving his boots beneath Melissa's bed, he opened the door and moved through the main room and into the yard. He needed to feel the depth of the water in the darkness.

The icy rain stung him as he stepped into the yard. He could hear the sound of rushing water, but it was still far enough away that he could breathe a sigh of relief.

* * *

When the door closed behind Lucky, Melissa let out a shuddery breath. She'd never felt so alone. Even telling him that she loved him hadn't been enough. Obviously he didn't feel the same way she did. She'd tried to resist him. When that didn't work, she'd given in to her own desire and pursued him. Was it her pursuit that had driven him away? Or had she pushed him too far in trying to make him something he wasn't? Why didn't he realize what a good man he was? Lord knows she didn't plan on this, but she'd learned that love happens in spite of what you plan. More than that, she learned that making love was glorious.

Her body felt as if it were singing. She touched her cheek and remembered how the stubble of his whiskers felt rubbing against it. Her nipples hardened and her skin twitched as it remembered how they'd been together. She'd never expected anything like this when she came to Silver Wind. First, the town had fought her, then the elements, and now the man who claimed her heart. Was she strong enough to keep going without Lucky? She forced herself to admit that she hadn't come to Colorado for her father; she ran away from the same things that had sent him to the West. She'd thought if she made his school a success, she'd be safe from all the failures of her parents' life together. In spite of what had happened, she knew now she could succeed, but she also knew her life would be empty.

Melissa folded her arms across her chest, hugging herself, trying to bring back the warmth and the closeness she'd just shared. Where was Lucky? He'd gone out into the storm in his bare feet, otherwise, she would have heard his boots clicking on the wood floor. She remembered what happened to his shirt when it was caught up in the current, remembered herself being dragged helplessly. What if he'd been swept away by the water? He might die.

Without a thought, she sprang to her feet and headed for the door. As she reached for the handle, the door opened and she collided with Lucky. She flung her arms around him and started to cry.

"What's wrong?" he asked, pulling her close.

"I thought something had happened to you," she said in a muffled voice. "The river might have swept you away."

"And you planned to rush out and save me?"

"I didn't plan. I just had to go."

"Seems to me we've been there before."

She curled up in his embrace, planting wild kisses on his chest. "You're all wet. You'd better take off your clothes and let me get you warm." She pulled away and unbuttoned his shirt and his trousers.

He chuckled and finished the job. "You know you're not wearing any clothes. It's very cold outside and it's raining. And you want to warm me up?"

"But I'm not cold anymore," she said.

"Neither am I."

She gasped with pleasure as he picked her up and fell into the bed with her, pulling her close to him. A sigh of pleasure was whispered into his ear as he drew up the covers.

This time their lovemaking was slow and gentle. Too slow for her. Each time she tried to urge him on, he stopped her. He kissed her throat, lingering there before moving down her body, touching her in places

she'd never known were sensitive. Time stretched out
as he teased every part of her into a trembling mass of
desire. She responded with a freedom she'd never
known until there was no stopping. When at last he entered her, she felt such a burst of pleasure that she cried
out. When the last tremor died away, he plunged into
her once more and filled her with his release. Finally,
inch by inch, he withdrew, and she knew a part of her
would go with him if he left.

The rain slowed to a gentle pace as if it, too, had
been fulfilled. Now it fell across the roof and slid down
the walls like silk. She wouldn't ask about tomorrow and
he didn't speak of it at all. Finally, lulled by the soft
whisper of the rain, she slept.

When the rain stopped he could hear the sound of her
breathing as she slept. The darkness gave way to a filmy
gray, as soft fingers of light reached through cracks in
the wall. He pushed up on one elbow and studied her
beautiful face, touching a curl of hair that fell across
one cheek. Soft, yet full of fire, Melissa Grayson was a
true woman of the West. She'd said she loved him. He
couldn't bring her the grief of being a widow. Claiming
to give her up by pretending he'd died would be wrong,
especially after she'd been ready to rescue him twice.
No, he had to be honest if he had any chance of making
things right.

She moved and pulled the blanket from her neck,
that neck he kissed so hungrily. He wondered if she
knew how much he wanted to tell her that he was in
love with her. But he couldn't, not until he had the right
to claim her as Lucky Lawrence. What would the

townsfolk do if he rode in tomorrow and confessed his deception? They couldn't hold her responsible; he'd make it clear that the fault was his. That was the only answer.

Now it was time for him to see what the storm had done.

18

—❦—

The house and the dormitories were surrounded by rushing water on three sides. Lucky had forgotten that the house sat on a slight incline until he looked out. The sky above the mountains was clear, but there was no way he'd get to town without fording a moat.

The door behind him opened. "Looks like we need a bridge." Bart limped to the porch beside him, steadying himself by holding the post.

"That would help," Lucky agreed. While Bart's arm was still bandaged, the dressing was gone from his head and the raw flesh along his cheek and neck was trying to scab over. The clothes he was wearing were too big and too short. Lucky guessed they must have belonged to Melissa's father.

Melissa stepped out on the porch and slid her arm around Lucky's waist. "Look at the school. It's all gone."

Bart nodded, looking toward where the school had

once stood. "Looks like it's been picked clean by buzzards. Nothing left but that platform for the teacher's desk."

"Never did understand that platform. More like a tower than a place for a teacher's desk. Why'd you build it so high?" Lucky asked.

"Wasn't me. Grayson built it. It was already here when he hired me to help finish the building. Look," Bart said. "I figure I owe you an apology. I never should have started that fire. Wouldn't have done it if I hadn't been drinking. But I did and I can't take it back. Mrs. Pickney—I mean, Mrs. Lawrence has lost her school and you and Aggie risked your life to save mine."

"Aggie?"

Bart grinned. "Yeah, well, she likes me calling her that. Never had a man call her anything special before. She thinks—I mean, I think I ought to build the school back, and I will. And there's this. I reckon I'm sorriest about this." He fumbled in his pocket and pulled out the waterlogged portrait of Melissa and handed it to Lucky. "This ought to be yours, I reckon. It belonged to her pa. I swiped it when he died."

Lucky took the portrait and looked into the face of the woman he'd watched this morning while she was sleeping. The artist had caught an impish look in her eyes, and an innocence that had been replaced by determination and wickedness. Her father had given her the determination but it had been Lucky Lawrence who'd made her into a wicked woman. He could understand Bart's reaction to the likeness.

"Are you sure, Bart?"

"Yeah, I'm sure. She don't belong to me. Never did.

Sorry I made trouble for her. Reckon we could shake hands and start again?" Bart asked. "I'd like to be your friend. Ain't never had nobody share their picnic with me before. Ain't never had nobody risk their life for me, either. I figure you and Miss Melissa and me and Aggie can do anything we set out minds to."

It wasn't the time to tell Bart what he had in mind, but it wouldn't hurt for Melissa to have someone around besides James to help her. And from what he was gathering, Miss Agnes Fulbright had Black Bart Jamison in control.

Lucky held out his hand.

It was two days before the water receded enough for Lucky to carry out his plans. He spent the daylight hours gathering pieces of lumber that could be used to rebuild the lean-to, and the nights making love to Melissa. He excused his actions by saying that she would have guessed that he intended to leave if he hadn't. Agnes had a broad smile on her face that widened every time she walked by and Bart gave her an affectionate swat on her plump rear.

Lucky was about ready to start into Silver Wind on foot when, on the third morning, the sound of a wagon approaching drew the four housemates to their feet.

"Hello?"

"It's James," Melissa said, and hurried to the porch. The others followed.

"You all right?" James called out. He was driving the wagon, but he was accompanied by the man who'd been Ellen's escort to school. The escort's horse was tied to the back of the wagon.

"We're fine," Agnes said.

"Almost got washed away," Bart added.

THE MAIL ORDER GROOM		263

James climbed down from the wagon, eyeing Bart. "You're up and about, I see. I'd have returned sooner but Miss Ellen was concerned that the water might— that it might not be safe." He blushed as he tied Arthur to the porch post. "I mean, I don't know much about driving this kind of wagon, but I'm learning. And Agnes, you'll be pleased to know that Miss Ellen is attempting to do the exercises to strengthen her legs."

"Then I trust you and Ellen had both a profitable and a pleasant visit?" Melissa said with a hint of the impish look Lucky had seen in the portrait.

"Indeed we did. That is, until a rider came this morning from town with a message. He and the colonel went into the library. After a while the colonel came out and sent me home. Said he'd call on us in a while and he'd appreciate it if you'd be here."

"The colonel's coming here?" Lucky frowned. "That sounds pretty strange. Who brought the message?"

"Cob Barnett, the telegraph operator, brought it."

Lucky's heart thumped. There was only one thing that operator could be bringing to the colonel. He'd inquired about Lucky Lawrence. This must be a follow-up report on the colonel's inquiry. One look at Melissa's face said she thought the same thing.

Were it not for Melissa and James, Lucky would tell Cerqueda the same thing his mother used to say: "Go to grass and eat mullet." In her mind that was a message to the lowest kind of person—pond scum. But there was Melissa and James. And now there was Agnes and Bart.

"Lucky?" Melissa said, coming to his side.

"That's it, then," Lucky said. "Tell Colonel Curtis we'll be here."

The mood was somber after the colonel's man left.

By some unspoken agreement, they went their separate ways, as if each needed to get ready for the encounter. James went to the dormitory to write some letters. Bart pulled a timber sliver from the mud and used it as a cane to balance himself as he walked back and forth, studying the layout of the remaining foundation of the school. Agnes and Melissa gathered the rain-soaked clothing to hang it on the porch rail to dry. Lucky put Arthur back in the corral and disappeared into what was left of the lean-to to search for feed.

October 30, 1888

MY DEAR MOTHER,

I know you must wonder where I went. I should have told you, but for once, I had to do something for myself. I'm in Silver Wind, Colorada, where I'm the Assistant Headmaster of Grayson Academy. At least I was, until it caught fire and burned.

I would not have you worry about my health, for a curious thing has happened. In this clear mountain air, my breathing problems have significantly improved. There is a young lady who also has health problems and I hope to help her overcome them.

My reason for writing is twofold: to reassure you of my well-being and to ask that you transfer some of my trust funds to the Dawson Banking Company in Silver Wind. I want to contribute to the school.

*Also, I'd like you to send me a black satin vest
with silver embroidery.*

Faithfully,
Your son, James

*Oh, if you should happen to hear that
I've taken a wife, it's simply a temporary
misunderstanding.*

Bart made his way slowly about the site of the demolished school. Fortunately, his burned arm was the left one. He could still wield a hammer, and wield it he would, lest he disappoint Agnes. In the beginning he'd thought that she was an odd-looking little woman; his ma would have called her a Rhode Island red "setting hen." He'd simply wanted her to go away. Then, moment by moment, she'd begun to chip away at his thorny exterior, forcing him to think back to the time before his life had hit bottom, badgering him to think about his future. Miss Fulbright became Agnes, who became Aggie, who became the woman he'd been looking for all along. She believed in him. Now he just had to repair the damage he'd done.

"Lucky seems worried," Agnes said. "And you're tiptoeing around like you're in a funeral parlor. What's wrong?"

Melissa held Lucky's wet trousers and shirt. She laughed as she laid them over the porch rail with the rest. "You mean, other than the fact that my schoolhouse was burned, then washed away? I'm pretending to be the wife of James Harold Pickney IV, scholar, when I'm really married to Lucky Lawrence, a gambler who thinks the only way he can protect me is by disappearing."

"Why would he be worried about protecting you? And what does the colonel have to do with any of this?"

Melissa sighed. "It's such a mess. Because of Ellen's interest in James, the colonel sent out some inquiries about Lucky Lawrence—since that's who he believes James is. I'm guessing Colonel Curtis got some kind of reply. And maybe the reply isn't good. You see, there's a killer out there looking for Lucky and Lucky's afraid I'll be hurt."

Agnes snorted. "Lucky would be long gone if he couldn't take care of himself. But I'm not so confident about James. All things considered, don't you think it's about time you got all this straightened out?"

"Past time," Melissa admitted in a low voice. "I just didn't want it to end. I don't want to lose Lucky, and when the truth comes out, I won't be married to him anymore."

Agnes put her hand on Melissa's arm and squeezed it. "Look, I don't know much about this kind of thing, but anyone can see that he's in love with you. He's a better man than he thinks he is. One thing I've learned since coming out here is that anything's possible. Don't sell him or the folks in Silver Wind short."

Melissa leaned against Agnes for a moment, then shivered and caught her wet hands in her apron to keep them warm. The sun was out but the temperature was definitely nudging them toward winter. She gave a grave look at the yard. It looked like the beach along the ocean after a stormy tide receded, all rippled layers of gooey mud and debris. The water was receding quickly, but it would be days before the students would be able to return, even if they could get the dormitory turned into a school, even if the town would allow her to continue.

She almost hoped that the colonel's announced visit meant that he'd found out about the transfer of names, that Ellen's infatuation was for a man who was a respectable teacher instead of a gambler. She could deal with that. Learning that Lucky was in danger was causing a pain in her heart. Confession was good for the soul, but she had no defense against the fear that was building in the pit of her stomach, a fear that seemed an omen. Lucky had disappeared from view, making the bad feeling worsen.

Agnes went back into the house and returned with a broom, attacking the mud drying on the porch with a vengeance. "I'm not a worldly person," Agnes said, "or I never thought myself to be one, but out here it seems to me that a woman can be pretty much what she wants. Out here, you can have your freedom if you're strong enough to demand it."

Durango, Colorado

Cerqueda climbed down from his horse, tossed the reins over the rail in front of the Durango Hotel, and adjusted his gun belt. The four men riding with him followed his lead.

Nobody seemed to be interested in their arrival. The town was a beehive of activity with the small mountain railroad huffing alongside the rock crushers unloading the ore, and traders and shoppers busily moving down the wooden sidewalks. Cerqueda caught sight of one slim, dark-haired young woman and he paused for a moment. She looked like Louisa. Then she glanced over her shoulder as if she were staring right at him, and he realized it was someone else. But he was close to finding her now, he could sense it, and once he did, she'd never get away from him again. Oh, he'd given up on making her his wife; she wasn't good enough anymore. All he wanted to do now was punish her and the gambler dressed in black, who stole her away from him.

Cerqueda retrieved a small cigar from his pocket and bit the end off before lighting it with a match. "Well, where is he, this informer who expects to claim my bounty? What's his name?"

"Nobody here claims to know anything about any reward," one of his men observed. "Reckon somebody brought us on a wild-goose chase?"

"Maybe," another rider said. "But maybe somebody got to him and he decided to move on. If your man is here, we'll find him."

"We'll wait," Cerqueda said with a snap of his head. "Let's go inside and get some food."

It took two bottles of whiskey and most of the night to find anyone willing to talk about newcomers to the area. And it was the off-duty depot operator who told Cerqueda what he wanted to know.

"Only man I heard about in these parts wearing all black and packing a pearl-handled pistol come in on the train from Denver. I didn't even see him, mind you. His name's Pickney. He's married to the schoolteacher up in Silver Wind."

"He can call himself whatever he wants. Just tell me again what he looks like," Cerqueda said.

The depot manager described Lucky perfectly. Cerqueda smiled. "That's got to be him. I'm surprised the town would approve of their schoolteacher marrying a gambler."

The informant looked confused. "Don't reckon they would have. Mr. Pickney is some kind of schoolteacher from back East."

"I don't figure Pickney's his real name. He's hiding from me." He tapped his pistol on the table and then aimed at the railroad employee. "I believe I'll just ride on up to Silver Wind and have a look."

There was a sudden silence in the saloon. Cerqueda stood and announced to the onlookers, "Pay attention, amigos. I'd take it unkindly if any of you tried to warn Mr. Pickney that I'm coming."

The saloon patrons nodded.

"Tell me how to get to Silver Wind."

The bartender shook his head. "You don't want to ride up there in the dark—not after all this rain we had. Some of the rail line even got washed out. Wait till tomorrow and they'll have the line repaired and you can ride."

"One more day won't matter," Cerqueda said. "Let's find us a room, *hombres,* and get some shut-eye. This will be the last good night Pickney will ever have. Bartender, tell that engineer not to leave without us. Tomorrow, we're going to take a little train ride."

19

After the noon meal, Lucky casually strapped on his gun belt, picked up Melissa's shawl, and asked her to take a walk with him. She nodded and let him drape the wrap across her shoulders.

Outside the day was gray, with a light wind that tugged at her hair and pulled loose strands across her face. Since the flood, Lucky had not shaved. He looked serious and foreboding as he headed toward the creek bank. They made their way through the debris that had been swept down by the flood. For a time neither spoke, as if they both were content to delay what they knew was to come. Finally, he stopped and turned to face her.

"You're wearing your gun," she said. It wasn't a question.

"Just a precaution. I don't know what's on the colonel's mind but you and I know this is about to end."

"Yes," she said softly.

"When the town learns what I did, you could lose your reputation and even the school."

"I'm not worried."

As if he hadn't heard her, he went on, "Because of me, you could even be in danger."

Melissa shook her head. "A person is always in danger. Agnes made me see something; here in the West, we can make a choice. It may take me a while, but I can rebuild the school and my reputation. I ... I just don't want to lose you."

"I'll take the blame for pretending to be James. He can take back his real identity and I'll be out of here before Cerqueda comes. He'll have no reason to harm you if I'm gone."

"But he won't give up, will he?"

"Of course he will, sooner or later."

She knew he was lying. "Will you come back?"

"I don't know."

He wouldn't. She'd already lost him. Lucky was an honorable man, no matter what he thought. Leaving her was the only way to protect her.

"You're certain that Cerqueda will come, aren't you?"

"I think he's already coming. Once the colonel sent out an inquiry on Lucky Lawrence, he gave away my location without realizing what he was doing. I have some time to make things right, but I have to go, Melissa. No matter what I'd rather do."

He reached out and touched her face. She closed her eyes, forcing herself not to collapse against him. She'd never imagined that it could hurt so much to lose a man. Perhaps if they hadn't made love it would be different. If she'd ever had any idea of the pain she now felt, she might have refused him. No, that was wrong.

She was lying to herself and the world. Lucky knew how she felt. If they were going to tell the truth, she must tell the others that she loved him. It might be the only way to keep him from leaving her. If Cerqueda came, they'd face him together.

"What I did to you was wrong," Lucky said. "I should have been a stronger man. I shouldn't have taken advantage of you."

"Wrong for a man to lie with a woman who loves him? I don't think so," she said softly. "That couldn't be wrong—unless he didn't care for her. I think you owe me that much, Lucky. Tell me that you cared a little."

He groaned, his breath turning into a rasp as he pulled her into his arms. "Care? Of course I...care." His mouth captured hers, sending a sharp pain through her. This kiss was one of great sorrow, of desperation, of good-bye. He'd been leaving from the beginning.

He wouldn't allow himself to say the word love, but he loved her. *I care.* His words rang through her in a rolling wave of joy that was greater than the passion she'd felt before. That release had been physical; this was a melting of the heart.

It was Mac who brought them back to the present. He'd begun barking frantically, circling the two of them and dancing back toward the house. Someone was approaching.

Lucky held her one more moment, then let her go. "It's time," he said.

She nodded and they went back to the house.

The colonel was not alone. He was accompanied by one of his men on horseback and Ellen, who was sitting anxiously beside him in the wagon, her face tear-stained and pale.

"Would you like to come inside?" James was saying.

"I would not!" was Colonel Curtis's sharp answer. "I'll say what I have to say from here."

"Please, Father," Ellen said, catching his elbow and shaking it.

"No more from you, child. I allowed a gambler with a bounty on his head into my house as a guest." He planted his gaze on James. "I forbid you to ever see my daughter again. I intend to see that Lucky Lawrence is run out of Silver Wind immediately."

Lucky let go of Melissa. "That won't be necessary, Colonel. I'm leaving as soon as I can."

The colonel frowned. "I'm afraid I don't understand, Pickney."

"I'm not James Harold Pickney IV, sir. *I'm* Lucky Lawrence. The man you're about to run out of town is the real Pickney, a respectable scholar from New York City."

Turning to Melissa, the colonel asked, "Is this true, Mrs. Pickney—eh, Melissa?"

"It's true." She caught Lucky's arm. "Reverend Weeks married me to James Harold Pickney, but no one knew that my husband was really Lucky Lawrence."

"James?" Ellen whispered.

James stepped toward Ellen. "He's right. I really am James Harold Pickney IV. I'm sorry I deceived you. When your town fathers gave Melissa an order to marry, she contacted me, thinking I would . . . I might be able to help her. I accepted her offer of marriage, and started out. Unfortunately, I became indisposed in St.

Louis, where Miss Fulbright agreed to accompany me
as my nurse, and was weeks late in arriving. I don't
know how Lucky came to be on the train the day I was
expected, but I do know he gallantly offered to become
her fiancé in order to save her school. Obviously there
couldn't be two James Pickneys, so when I arrived, I became Lucky Lawrence."

James straightened his spine and jutted out his chin.
"Three life-altering events have happened because
Melissa wanted my help: first, I came out West; second,
I was allowed to be the kind of man I always dreamed of
being, even if it was just for a while; and third"—he
walked around the buggy to Ellen's side and took her
hand—"I met Ellen."

"Daddy," Ellen pleaded, "I told you you were wrong
about Lucky...James. You have to do something."

"I hate to break up this tender moment," Bart spoke
up from the doorway, "but did you just say bounty on
Lucky? Who's offering it and how much is he worth?"

"A man named Cerqueda is offering five hundred
dollars," the colonel said. "Jamison, what are you doing
here?"

"Making use of the best nurse in the West while I get
well. Then, I'm guessing that I'll end up back in jail for
burning down the schoolhouse."

"This is a disaster, all right," Colonel Curtis said.
"Still, I'm a fair man and I'll find a way to repair whatever damage I have caused."

"You are a fair man, and you can't run Lucky out of
town without knowing why he's being hunted," Melissa
said.

"I *know* why Cerqueda is coming—because of me.
Lawrence, when I saw *Mr. Pickney* here getting a little

too involved with my daughter, I sent out some inquires through Sheriff Vance about a gambler I thought to be Lucky Lawrence. Now I find out that a sheriff in some little town down in Texas was doing the same thing. A Mexican named Cerqueda has offered a reward to anyone who can tell him where this gambler is hiding. What I don't know is why."

"Tell them, Lucky," Melissa urged.

"Cerqueda is a Mexican gambler who dabbles in horse stealing and other things that give him power and wealth. He saw a woman he wanted down in Texas. When she refused to have anything to do with him, Cerqueda deliberately set out to break the girl's father, Louis Hidalgo. Hidalgo was an easy target. He'd just lost his wife and had begun drinking heavily. Cerqueda befriended him and enticed him into a high-stakes poker game where he eventually lost his ranch. Cerqueda dealt him one final hand in which his daughter became the bet. If Hidalgo won, Cerqueda returned everything."

"He lost," Melissa said.

"Hidalgo ended up in New Orleans. He heard I was a gambler who traveled around. He hired me to rescue his daughter. I found Cerqueda and the girl in Santa Fe. We played poker. This time, I won; but Cerqueda didn't see it that way. We had a difference of opinion. Cerqueda was hurt. I sent Louisa to her father and Cerqueda came after me. He's killed two men that I know of since, maybe more."

The colonel let out a deep breath. "And now he's coming to Silver Wind. According to Cob Barnett, Cerqueda and his gang arrived in Durango yesterday, asking questions about a gambler dressed in black. If the road and part of the track hadn't washed away, Cerqueda and his gang would probably already be here."

"Then there's no problem," James said confidently. "All he has to do is look at me and he'll know I'm not the man he's looking for."

"But they might shoot first and look later," Ellen protested, releasing her father's arm and clinging to James.

"And sooner or later, they'll learn that the man who pretended to be Pickney is the real gambler," Bart said. "Believe me, you can't hide from what you are."

"But you can change what you are, Bartholomew," Agnes said confidently. "And we can find a way to protect Lucky if we just put our minds to it."

There was a long silence as the enormity of what happened sunk in.

"I still don't understand how Lucky came to marry Melissa," Bart said.

"Melissa didn't know what I looked like," James answered. "She just knew which train I was arriving on."

"When Lucky got off," Melissa said, "everyone assumed he was James and the marriage took place before I found out he wasn't."

"I could have stopped it," Lucky admitted, "but I figured if she was marrying a man named Pickney, I could be him until Cerqueda gave up. That would give Louisa time to get to safety. I didn't plan to cause such a problem or to hurt Melissa. I can't take a chance on putting her in danger. That's why I have to go."

"And you think leaving will make everything all right?" the colonel asked.

"No. He's a man bent on revenge. He won't be satisfied unless he gets me."

The colonel's horse shifted his weight impatiently. "Whoa, boy." Colonel Curtis studied the reins for a moment, then said, "You know, Miss Agnes is right about one thing. Somewhere along the way we've gotten soft. The women out here are the courageous ones. Miss Grayson was determined to choose her own husband. Miss Fulbright saw something worth saving in *Bartholomew,* and my Ellen seems to want to walk again. I think I'll leave my daughter here with you while my hand and I ride into town to discuss this with the bunch of fools that started it."

"I'm going with you," Lucky said.

"If you don't mind, I'll come along too," Bart said, climbing into the colonel's wagon. "What about you, Pickney?"

James had already removed Ellen's chair from the wagon and planted her in it. He pushed her to the porch, then climbed in beside Bart. "Wait," he said, and dashed back into the dormitory, returning with his gun belt and his ten-gallon hat. "Don't worry, men, you can count on me."

The sun came out as the colonel's buggy disappeared around the abutment. Melissa, Agnes, and Ellen watched from the porch as the five men disappeared from sight, Mac trailing along behind.

"What's going to happen?" Ellen asked.

"I don't know," Melissa said after a time. "But I know one thing, Agnes is right. As women, we have a stake in this and we can't do a thing out here. Ellen, if we can get you into our wagon, can you ride there?"

"I'll ride Arthur if you get me on him," she said with certainty.

The colonel summoned Alfred Sizemore, Mayor Dawson, Reverend Weeks, and Sheriff Vance to the church—the same place they'd handed down Melissa's directive to take a husband.

"Now, Lawrence, you tell them our situation."

Lucky stood, drawing the men's puzzled attention away from James. "I'm Lucky Lawrence," he said. "The man you know as Lucky is the real James Harold Pickney IV."

A collective gasp came from the crowd.

Reverend Weeks looked stunned. "I . . . I don't understand."

Lucky repeated the sequence of events, adding that his presence now threatened the safety of the town. "At first I thought I'd just leave, but Cerqueda is a hot-tempered murderer. Leaving would put the town in danger."

"Did Melissa know about this?" someone asked.

"This wasn't Melissa's fault. She didn't know I wasn't Pickney. She'd never seen him."

"You let me perform a marriage ceremony so that you could hide from a killer, knowing that you'd be ruining an innocent young woman?"

"At the time, I was trying to protect another young woman. I stepped off the train and you just assumed I was Pickney. Melissa seemed to be on the verge of being tarred and feathered and I didn't figure it would hurt anything if I helped her out. How was I to know that you were performing the marriage ceremony then and there?"

"Why wouldn't you think that when she was wearing a wedding dress at the time?"

"Trust me," Lucky said, "I didn't recognize that as a wedding dress. But that's no excuse. Things just got out of hand. I never thought the real groom would turn up and pretend to be me."

"Never mind that now," Mayor Dawson said, assuming leadership. "The important thing we have to deal with is how to protect ourselves from a killer heading for Silver Wind."

"So, what are we going to do about this Cerqueda?" Sheriff Vance asked. "Fights and scuffles are one thing, but facing a real killer—that's something else."

The men looked at each other helplessly, none of them ready to speak the truth; Sheriff Vance couldn't even break up a dogfight.

"Let's just hope he doesn't come," someone offered tentatively.

"He'll come," Lucky said. "It's a matter of restoring his honor and his reputation. If he's in Durango now, we'll see him by morning."

There was a long moment of silence.

Finally, the minister said, "I think you have to take the responsibility for Cerqueda, Lawrence. In the meantime," he added with authority, "you can't continue to pretend to be her husband. I think you'd better plan on sleeping down at the jail."

The mayor agreed. "Yes. If you stay in town, she'll be safe."

"Of course, there's the matter," Reverend Weeks

said, "of who Melissa is married to and if the marriage is legitimate."

"I think we're going to have to get a legal ruling," Alfred Sizemore said. "In the meantime, I agree, Lawrence, if he comes it's up to you to face Cerqueda. Then we'll decide about Miss Grayson. She may not be Mrs. James Harold Pickney IV, but she's not Mrs. Lucky Lawrence, either."

"Then we have a problem," Melissa's voice rang from the back of the church. She strode down the aisle followed by Agnes and Ellen, who rolled her own chair.

"What do you mean?" Mayor Dawson asked.

"Because I'm expecting a child."

The mining train didn't come, but Cob Barnett brought a second telegraph warning Sheriff Vance that the train would be arriving in the morning and Cerqueda and his men would be on it. Agnes, Ellen, and Melissa refused to return to the school, and took rooms in the hotel instead. After a supper of which they ate little, they had come to no conclusion about how to handle the approaching danger. Word of the trouble spread, and merchants began closing and locking their doors.

Too many eyes made it impossible for Lucky and Melissa to speak privately. Finally, it was decided that Lucky would keep watch and face Cerqueda alone when he came. Bart's plan to wrangle a room from Sable met swift opposition from Agnes, who arranged rooms for the colonel, James, and Bart.

Lucky couldn't have slept if he'd wanted to. He didn't trust Cerqueda and spent most of the night pacing the sidewalk from one end of town to the other. He wasn't afraid to face Cerqueda, but the men traveling with him presented a problem.

By morning, little groups of residents and miners gathered in the alleyways and in front of the businesses, speaking in low tones. Mayor Dawson called a second meeting of the town fathers and the parties involved. Cob Barnett was sent from the meeting to remain at the depot to keep watch for riders and listen for the train.

Cob protested. "Suppose he's angry and looking for trouble?"

"Then send him to me and you can collect the reward," Lucky said as he checked his gun to make certain it was loaded properly.

Colonel Curtis addressed the group. "After much deliberation, we believe that Mr. Lawrence may have been right about leaving town. We'll provide a horse for both him and Mr. Pickney to ride north through the mountains. If Cerqueda comes and finds that the man he is looking for isn't here, he'll be forced to leave."

"But, Father..." Ellen began.

"The decision is made," the colonel said. "Let's get the women back to the Academy."

Melissa stood. "There could be another way. I, too, have been thinking. Wouldn't it be a federal crime for that killer to fire at an officer of the law in Colorado?"

"It would," the sheriff agreed. "But I don't think a man who's already killed two men is going to listen to me."

Lucky nodded. "No, but he'll listen to me. As I said last night, facing him is the only way to stop him once and for all."

"Fine, you can have my job and my badge," Sheriff Vance said, and handed it to Lucky. "Any objections?" he asked as he pinned it on his vest.

There were none.

"Are you crazy, man?" Bart asked incredulously.

The train whistle made Lucky wonder the same thing as he stood and started toward the door, then turned back to face the town elders. "Melissa is my wife, no matter what anyone says." Then he turned back to Melissa "I love you. I may not have been able to protect the other women in my life, but I'll protect you. Wait in the church."

Melissa looked around at the men watching slack-jawed as he left. "You're just going to let him go by himself?" she asked. "Never mind. I'll go."

"And I will too," Agnes said. "Somebody give me a gun and tell me how to use it."

"Sit down, Aggie," Bart snapped. "I'll go."

"And me," James chimed in.

The minister caught Melissa at the door and held her back. "You're carrying his child now. You have to think of the baby."

The streets were deserted when Cerqueda and his men left the train and started up the street. The shutters on the windows had been closed and there were no horses in front of the buildings. As the intruders' boots hit the dried ruts left by the rain, the chinks of their spurs rattled ominously through the silence.

The minister moved to the front of the church, knelt at the altar, and said a prayer. Melissa, holding her shotgun in one hand and fingering her derringer in her pocket, moved to the window. She closed out his words, focusing all her concern on the man she loved. She could see Lucky open the churchyard gate and step into the street, where he walked toward the depot—alone.

When the four outlaws reached the halfway point, they stopped and whipped back their dusters to free their guns.

At that moment, Lucky stopped and laid his hand on his pistol.

"There's no way Lucky can handle four men," Melissa said, her brain racing to come up with an answer.

Even from where she was, Melissa knew when the Mexican smiled that he'd seen the sheriff's badge pinned to Lucky's coat.

"Heard you were looking for me," Lucky said.

"Sí," Cerqueda said with a broad grin. "Looks like I've found you, Sheriff Lawrence. Where's my Louisa?"

"Where you'll never find her."

"Oh, I'll find her and you'll help me, or you'll die."

"I might. But then you'd never know where she is. Would you?"

Cerqueda frowned and looked around. "Don't be a fool, gringo. This is as far as it goes. Unless you want others to die."

"I don't think we're prepared to let that happen," the colonel said as he, James, and Bart exited the church and came to stand beside Lucky.

Cerqueda slapped his knee and laughed. Then he took a step closer. "An old man, a walking skeleton, and a...what are you?" he asked James. "A medicine-show dandy?"

"And three women," Melissa said, her shotgun in her

hand. She was flanked by Agnes, now flourishing the derringer, and Ellen, pushing her own chair stoically.

"I understand that you're a man who likes to hurt women," Ellen said bravely. "How do you feel about one who can't walk?"

"Melissa, get the women back inside!" Lucky snapped. Fear, like he'd never known, jabbed his chest. He should have known that Melissa would be right in the middle of the problem. With her eyes flashing and her chin lifted high, she was the most beautiful woman he'd ever seen.

Cerqueda's men looked at their boss. "Can we have the women when we're done?" one of them asked.

"Not unless you want to take on the whole town," Cob Barnett said, stepping into the street to join Lucky. One by one, every man in town appeared, holding rifles and pistols. They surrounded Cerqueda. Lucky swore. They meant well, but any shot could hit one of the townspeople—not that Cerqueda would care.

"Got no business with the rest of you fellows," Lucky said to Cerqueda's cronies. "I'm the sheriff here now, and I'm about to arrest the man you're following for murder. Unless you want to go to the gallows with him, you'd better get on that train and head back where you came from."

The three men accompanying Cerqueda didn't argue. They turned and fled. Cerqueda's rage was evident, but when he realized there was no way out, he pulled his gun, almost as if he were daring Lucky to shoot. Lucky drew his weapon. At the same time, James whipped out his pistol and pulled the trigger.

The jolt of the gun firing caused James's hat to slide down his face and cover his eyes. Lucky was stunned when Cerqueda's gun slammed to the ground and fired, striking Cerqueda in the chest. By the time James got his hat on straight, the crowd was cheering and Cerqueda lay crumpled in the street, killed by his own bullet.

Ellen caught the arms of her chair and pulled herself to a standing position. "James, you did it." Colonel Curtis was shaking James's hand and Bart was examining Cerqueda.

"What are you doing?" Agnes asked.

"Just making sure he isn't playing possum," Bart said. "I don't think we want James to have to shoot again."

Agnes smiled. "Just think, our James got the bad guy. I have a feeling that he's going to retire from the life of a gunfighter if Ellen has anything to do with it. And I'm sure Lucky will see that he gives up his weapons."

Bart helped lift Cerqueda and carry him to the depot. The mayor said they'd put him on the train with his cohorts and ship him down to Durango until they could contact the federal marshal.

Melissa turned to Lucky, her heart thumping wildly. "What now, Sheriff Lawrence? Looks like you and your men have saved the town. Now that you have the means to support a wife, want to get married?"

"Sorry, lady, I'm already married. My woman's gonna have a baby."

Melissa put her arms around his neck and whispered in his ear, "Not yet, but you'd better give me one or I'll tell everyone that you're trifling with my affections. And you know what happened the last time the men of Silver Wind caused trouble over me."

* * *

The next week, Bart turned up at the school with a pump.

"What are you going to do with that?" Lucky asked.

"Well, I got to looking at that platform Grayson built and it's full of water from the flood. Thought we'd pump it out and see what's down there before we cover it up."

"Why would you want to waste time doing that?" Melissa asked. "Besides, we may decide not to rebuild the school there. I'm sure that wasn't the first flood we'll experience."

"Maybe not," Lucky said, "but let's have a look. I'm willing to gamble on a little wasted time."

"I thought you were through with gambling," Melissa said sternly.

"Nope. I gambled that the courts would rule you were a free woman and I won. There's nothing wrong with taking a chance now and then if the stakes are high enough."

"And I'm still a free woman, until next Sunday."

"And I'm still a gambler until then. Let's go check it out, men."

James, still wearing his boots and gun belt, swaggered out the door, following Bart and Lucky. He wasn't allowed to wear them to the ranch, but he didn't need them. In Ellen's eyes, he was already six feet tall.

After two days of pumping, they had emptied the hole beneath the platform. Lucky was only too glad to have some physical work to do; anything to keep his hands off Melissa. In spite of her whispered request, he'd promised the men in town not to touch her until she was legally his wife.

"Looks like there's a ladder down there," Lucky said. "What do you suppose Grayson was doing?"

"Why don't we get a lamp and have a look?" Bart suggested. "Be nice if he had found a vein. The colonel's mine is playing out. About all he's got left is coal."

Carrying Melissa's oil lamps, they entered the narrow, moist cavern and moved cautiously down the slick ladder one rung at a time. They had no way of knowing what lay at the bottom or how safe the wooden beams were. Finally Lucky's feet reached an outcropping narrow enough for only one man.

"Hold up, Bart."

He held up his lamp and saw it, a vein—a shiny gold vein that caught the lamp's flame and blinked like sunlight.

"Do you see it, Bart? That's why he built the school out here. He was hiding his claim."

"Hot damn! We're rich!" Bart exclaimed. "Lucky son of a—"

"No," Lucky corrected, "Melissa's rich." And suddenly he realized that could change everything. A schoolteacher and a sheriff were one thing, but Melissa had just become one of the wealthiest women in the West. She could do better than an ex-gambler. He wished he'd never gone down there.

"Here," Bart called out, "take this knife and dig out a chunk or two. She needs to know she's rich."

Minutes later they were on the surface. "Melissa, Aggie, James! You're not gonna believe what's happened," Bart was yelling.

Melissa came to meet them, followed by the others.

"Well, we've had a snowstorm, a fire, and a flood. What's left, an earthquake?"

Bart danced around like a court jester. "No, ma'am. You've struck it rich. Your daddy found what looks like a vein of pure gold."

Agnes rolled her eyes back. "Don't be a fool, Bartholomew. If he struck it rich, why didn't he tell Melissa?"

"He didn't want anybody to know. Prospectors are killed for even thinking they've found a vein. It was safer for Melissa to say the gold he found washed down from the mountains.

"This didn't wash down," Bart said. He held out the chunks of ore.

Melissa took them, rubbing them in her hands. She looked at Lucky, who was strangely silent. "Is it really gold?"

"Bart's the miner, not me. But I think it must be. That's why your father built the school where he did, to conceal the mine entrance. You're rich, Melissa."

Melissa closed her fingers around the ore and held it against her chest. "You did it, Father. You really did it."

After a time, she nodded her head and said, "Bart, pull out enough to rebuild the school and cover the mine again. So long as you remain silent about its location, we will all share in what's there. Can I trust you to keep the secret?"

"Share the gold?" Bart repeated in amazement.

"All of us? We're going to be gold miners and teachers?" was James's proud comment.

"Not only teachers," Melissa said, "but we'll build a school for students who have health problems like you did. With Bart to mine the gold we need, Agnes to look after our boarding students, and James to teach them, one day Grayson Academy will be famous."

"Yep," Lucky said, "it looks like you got everything you wanted. I'm happy for you."

Melissa shook her head. "Not quite. If it hadn't been for you, Lucky, none of this would have happened. I wouldn't have fallen in love with you. Bart wouldn't have burned down the schoolhouse. Agnes and James . . . well, who knows."

"You don't need my help," Lucky said. "I'm not a miner and I'm not a teacher."

"I have a miner and a teacher. You're going to be my husband and you're going to keep Silver Wind the kind of place where we can raise our children. I love you, Lucky Lawrence, and I can't do it without you."

"You could still marry James," Lucky said.

"No way. I have someone else in mind," James protested. "I just have to convince her father."

Lucky went on, seriously. "Well, there's Bart. After all, he wanted you first and he found the gold."

"And he's spoken for!" Agnes snapped.

"But I'm no scholar, Melissa. You need a man who challenges you, who stimulates your mind, who is equal to the position you'll earn in Colorado."

Melissa held out her hand. "I love you, Lucky Lawrence, and I intend to marry you on Sunday. You hold my heart, that's all that counts."

EPILOGUE

— ❧ —

The whole town turned out to watch Melissa Grayson get married for the second time. Agnes and Ellen were to be her attendants. James and Bart were to stand up with Lucky.

Lucky still voiced great reservations about the marriage, about being the husband of the owner of the biggest gold strike in the San Juans, even if nobody knew about it yet. Melissa continued to insist that the mine had to be protected for their child and so that the town could benefit. Lucky was the only one who could do that. He was now the sheriff, and like it or not, he was about to be partner in the Grayson Academy and Gold Mine.

But it was Melissa's visit to the dormitory that sent James and Bart for a midnight stroll. She didn't have to use her derringer or the length of rope she'd brought, to convince Lucky that he couldn't leave. So there he was, standing at the front of the church, his fingers crossed that she wasn't going to change her mind. Melissa had sent for a husband. He'd been looking for a woman. They'd both gotten their wishes in a way they had never expected.

James pushed Ellen down the aisle and took his place beside Lucky. Agnes, holding Bart's arm, came next. They separated, Agnes beside Ellen and Bart next to James. At that moment the Widow Cassidy, at the organ, raised her arms and let them fall dramatically in a crescendo of sound. Then, as if she'd gained their attention, she began to play a hymn that brought the congregation to their feet. All heads turned to the doorway and Melissa stepped inside the church.

No borrowed wedding gown this time, she was a floating vision of light and beauty as she walked toward Lucky. Any concern he still felt, disappeared as he saw the look in her eyes. "I love you," he whispered as he came to stand beside her.

Melissa smiled. "I know."

The Reverend Weeks began the ceremony. "We are gathered here to join this woman, Melissa Grayson, to this man—what is your given name, Lawrence?"

"Lucky will do, Reverend."

The minister raised his gaze to Melissa. She nodded. "Lucky's perfect."

In ten minutes Melissa Grayson became Melissa Lawrence, and Lucky had finally found his place in the world.

Two hours later they'd had refreshments and the good wishes of every permanent and temporary resident of Silver Wind.

"Let's go home, husband," she said.

"Arthur's been harnessed and ready for a half hour, wife."

It was almost morning when Melissa leaned on one elbow and looked down into the face of the man she'd married. "Our son is going to be just like his father, a man on a pilgrimage, a knight, a beautiful, loving man. We'll call him . . . what is your real name, Lucky?"

"I never told you, but my mother was a scholar too— before she had to turn our home into a boardinghouse to support us."

"So, what kind of scholarly name did she give you?"

"We absolutely are not going to name our son after his father."

"Your name, Lucky. If you don't tell me, I'm moving your pallet back to the loft."

"All right. But don't laugh."

"I won't."

"My name is Harold Byron Lawrence."

"*Childe Harold?*" She collapsed against his chest in laughter. "*Childe Harold?* It has to be fate."

"You promised."

"I'm sorry."

"I'm crushed. I can't trust you, Mrs. Lawrence. I think we'll just have a girl. We'll name her Melissa."

"Whatever you say, Lucky. Whatever you say."

She didn't tell him then, but she had a strong sense there'd be a boy and a girl. The first boy would be James *Harold* for his father. But they would call him Harry. The first girl would be named Rainey for Lucky's sister. After that, well, they'd just take a chance.

After all, her father had been a prospector and her husband was a gambler. And she...she was a woman awakened. And tonight was the beginning of fulfillment.

"Lucky, I'm cold."

"Want me to build up the fire?"

"Oh, yes." She kissed him and felt the flame begin.

ABOUT THE AUTHOR

Since Bantam published her first romance in 1988, bestselling and award winning author Sandra Chastain has published forty-seven works, including novels, novellas, short-story collections, and a collective novel. She lives right outside of Atlanta and considers her life to be just about perfect, with her three daughters and four grandchildren close by.

Sandra enjoys hearing from her fans. You may write to her at P.O. Box 67, Smyrna, GA 30081, or go to her website at SandraChastain.com.